Southern Hart

A MAX PORTER PARANORMAL MYSTERY

Stuart Jaffe

Southern Hart is a work of fiction. Names, characters, places, and incidents either are the product of the author's imagination or are used fictitiously, and any resemblance to any persons, living or dead, business establishments, events, or locales is entirely coincidental.

SOUTHERN HART

Cover art by Mari Morgan

ISBN 13: 978-1-963517-11-8

First Edition: December, 2023
First Hardcover Edition: February, 2024

For Bob Payne

enjoy your agriculture

Also by Stuart Jaffe

Max Porter Paranormal Mysteries

Southern Bound
Southern Charm
Southern Belle
Southern Gothic
Southern Haunts
Southern Curses
Southern Rites
Southern Craft
Southern Spirit
Southern Flames
Southern Fury
Southern Souls
Southern Blood
Southern Graves
Southern Dead
Southern Hexes
Southern Hart

Nathan K Thrillers

Immortal Killers
Killing Machine
The Cardinal
Yukon Massacre
The First Battle
Immortal Darkness
A Spy for Eternity
Prisoner
Desert Takedown
Lone Star Standoff
The Puppeteer
Blowback
Prime

The Ridnight Mysteries

The Water Blade
The Waters of Taladoro
Waterfire

The Parallel Society

The Infinity Caverns
Book on the Isle
Rift Angel
Lost Time
Pages of Glass
The Bold Warrior
City of Infinity

The Malja Chronicles

The Way of the Black Beast
The Way of the Sword and Gun
The Way of the Brother Gods
The Way of the Blade
The Way of the Power
The Way of the Soul

Gillian Boone novels

A Glimpse of Her Soul
Pathway to Spirit

Stand Alone Novels

After The Crash
Real Magic
Founders

Short Story Collection

10 Bits of My Brain
10 More Bits of My Brain
The Bluesman
The Marshall Drummond Case Files: Cabinet 1
The Marshall Drummond Case Files: Cabinet 2
The Marshall Drummond Case Files: Cabinet 3

Non-Fiction

How to Write Magical Words: A Writer's Companion
For more information, please visit ***www.stuartjaffe.com***

Southern Hart

Chapter 1

THEY WERE ALONE. That had once been commonplace, but since moving to North Carolina, since freeing the ghost of a 1940s detective from a witch's curse and starting the Porter Agency to investigate the paranormal, since adopting two homeless boys and guiding them towards adulthood, since caring for his mother who had moved to Winston-Salem to be closer and more involved, since dealing with the endless parade of strange and bizarre events, Max and Sandra Porter had spent little time alone. But the next few days promised otherwise.

With his senior school year closing in for J, and with PB preparing to hit the road for whatever fortunes he may find, the Sandwich Boys had decided to take Max's mother for a mini-vacation, a last hurrah, into the Appalachian Mountains. Sounded like a strange destination for this group, and Max suspected the itinerary had been dictated by his mother. The moment the plan was announced, Max bought an expensive bottle of wine and set it aside. Ten minutes after PB's car drove away, Max stepped into the bedroom with his special bottle of wine and his special smile.

"We've got a few wonderful days ahead of us. You think it's too early to open this up?" he said, the old floorboards of the tiny house creaking as he set the bottle on the edge of the dresser.

Sandra had curled on the rumpled bed, reading a book on the materials and color usages of witchcraft candles. She set it down, tapped on her phone a moment, and then grinned. A sultry tune filled the air — *Wicked Games by Chris Isaak.*

"Not your usual pick for music."

"A little change from the usual," she said, sliding to her feet. She opened the accordion door of the closet and pulled down a slinky, blue satin piece of lingerie.

"That's new."

"A little change from the usual."

Max grabbed his wife by the waist and pulled her close. He pressed his lips against hers — gentle and full of promise. "I love it when we're thinking the same."

"Then what am I thinking?"

He chuckled. "That you want me to get a corkscrew and open that wine. Give you a few minutes to put that on." He made a show of thinking, scratching his rough cheek. "Maybe I should shave, too?"

With a peck on the tip of his nose, she said, "We *are* thinking the same." She paused to gaze around the room.

Max said, "Don't worry about Drummond. He's been extra moody lately, but last night, I got him to tell me why."

"How did you manage that?"

"Everybody likes to talk about themselves — even the stoic ones. They just need the right conditions. Or they let it slip out."

"Okay, ghost whisperer, what's wrong with him?"

"His on-again, off-again girl in the Other — Miss 1800s — she hasn't spoken with him in days. He leaves messages, but she doesn't respond."

Sandra giggled. "Ghosted by a ghost."

"He'll get over it. From everything I know about how he lived, he knew every good looking waitress in all of North Carolina. But there have always been a few that caught his heart, and I'm guessing he really liked this one."

"Well, I really like the one in my arms."

"Hate to break it to you, hon, but I'm not a waitress."

She pulled him close for another kiss. "Let's stop talking about the cold dead and get a little living warmth going between us."

"You are the smartest lady I've ever known. I'll get the corkscrew."

Slinking toward the bathroom, Sandra said, "I'll get into

something more comfortable." She tossed the lingerie over her shoulder and snickered. "Well, into something different anyway."

With a hearty laugh, Max headed to the kitchen. Though only a handful of steps, his lips still had time to tingle from her kiss. He rubbed his stubble, wondered if she had been serious about him shaving or if that had been merely teasing, and reached for the utensil drawer with the corkscrew.

The pale ghost, Marshall Drummond, the dead detective that had changed Max's life immeasurably, slid through the back wall of the house. "Hey, partner, you need to —"

"Whoa!" Max dropped the corkscrew, and it clattered on the floor. Spreading his hands on the kitchen counter, he took a deep breath. "I swear you're going to kill me when I'm older. You'll just pop in and BAM! I'll have a heart attack."

"Enough dramatics. You've got —"

"I don't want to hear it. Whatever your issue with Miss 1800s, I'll be glad to help you work it out later. But right now, Sandra and I need to be adults. Alone."

"No, pal, it's not that."

A horrifying two-note chime rang out — the doorbell.

"What now?" Max said.

Drummond removed his fedora. "I've been trying to tell you that a big guy showed up. I checked his car for some ID. Looks like he's Cecily Hull's new assistant."

The doorbell chimed again. Max glanced down the hallway toward the front door. "Crap."

He walked the short hall, through the small living room, and to the door like a convict approaching the gallows. His heart sank and his nerves ignited. Cecily Hull not only strived to regain her family's former power controlling all use of magic in North Carolina, but she also paid the Porter Agency a retainer — something he had hated but needed until recently. She had never truly called on them before. A tiny matter here or there. Nothing they couldn't handle, and nothing requiring an unannounced visit from an assistant. In the past, Cecily simply picked up the phone.

"Sorry to interrupt your afternoon," Drummond said, floating behind. He clearly wanted to add further comment but held back.

Max left it alone as he opened the door to find a man pushing seven feet tall, gaunt, wearing a tailored suit and a grim expression. The man flicked his hand out, offered a slight tilt — which could have been a bow or just the need to lower from his height — and displayed a business card in his palm. The heavy paper rectangle looked tiny in the man's massive hand.

Picking it up, Max read:

LYLE VAN HORN
HULL ENTERPRISES
ASSISTANT TO THE CEO

"What can I do for you, Mr. Van Horn?" Max said, trying to ignore the sense of doom floating around this man's head.

With a voice deep enough to tremble the sea floor, Van Horn said, "I am to escort the members of the Porter Agency to an urgent meeting with Cecily Hull."

"If it's so urgent she could have called us. I mean what if we weren't here? Would you have meandered around the city looking for us?"

"You are here, and I am to take you to meet with her."

"You're new, and I appreciate that you want to do a good job for your employer. But this is not how we do things. I've got plans for today. If she wants to meet, she can make an appointment. Or if it's truly an emergency, she can pick up the phone and call."

Max moved to close the door, but the huge man placed his huge foot in the way.

"I am to escort the Porters to meet with Cecily Hull."

Drummond said, "I'd offer to freeze this guy's brain, but I'm not sure he's playing with a full deck."

Max knew he had only two reasons to be belligerent, but they were good reason. First, he made it a point to always challenge Cecily Hull at every step. Otherwise, she would get the idea that she could control him, and that would lead to an ugly, horrible outcome. Second, and most importantly, he wanted to spend the day with his wife.

From the bedroom, he heard Sandra call out, "Max? Where are you? I'm ready."

Van Horn's mouth rippled into a sneer. "I have been given strict orders, and I will see them through."

Max's shoulders dropped. He let go of the door and fought back the urge to shout. "Wait here," he said to both men. "I'll be right back with Sandra."

Chapter 2

DESPITE VAN HORN'S PROTESTS that everyone travel in his Mercedes, Max insisted on following in their own car. Van Horn finally agreed only if Sandra sat in the back of his car. During the entire drive, Max spotted Van Horn checking his rearview mirror repeatedly as if he thought Max might ditch his wife. Perhaps something urgent had truly occurred.

Drummond bounced between the cars, keeping an eye on both of his partners and delivering messages to bring Sandra and Max up to speed. This became invaluable when Van Horn took the on ramp for US-52 South, driving away from the city instead of toward the Hull offices downtown.

"Yeah, Sandra asked about that," Drummond said when he appeared in the passenger seat of Max's car. "She noticed right away. Startled Van Horn, I think. He's an odd duck to say the least."

"Did he respond at all?"

"Said recent events have caused Ms. Hull to temporarily relocate."

"What does that mean? What events?"

"She asked. He didn't answer."

Max peered ahead and caught Van Horn peering back through his mirror. As Hull's assistant, the man could have been warned about Drummond — most definitely was warned — but the way his eyes pierced across the highway suggested more.

"Do you think he can see you?"

Drummond's face locked forward like he did when on stakeout — not wanting to miss a single movement of the target. "I had the same thought. If he can, he's doing a good job of not giving the fact away too easy. Doesn't look directly at me.

Doesn't startle when I start talking or appear in his car. Doesn't even react to a nasty jibe or a pretend off-hand comment about him or Hull."

"You were testing him?"

"Absolutely. But I didn't get a firm result."

"Then get back to Sandra and keep trying."

"Don't worry. I won't let anything bad happen to her." He vanished, his pale glow appearing next to Sandra in the car ahead.

About fifteen minutes later, they took Exit 92 for Route 8, a small road that led them into the northern tip of Lexington — an area he had not been back to since dealing with the witch, Madame Yan. The speed limit dropped to a crawl, but that was the only familiar part of the road. Madame Yan's trailer was off a side street opposite Speedy's Barbecue — a Lexington institution for decades. Only Speedy's wasn't there. In fact, Speedy's, Sonic, a gas station, and several other buildings — they were all gone. The entire strip had been leveled for the construction of something new. A few signs promised that the stores had relocated, but the empty lots looked so strange, so dead, Max could feel the chill of a graveyard.

These thoughts and the nervous energy that brought them about would not help him or Sandra now. He took a deep breath and refocused on Van Horn's car.

Near the end of this dead strip, they turned onto one of the former alleyways — now simply a piece of pavement amongst a flat, dirt lot. When they reached the back, they parked before a thin stretch of trees. Homes could be seen on the other side.

Van Horn exited, opened the door for Sandra, and walked with her toward the tree line. Drummond floated nearby as Max hustled to catch up.

On the opposite side, they approached an empty home on the end bearing a FOR SALE sign in the front lawn. Van Horn unlocked a side door, and they stepped into the garage. Bare metal shelves lined the cinderblock walls, and the concrete floor looked smooth and clean. No oil-leaking cars had been parked in here yet. In the center of all this emptiness, Cecily Hull sat at an ornate wood desk with her head buried in her laptop.

When she heard them approach and lifted her head, Max saw a woman who had not slept in days. "Good job," she said, nodding to Van Horn. He bowed and slid back out of view. "Please," she said, indicating two plastic folding chairs in front of her desk.

Max gestured to the surroundings. "New assistant, new office space, no bodyguards — what's going on?"

As Sandra sat, she said, "No wards, either. I don't sense any magic in here."

"Also, not a ghost in sight," Drummond said. "Except me."

Max eased into his chair and noted Cecily Hull's silence. She stared back at him, her clothes askew, her hair a bit tangled. He thought the word *haggard* but rejected it. *Rattled.* That's what he saw. Cecily Hull looked rattled, and he had rarely seen that.

Lifting her chin as she folded her hands on her desk, Cecily said, "Madame Ti is missing."

Max couldn't help himself. He laughed. "You've lost your witch?"

With a gentle slap on his thigh, Sandra said, "What do you mean *missing?* Has she been kidnapped?"

Cecily offered a weak shrug. "She's gone. I haven't heard from her in over a week, and I can't get ahold of her on the phone. No response to texts. Nothing. But her things are still at her place. She didn't pack up and leave. She wouldn't have, anyway. Not when we're closer than ever to gaining control of North Carolina magic." Her sunken eyes narrowed. "Something bad has happened to her. Somebody is already making their move."

"You think this is an attack?"

"It is impossible to rise to the top without making enemies. And in our world, enemies are of the most dangerous variety."

Drummond said, "You gotta be kidding."

Max held back a laugh — partly out of respect, mostly because it might cause Cecily to shut down. Still, unless she had made great strides of power recently, he had to agree with the ghost. He didn't see how Cecily could think the Hulls were close to regaining anything. They had money, they had some control, but all the evidence he had seen — including the cases he had dealt with in the last few years — suggested she had a long road ahead. He had no doubt she had the tenacity to win, but he saw the finish line years away. Perhaps decades.

"What *enemies* are you referring to?" he asked.

"The Brotherhood of the Rising, Haven House, Sister Sadie, take your pick."

Big enemies, indeed. And all different. The Brotherhood sought to supplant witchcraft with ancient rites and power long forgotten — even by witches. Haven House was a strong coven led by three unnaturally old ladies who also ran a witchcraft library that probably held all the tomes the Brotherhood wanted. And Sister Sadie — the less Max thought about that insane witch, the better.

Cecily gestured outside. "I've even heard rumor that Madame Yan might be the cause. But we checked her home, and if she's back, she has not returned here."

"So, Madame Ti has been taken, and it could've been anybody. You fire everyone, hire your charming new assistant, and set up shop in this empty house."

Sandra said, "Now you want us to work the case because we're the only ones left you can trust."

"You could go to the police."

"Don't be stupid," Cecily said. "They have a hard enough time with a standard missing person's case. What are they going to do against witchcraft? Not that they'd believe it, anyway. Besides, I pay your retainer for a reason. Might as well get my money's worth."

"We can return those funds."

A dark spark lit in the recesses of her eyes. "Even if you don't need my money anymore, do not start thinking that you do not need me. I may not control all the witches in this state, but as a Hull, I do have plenty of power. Some of it a more mundane, political type of power that can make daily life difficult for you." Sitting straighter, she tapped at her keyboard for a second and her lips formed a malicious grin. "That's right. You have been hunting for offices again. Finally have the money to move into a real space instead of operating out of your kitchen. Well, one call from me, and you will find all real estate opportunities have vanished. Like magic. Nobody in North Carolina will be willing to buy, rent, lease, or even barter with you."

Max clenched his jaw. Clearly, she had fallen from the full power she once held, but how far? Could she really screw them over in finding a new office, and would she really be so petty? He wasn't sure about the former, but he had no doubts about the latter.

Before he could respond, Sandra leaned on his shoulder and whispered, "It won't hurt to look."

Drummond added, "Besides, if Hull is right — and really, who else but a witch would dare to kidnap Madame Ti — then we want to know about it. We need to be ready for whatever that means is coming."

Rising to his feet, Max glared at Cecily. Despite her disheveled appearance, she eased back in her chair, folded her hands, and returned his glare.

"Fine," Max said, sounding more like a petulant child than a seasoned investigator. "We'll look into this."

Chapter 3

LESS THAN AN HOUR LATER, they stood before the metal door that led to Madame Ti's hideaway beneath the city sewer system. Van Horn had attempted to accompany them, but Max insisted his presence would interfere with any paranormal energy they might pick up on. Utter horsecrap, but Cecily didn't argue the point. Perhaps she didn't know what she should about the world of ghosts and witches. Perhaps she suffered from too much stress and didn't see the upside of another fight. Either way (and possibly a few others), Van Horn stayed behind.

"This place," Sandra said, as they gazed at the empty shoe cubbies, "it's just as creepy as it was before."

"But somehow less at the same time," Max said.

"Maybe even a little more."

"Yet not so much."

"Are we fighting?"

"Not at all."

"Then what is this?"

"The place feels like both of us are right."

The only other time they had been here, they had been blindfolded and forced to come. Madame Ti had designed the entire experience of entering to impose a mystical, intimidating aura. Now, empty of her presence, a sense of danger abounded yet coupled with a general calm that left Max out of sorts. Like being in a horror movie, he kept walking through this empty room thinking a cat would jump-scare him at any moment.

"We're not taking off our shoes this time." Max didn't know why he said it. The words blurted out and echoed in the cavernous area.

Drummond said, "No point in waiting around, and you don't

have to knock this time. Let's get this over with."

Max wanted to point out that Drummond stalled like the best. After all, he could have passed through the wall at any moment yet remained back. But before Max spoke, Sandra yanked the metal door open and led the way.

The eerie emptiness continued. The main room consisted of a wide, domed shape — so wide, that in the dark, one could not make out the walls. But with their flashlights and three of four white candles mounted on long gold poles in the middle, Max and his team could see it all clearly. The thick, Turkish rugs that covered the cold concrete floor, the silk strips hanging around the central section of wide, colorful pillows, the extra-large, teal pillow with an indent from where Madame Ti dominated the room — all of it had lost the threat Max had expected while also acquiring a foreboding unease. Something bad hung over this room. Just not the evil witch Max had known it for.

Drummond drifted toward Madame Ti's perch. "No signs of struggle that I can see. I don't think this is where she was abducted."

Max said, "Unless they fixed it up after — to throw us off any trail they may have left behind."

"When you kidnap somebody, that person usually doesn't like it. They tend to be uncooperative. Doesn't leave much time for tidying up."

"They could've brought someone along to clean afterward."

"A post-abduction maid? Not likely."

Running his flashlight across one pillow then another, Max had to agree. Not one item looked out of place. Not one piece of fabric torn or disturbed. If Madame Ti had been attacked here, she didn't fight back at all — and that was not the witch he knew.

"We should call Osorio," Sandra said. "See if the police got any reports in the last week that match up with the abduction. If she was taken at a parking lot or in an alley, somebody may have said something."

Max tapped a note onto his phone to remind himself later.

"Look here." Sandra had found a closet door on the left side. It overflowed with stacks of old magazines and newspapers.

Sifting through Madame Ti's closet of treasures, Max found several old maps of Winston-Salem, a box of snow globes from around the world, a shelf of golf magazines, and two plastic containers filled with marbles and rubber bands. In the stark cast of the flashlight, these objects had a pale, clinical quality. They seemed like an improper display at a bizarre museum.

"Witches and their hoarding," he said. "I'm glad you haven't started that."

"There's still time."

"Don't even joke."

"I have been thinking about what to do with the kitchen alcove once your desk is no longer there. Might make a good place to stash stuff."

"If you do that, I'll be forced to paper the kitchen walls with photos of my mother."

"You wouldn't dare."

"She'd look at you every day."

"Okay, I give up. You win. I won't be a hoarding witch."

Max nudged her shoulder. "And people say a witch can't compromise."

"Don't push it, funny man."

"Hey, you two," Drummond called from the opposite side of the room. "If you're done playing at cutesy-banter, I've got something."

Max and Sandra hurried over, their steps sounding dull against all the thick rugs. Before they reached the ghost, Sandra pulled back. "Oh," she said.

"Oh, what?" Max asked.

With the tone of a plumber discovering a leak in the ceiling, Drummond pointed to a metal safe imbedded in the wall. "Wards. On all sides of this thing — so you can't just rip it out of the wall and go in from the back or the bottom."

"It's more than that," Sandra said. "There's a spell-lock on this safe, too. Maybe more than one. I can feel the energy pulsing in the air."

Max gave his wife's arm a squeeze. "Seems obvious that there's something important in there. Something Madame Ti didn't want others to have access to. You think you can crack it?"

"Do you really have to ask?"

He kissed her cheek. "You need anything?"

"Help me clear these rugs out of the way."

After they removed several Turkish rugs, Sandra lowered to her knees and opened her bag. Though she never traveled with a full supply of witchcraft paraphernalia, she always maintained the bare minimum required to cast most basic spells.

"Won't you need something stronger?" Max asked.

"Spell-locks are different than traditional spells. They tend to be a lot like locks on a bedroom door. Most only need the equivalent of a hairpin to pick open — a common item that has the correct shape. Same here. All the basics of witchcraft will give me what I need. It's up to me to figure out how to shape it so that it'll fit the lock and crack it open."

From her bag, she removed a thick piece of chalk and drew a casting circle on the concrete. She spent a few breaths observing the metal safe, then nodded. To Max: "This is going to be a lot of trial-and-error. I might get it in a few minutes, if I'm lucky, or it could take hours. You should keep searching. See if you can find anything else worth our time."

Max hesitated. Drummond must have noticed because he said, "C'mon, partner. Your wife is being too polite to say that she wants us out of her hair so she can concentrate. Let the lady do her work."

With a nod of his own, Max finally walked away. As he resumed the search of Madame Ti's abode, he couldn't stop from snatching glances in Sandra's direction — just to make sure. After all, they had dealt with all kinds of spells in the past. Protection spells on doors and buildings, for one, and they could be nasty things — vindictive, even. If Sandra uncovered something malicious, Max wanted to be ready to jump to her rescue.

But Sandra displayed no fear. Her expression reminded Max of the few times they put together a jigsaw puzzle — a determined level of focus as she hunted for the proper piece.

That eased the tense stiffness running through his back. A little.

He ambled toward the center of the room where Madame Ti's indented pillow rested next to a miniature desk — a serving tray mounted on four wooden legs no more than a few inches off the floor. Several papers cluttered the desk, and a closed laptop sat upon a manila folder. In the corner, a coffee mug — *World's Greatest Witch* had been painted on the side and a mouth-shaped stain marked the lip of the mug.

Sifting through the papers, two stood out. The first — an overdue notice on her credit card bill, maxed out at over ten thousand dollars. The second — a list of five names with dates next to each name. The dates spanned the last week and a couple marked the next two days. The names — Emily Dodson, Rosita Stakson, Michon Charee, Sung Park, and LaShanna Mill — meant nothing.

"Hey, Max," Drummond called from a doorway deeper in.

Pocketing the list, Max ambled across the office. He peeked at Sandra. She hunched over her casting circle, rubbing away several symbols before drawing new ones with controlled precision.

When he finally stepped through the doorway, he found Drummond hovering in the middle of a well-designed kitchen. White and gray tile, two chrome islands with deep sinks, a six-burner gas stove, a walk-in freezer, and an impressive array of knives — the room gleamed like the workspace of a professional chef. Or the television set of a celebrity.

Drummond floated near two storage cabinets that ran perpendicular to the wall. Max's neck and shoulders tensed. As he approached, he pictured Madame Ti's crumpled corpse rotting at the bottom of those cabinets. But when he reached out to open one, Drummond shook his head.

"Not that," he said. "Look behind them."

Max peered around the back edge of the cabinets. On the floor, he discovered a well-worn mattress with a head-stained pillow and several colorful blankets twined around each other. Between the mattress and the wall, a few personal items — toothbrush, nail file, eye drops — sat atop a paperback novel.

Cocking his head, Max read the title — *Bubba the Monster Hunter by John G. Hartness.* He didn't know the author, but the title made him snicker. That momentary amusement vanished as Max lifted his gaze to the row of multi-colored wigs hanging on nails in the wall.

"What was her name?" he said, picturing Madame Ti's assistant who changed personalities with each wig.

"Ruby. And did you catch that two wigs are missing?"

Max hadn't. But he saw it now — two empty nails on the far end near the corner. "So, Madame Ti *and* Ruby are missing."

"Ruby had time and mind to take two wigs. Probably not going to happen during an abduction. But her job is to take care of Madame Ti's needs, right? What would you do if your boss, one of the strongest witches alive, gets abducted under your nose?"

"Start looking for a new job — in a new country."

"But if you can't afford that, then you'd hide."

Max stared at the mattress and wigs a bit longer. "Do you remember her as particularly bright?"

"I remember her having plenty of space in her attic."

"Not the kind of mind that's going to logically work out her next steps, plan an escape, anything like that."

"More likely she'll go on instinct. I'd say first thing she'd do is run home, but it looks like this was home."

Surveying the kitchen, Max wondered if they would be lucky enough to find Ruby concealed behind a stack of plates in the cupboard. Drummond must have thought the same because, without prompting, he swished through the entire kitchen, sliding his ghostly head through all the cabinets, drawers, and cupboards. The walk-in, too.

"Not here," he said.

Max pulled out his phone. "Might as well go straight to the source. Ruby works for Madame Ti which means —"

"Ruby works for Cecily Hull."

After a few rings, Max heard a voice he had hoped to avoid — Van Horn. "What are you bothering us with, Mr. Porter?"

"I need to speak with Cecily. Right away." He had tried for

confident authority. He heard whiney brat.

Apparently, Van Horn heard it, too. "I am here to field her calls so that she may continue unimpeded in her important work."

"Did you forget about the whole *urgent* thing from earlier today? Clearly, Cecily thinks my task is important enough to send you hunting us down. Well, now we're doing the work, and I need her to answer a few questions."

"What are those questions?"

"That's between me and Cecily."

"Not if you wish to speak with her."

Max covered the phone, closed his eyes, and spit out a few choice words. With a deep breath, he recomposed and brought the phone back to his ear. One last effort: "I completely understand. You were hired to insulate her from daily reports and other such nonsense. You're like a firewall, and I salute you for it. Mustn't be an easy job. But in this case, you're obstructing us from doing the exact thing she hired us to do. I need some information —"

"If you would stop trying to get around me and simply say what you need to know, then perhaps I can help."

He glanced at Drummond. The ghost shrugged. "Fine," Max said. He explained about Ruby and that they needed to know if she had a place to live outside of the kitchen. An apartment or a house.

"Not that I am aware," Van Horn said. "However, if you will kindly wait, I shall consult our files." Four minutes later, he returned to the phone. "Our file on Ms. Ruby says that she had a cot and dresser in both of Madame Ti's offices."

"Both?"

"Certainly, you wouldn't expect the head witch of North Carolina to conduct all her business beneath the sewers. Plenty of meetings would find that counter-productive."

"Okay. We'll check the other office. Give me the address." When Max heard only silence, he bit back several choice comments and simply added, "Please."

Chapter 4

MADAME TI OWNED SEVERAL PROPERTIES throughout Winston-Salem including office space by Corpening Plaza. She also rented a private suite at the O. Henry Hotel in Greensboro, the former headquarters for Mother Hope and her witches, the Magi. But through Van Horn's lackluster description, he made it clear that Cecily Hull had recommended the least illustrious address — Maryland Avenue, a side road off East 5th Street. A simple house on a patch of land near the edge of the city. Only a few miles from Max and Sandra's home. A fact Max tried to ignore though it wriggled in the back of his head with recurring annoyance.

As a team, they had decided that Sandra needed to crack that spell-lock. She would be safe alone. Whoever took Madame Ti had already done all they intended in the office under the sewer. It made no sense that he or she would return.

"Besides, doll," Drummond said with a click of his tongue, "I've seen you fight. Nobody should mess with you."

Strolling up the brick-lined path to the small Maryland Avenue house, Max wished he had some of Sandra's power at his side. He had Drummond, of course, but the ghost's accurate point echoed in Max's head. Sandra was strong. A stronger witch than most realized. And they were tracking down a person or persons willing to abduct a witch even stronger than Sandra. To Max, that suggested destructive insanity in the culprit or devastating power. Either way, he had no desire to ring that doorbell without a good witch at his side.

"Relax," Drummond said as they stepped onto the porch.

"Look around you. This is a quiet neighborhood of people working hard to make a living. Nothing more. Not the kind of place Madame Ti would use to be casting spells or cursing enemies. She likes the moodiness of the sewer or the opulence that Hull money can buy her. This place — this must be like a guest house. When she has witches come from out-of-town and wants to give them some privacy."

"You really believe that?"

"Mostly. I'll tell you something I'm sure of, though. If Ruby is inside, she's cowering under a blanket or curled up on the couch watching television and drowning her fears in food and alcohol."

Max shivered. "Let's hope you're right." He rang the bell and, out of habit, knocked on the door. It pushed open. "Oh, crap."

"Stay here." Drummond flew through the wall into the house. Seconds later, he returned with his brow locked low. "She's alive, but be prepared — it's not good."

Max entered a home with a similar layout to his own, including a front door that opened into the living room. The curtains had been drawn closed, the furniture pushed aside, and the lights doused. A haze of incense fogged the room with its unique fragrance.

Ruby sat on her knees at the head of a large casting circle painted on the wood floor. Green and white candles ran the perimeter, their flames flickering the room in shadows and amber. If that had been the limit, Max would have questioned Drummond's assessment. After all, they had entered plenty of witch rooms with plenty of casting circles. But, of course, the situation did not stop there. Large, vertical strips of witch symbols had been painted on the curtains and walls. Where those strips reached the floor, they continued straight toward the casting circle. Three bowls filled with a thick liquid sat in the center of the circle. Probably blood. But worst of all — Ruby herself.

She wore a half-green/half-white wig, a black shirt, and black jeans. Even in the dim lighting, Max could see that every scrap of her skin had symbols drawn on it. Vertical lines of script in ancient languages covered her like terrifying tattoos. When she lifted her head, he saw those lines continued along her face as well.

"Close the door," she said with a slight accent as if she had spent years in a foreign boarding school. What country wasn't clear, but Max knew that with a different wig, Ruby could sound Southern, British, or any of dozens of other possibilities. The accent didn't bother him as much as the unnaturally deep tone.

As Max shut the door, Drummond said, "Keep her talking. See if you can get anything sane to come out of her mouth. I'll search around."

Ruby rubbed her hands over each other and on her knees as if trying to work out sore muscles. When she paused, however, her fingers tremored. "You're Mr. Porter," she said.

"That's right. Your boss's boss, Cecily Hull — she asked the Porter Agency to look into the disappearance of Madame Ti. You're aware she's missing?"

With a snorting laugh, she said, "Do you think I'd draw all of this on a whim?"

"Then you know who took her. I'm assuming this is all protection spells of one sort or another, and anybody bold enough to go after Madame Ti has got to know their way around a casting circle, so you must know who you're up against."

"They left me." She looked at her hands. "They left me."

"You were there?"

Drummond paused to glance back at them. "Press her on that."

"Of course, of course, I was. I'm always to be next to Madame Ti. Except now. When I'm not." She sniffled. "Except now. When she's … when she's been …" Her body quivered and short sobs escaped her mouth.

"If you help us, we can find her. We can stop those who are harming her."

Rolling her head back, she laughed — a languid sound, a drunken sound. "You can't do anything. You never could. I've watched you and your little wife poking around our world. You think you understand magic and witches and all we are, but you know nothing." She spit at his shoes. "Madame Ti is the kind of witch that unlocks all the secrets the world tries to hide. Madame Ti can change reality. Madame Ti is a real witch. And I serve her. I'm important to her. She needs me, and … and …"

"And they left you behind. They took her but didn't think you were necessary. I know what that's like — to be underestimated, unappreciated. When it comes from your enemies, sometimes it stings worse. Almost like you expect your friends to take you for granted, but your enemies — they should know best of all what you're capable of."

Max thought his little speech had worked. He swore he caught a spark of something behind her eyes. But then she let loose another long laugh.

"You know nothing."

"I won't argue with that, but I'm trying to understand. Tell me who you saw. Who snatched Madame Ti away but left you behind? The Brotherhood? Or maybe it was Sister Sadie?"

Ruby snapped her focus onto Max, and as she opened her mouth, Max's phone chimed — Sandra. He waited. Hoped that Ruby would speak, but she made a throaty clicking sound and shook her head.

Turning away, Max answered. "Tell me you've got good news."

"I broke the spell-lock. That's good, I guess," Sandra said.

"Then why don't I feel happy?"

"Because Madame Ti's safe was empty. All the things she would have put in there — the spellbooks, the artifacts, anything of value to a witch — it's all gone. Whoever took her knew exactly where to look and what to grab. We are definitely dealing with witches."

"Not the Brotherhood?"

"Not in the state we left them, and not with the limited knowledge they have. They were children playing with big guns. But this — well, think about that safe. Warded. Spell-locked. But most of all —"

"Empty."

"Exactly. Why would they go to the trouble of casting spell-locks and wards on something they knew was empty? Only one reason I can think of."

"Yeah. To stall us." Max caught Drummond watching closely, and the shared concern that bounced between them confirmed that the ghost had been able to hear the conversation clear enough. "We need to regroup. Take a step back and look at what we have before we go headstrong into whatever this is turning out to be."

"I'll pack up here and meet you back home. Be careful, hon." Sandra cut the call.

Pocketing the phone, Max glanced over his shoulder at Ruby. The witch symbols on her face, her wide-eyed fear, the shame of not being worth abducting — he thought he could push a little harder and get her to crack. All they needed from her was a name — a witch, a coven, a clue. Anything.

But before he could speak, Ruby said, "A war has begun." While the words sounded overly-dramatic, Max couldn't deny the prickling of his skin. With a smooth rocking motion, Ruby rose to her feet. "A war has begun, and you don't even see the tanks." She stepped over the candles and into the circle. "You stand in the middle of the battlefield oblivious that you are already dead." She reached symbol-covered arms out wide. "You're a ghost, but you don't know it yet."

Inching back, Max felt a ghost-chill across his back. Drummond had floated next to him. "Partner, I'm thinking you should leave now."

"Not a bad idea." Max moved for the door yet always keeping his eyes on Ruby. Never turning away.

With a full-throated roar, she said, "I will never fail you! I will always sacrifice for you!"

She swirled around the circle, knocking the three bowls over and followed up with each candle. As Max watched the liquid spread from the bowls across the floor, his mind noticed that it did not move like blood — far thinner and faster. Like a blue tongue snapping out, flames ignited upon the liquid, rushed across to the furniture and up the walls, devouring the room in fiery seconds. Thick curtains of smoke filled the ceiling, and

Max's brain finally registered the smell — gasoline. Not bowls of blood, but of gasoline.

"C'mon, move it," Drummond barked, his voice barely loud enough against the growing roar of the fire.

Intense heat pressed out as the flames turned the dark room painfully bright. Max yanked the door open — the knob already hot though the fire had yet to reach that wall. He took one step but stopped. "We can't leave her."

Ruby spun in the center of the casting circle with her head arched back and a bright smile reflecting the fire. Her wig had fallen to the floor, and her shaved head bore the markings that covered the rest of her.

Drummond said, "She ain't coming willingly. She wants this to happen. Might even be part of a spell."

But Max couldn't walk away from her. Suicide or ritual — it didn't matter. She didn't have to die.

"I've got to do something." He rushed into the inferno.

"Yeah," Drummond said. "Right with you."

Together they scurried into the blaze. Squinting against the flames, coughing against the smoke, Max found the small house had elongated as if in a nightmare. He saw her dancing in circles ahead, but the fire forced him to take careful steps so as not to fall through the disintegrating floorboards.

Ruby laughed when Max wrapped his arms around her waist and lifted her over his shoulder. No struggle. No fighting. That small blessing made the difference — and made Max wonder later if she ever truly intended to die here.

Turning toward the exit, he discovered his path blocked off. The outer-wall to the front of the house had become a blast of flames. The fire choked the air. Crackles and sputters of sparks flashed to the side. Max spun in one direction, then the other. Everywhere he looked, he saw orange and red and blinding yellows. His body soaked in sweat, his skin tightening under the heat.

Cooking. I'm cooking.

Drummond whipped around him, and the cold, ghostly air gave a small respite. Each time Drummond passed by, Max could grasp a breath. But it wasn't enough.

"Hang on," the ghost yelled. "Help's coming."

Drummond spun faster, trying to wave off the fire on all sides. But the hungry flames would not be satisfied. Max wouldn't last much longer — he could see that.

Ruby spread her arms like wings. "Make me a bird. Make me a phoenix."

A strange shape walked through the flaming walls and approached. Max pulled back, unsure if Ruby had summoned some creature of fire. But he heard a siren and noticed the figure put out a hand. A firefighter. He said something to Max and Max nodded and the man guided them out of the house. The cool air enveloped him with a welcome embrace. Somebody lifted Ruby off Max's shoulder. Somebody else walked Max to an ambulance.

"Tell Sandra I'm okay," he said. He must have said it a lot because one of the somebodies tried to quiet him down.

"Don't worry. I'll tell her." Drummond started to vanish but came back. With a flick of his hat, he said, "You did good in there. Saved a life tonight."

Max coughed until he spewed out a chunk of soot.

Chapter 5

FOR SEVERAL HOURS, Max told the story over and again. First, to the firefighters. Then to the EMTs. Finally, to the police. Each time, he stuck to the basic truth while avoiding the complete truth — that the Porter Agency had been hired for some private research, and that research brought them to this house for a visit with Ms. Ruby. She was distraught, babbling about witches, but Max did not believe she intended to kill herself. If any of the firefighters had been from the department the Porters had helped a few years back, things might have been more complicated. Although, even after facing ghosts in their stationhouse, they probably had dismissed the supernatural since then. Max kept the tale going that the fire had been an accident caused by too many candles and not enough common sense.

The various authorities swallowed the story. They had little choice. Ruby had been carted off to the hospital and was in no condition to talk. Max had the only story on offer, and even when Ruby could speak, Max knew the police wouldn't believe much of what she had to say. They barely believed him until one officer recognized Max from his television appearances.

Moments later, Max stood next the officer while a few selfies were taken. He tried to smile, tried to look in decent shape, but if he breathed too deeply, thick gobs of black goo shot up from his lungs. Thankfully, by the time he was permitted to go home, the worst of it had passed.

Drummond stayed with him through the drive back. He hovered in full-on mother hen mode until Max pulled into the driveway. After that, Sandra took over. She rushed out of the house, hugging Max fiercely while simultaneously threatening to kill him should he ever try to be a hero again. A few more minutes of hugs and kisses, threats and admonishment followed.

At length, Drummond said that Sandra could handle the idiot for the rest of the night. He had to get to the Other. "I've lost a lot of my contacts, but I can still find out a thing or two — especially news as big as anything about Madame Ti. If Ruby is right and a witch war has started, then Madame Ti may have been the trigger point, may have been the first casualty. If she's dead, murdered to start a war, I guarantee that witch will not have any interest in moving on. She'll be somewhere in the Other, and if that's the case, I'm the one who can find her."

When he disappeared, Max put his arm around Sandra, and they entered the house. "You really think that's the only reason he's going to the Other?"

With a shared grin, Sandra said, "I suspect Miss 1800s is still a factor."

Stopping in the kitchen, Max opened the refrigerator. As he reached for the wine, Sandra said, "Now?"

"Absolutely now."

"We have a case to work."

"We'll always have a case to work. Sometimes we'll be in a lot worse shape than some bad burns. Besides, it's our anniversary."

"It is not."

"Then a birthday or New Years. I don't care. I'm not waiting another year to be alone with you. Let's get drunk, fool around, and we'll start on the case fresh in the morning."

She paused. Max knew that pause well. She weighed out the possibilities and watched Max's reaction like a poker ace. He wondered if all wives learned that pause or if it was something unique between them. Well, he knew his part. He kept stoic. Even though she knew exactly what he wanted, he still put on a nonchalant air — partly out of pride, partly to limit any pressure she might feel, partly because that was the way they played the game.

With a grin, she rubbed his arm. "Go get the corkscrew." She sauntered into the hall, adding more sway to her hips than usual.

Once she slipped from view, Max dashed to the kitchen counter and yanked open the drawer. As he banged the various utensils aside in his search, he caught a whiff of charred wood coming off his clothes. Orange-red flames flashed in the corner of his eyes. He saw the blisters on the back of his hands.

Shaking his head, he pushed away those flickering images. He had been scared before — terrified, even — but that fire had been the closest to death he had ever come.

No. That's not true, he thought. After all, he had been turned into a ghost once, separated from his body, with no clear way back. Now that he thought about it, he had risked his life on numerous occasions — had come close to dying on several of them.

"I've been rattled by a few, too," he whispered.

He plucked the corkscrew from the drawer. Wine. Wine and Sandra and a life-affirming evening. That was what he needed to set his brain right.

But when he turned to get the wine, he caught a glimpse down the hall. Sandra stood in front of the Sandwich Boy's bedroom door. He walked up behind, careful not to startle her, and joined as she gazed in.

PB and J had outgrown the room. Small even for one young man, the two had shared the space for several years. Posters of cars covered the walls over PB's bed while J's side had an odd mixture of Beyonce, Babymetal, and Albert Einstein. PB's bed was a rumpled mess while J's had been made smooth and tight. Yet J's desk displayed piles of clutter and PB's — his was empty. Cleared out. Packed into boxes that had been stacked against the wall. His side of the closet had been emptied, too.

"I still can't believe he's leaving," she said.

Max placed the corkscrew in his pocket. "It seems like they just got here. At least, we have J for one more year. And it's not like we won't see them again. They'll come back to visit."

"I don't visit my family."

"You don't like your family. These boys love us." He nudged her shoulder until she faced him. "What's going on? A little empty nest feeling or what?"

She shrugged. "Maybe. Or maybe PB's not ready to go off on his own. Maybe we haven't done a good enough job and —"

"Honey, he lived on his own long before he met us. He'll be fine."

"But he's such a part of our life. How can you be okay with this?"

"I'm not, but I don't see that it's our choice. He's an adult now. It's right for him to move on."

Her eyes flared. "Bad choice of words."

"Sorry. How about — it's right for him to head out on his own?"

"Better."

"Besides, at its best, life provides balance, stability. After J leaves, our lives will become less hectic, less unpredictable. It might feel a little bumpy at first, building new routines and such, but in the end, we'll find our peace. After all, we've got us."

"I know all that. I do. But it seems like it'll be so quiet. So lonely."

"We won't be alone for long. My mother will insist on moving in."

Sandra's eyes flared wider. "I'll kill her first."

With a laugh, Max pulled her into a long hug. When they stepped back, however, Sandra did not let go. She looked into his eyes, and electricity built between them.

The kiss that followed tasted of fear and longing, need and desire, tension and hope. Between their lips, Max found their early-days of fumbling romance, their constant-present of snatched moments, and their unseen-future of quiet comfort. She was all of it to him.

He placed his hand on the small of her back. "I love you," he said.

"Of course, you do. I'm quite lovable." She kissed him again as she made a gentle purr. "In case you're in doubt — I love you, too."

Max's phone rang. He tamped down the urge to rail against the universe and simply let his head droop. Sandra kissed his forehead and tutted as she stroked his back.

"Stop that. I'm not a baby." He fished out his phone. "Just disappointed." But when he saw the caller ID, all teasing flowed out like a receding tide. Osorio.

"Hey, boss," Osorio said, the rumble of the police station in the background. "I've got something y'all need to see."

Setting the phone on speaker so that Sandra could hear, too, Max said, "Since you're calling us this late at night, I'm guessing it's important."

"Maybe. I'm hoping it's all a show, a costume more than the real thing, but by the look of the place, I figured it'd be best to get you there right away."

"*Right away* as in tonight?"

"I can't exactly walk you onto a crime scene in broad daylight. If I didn't lose my job, I'd be a laughingstock for years. Maybe forever."

"Crime scene? What exactly do you have going on there?"

Osorio hesitated, and in a lower voice, one clearly meant to hide his words from his fellow detectives, he said, "A dead witch."

Chapter 6

DISPLEASURE AND INQUISITIVENESS spun circles in Max's brain during the drive across town. Most people had gone to sleep leaving the roads open — a good thing since recent events had sapped his concentration. If he wasn't thinking about his fumbled attempt at romance, if he wasn't thinking about Ruby nearly burning to death and taking him along for the ride, then he thought about the quake in Osorio's voice. That man had endured a lot since meeting the Porters. Most notably, his hand had been cursed to destroy nearly all it touched. Now, what would have been the case of a murdered woman with an interest in the occult — interesting but not unique — took on a new range of possibilities. Ones that meant calling the Porter Agency.

Nestled amongst a line of lower-middle class homes, Max found the address — a house that had been used for both living and work. A sign out front read *Ms. Jennie's Hairdresser.* He parked on the street, and with Sandra at his side, they met Osorio near the yellow-taped entrance.

"Sorry to bring you out so late," the police detective said, adjusting the shoulder strap of his leather satchel. His brown slacks and white shirt bore the rumpled lines of a long day, and the bags under his eyes fared no better, yet he managed a warm smile. "I have to admit, despite the few things I've already seen with you two, this stuff still bothers me."

"That's good," Max said. "It bothers us, too. The time to really be afraid is when you start getting complacent about it all."

Gesturing to the house, Osorio said, "We'll have to go around back. A murder on a quiet street like this gets noticed. I wouldn't be surprised if a few gossipy types or night owls are sneaking peeks at us right now."

"Can we wait?" Sandra said. "Drummond's not here yet."

Osorio shifted from one foot to the other on the dark, cold street. "I didn't realize that he would be coming, too."

"You'll get use to him. I mean, just because you can't see him or hear him, doesn't mean you can't know he's around. You'll feel the cold spots, at the least."

"It's okay with me if I never feel him. I'm not eager to start seeing ghosts like you. Not all of them or just one of them or anything." He raised his leather-gloved hand. "This was enough." He always wore it to protect those he loved, but it was a hefty price to learn the reality of magic, witches, and worst of all, curses.

"I haven't given up on that. One thing about magic — anything that it can create, other magic can undo. I'm still searching, but I will find a spell to break that curse on you."

Whether Osorio believed her or not, Max knew she had spoken the truth. But, of course, he had a front row seat watching her put in the work. Between cases, she often spent time scouring the online witch community, sending out feelers, reviewing old chat threads, and even sifting through old archives reaching back to the early BBS days of the internet. At the same time, she had handwritten requests to various occult bookstores dotted throughout the world — ones that handled legitimate witch tomes. They all were on the alert to notify her of any titles that might help with such an ancient, botched curse.

"Don't worry," Max said. "When Sandra gets determined about a thing, you can't stop her. And she's very determined to help you."

Osorio quivered a smile, but his eyes darted back to the hairdresser's place. He swallowed hard as he watched the building.

"Is it that bad in there?"

"It was." Osorio rubbed his gloved hand. "Wait here."

As Max watched the man fast-walk back to his car, the air chilled behind him, and the familiar tones of a ghost detective said, "What are we standing around for?"

"Osorio forgot something," Sandra said.

"Well, I don't have to wait. I can search the whole house before you even reach the front door."

"We're going through the back, and you should wait, too."

"Why? Usually, Max loves sending me into danger ahead of him."

"Very funny," Max said, turning toward Drummond. The icy visage facing back held no amusement. "What's the matter? You look —"

"How? How exactly do I look?"

Max choked down his comment and glanced at Sandra. She shrugged.

"Everything okay in the Other?" she said.

"Peachy. Madame Ti is not around messing with the afterlife, and no word about her, either."

"That's not what I meant."

Drummond cinched his coat lapels up and lowered his hat. "There's nothing else in the Other worth talking about."

Osorio returned with a file folder in his hand. "I see you two talking with thin air, so I'm guessing the undead member of our team is here."

"Tell him to watch his mouth," Drummond said. "The term *undead* is frowned upon."

Gesturing for Osorio to lead the way, Max said, "He's here. He's also in a mood, so I'd be careful with what you say."

Without another word — though several uneasy glances did occur — Osorio guided them to the backyard and up to a laundry room entrance. From the outside, the house did not project any sense of horror, murder, or witchcraft. Rather, it looked much like the others on the street — a simple, one-story home, painted tan with black trim, more wide than deep, with a waist-high chain-link fence around a shabby yard. The back of the building continued the same. Stepping into the laundry room, however, changed everything.

Though the narrow room looked like any small laundry dominated by a washer and dryer, Max winced at the stench of decay and the lingering odor of long dead candles. Witch candles. Wax laced with incense, herbs, and other items he didn't want to consider.

"In here," Osorio said, leading them into the connecting kitchen.

Drummond straightened as he drifted aside. "Damn. We've seen this before."

Indeed, one look and Max's stomach twisted. The entire kitchen — floors, walls, cabinets, ceiling — had been covered in symbols that converged on a casting circle in the center of the room. A ring of black and red candles surrounded the circle. Most had melted to the floor. The notable difference from Ruby's display — the thick bloodstain marring the center.

As Sandra grabbed photos on her phone, Max and Drummond stuck to the back corner and watched. In color, the dark splotch on the floor looked more like burnt linoleum than blood. In pattern, it looked more like spilled paint. But the emotion of the stain — if such a thing could have an emotion — screamed rage. The witch that died for this spell did not do so willingly.

"You think that was Madame Ti?" Max said, keeping his eyes on the crime scene.

Drummond said, "Does it really matter? It's one less witch in the world."

"You are full of charm tonight."

"Sorry I can't put on a show of smiles all the time. Y'know, just because I'm dead doesn't mean I can't have a bad day. Let's finish this up. I've got places to be."

Osorio opened his folder. "The body was discovered after a call came into headquarters on a noise complaint. We sent a patrol unit over, and by the time they arrived, they found the house much like we did outside — dark, abandoned. One of the officers was bothered enough by the inconsistency — a noise complaint where nobody was and no immediate evidence that there had been anything going on — that she suggested they inspect the surroundings before knocking on the door. Looking for probable cause to enter without a warrant, most likely. Eager officer crap, but in this case, a good instinct."

"What got them inside?" Drummond asked, and Max relayed the question.

"When they came around back, they saw a flash of light. Described it as *'similar to a muzzle flare but no sound.'* They figured it was enough and readied to barrel down the door. But before they did that, the lead officer followed her good instincts once more and tried the doorknob. Laundry room entrance was unlocked. They came in and found this. Well, more than this. Take a look."

One by one, Osorio pulled photos from the file and handed them to Max and Sandra. Each one more gruesome than the last, they showed the victim in blood-soaked detail. A woman, nude except for a black cloak, with her wrists tied behind her back and her feet bound with coarse rope. She had been placed in the center of the casting circle, and the witch symbols continued onto her skin. But where Ruby had drawn them down her own face, this witch had no available surface on her face. Her facial skin had been removed — with skill, judging from the fine edges near the scalp. But she still bore the witch symbols on her body. They had been carved into the arms and legs. Everywhere. Presumably, the chest, too, but Max couldn't tell for sure because of the most horrifying detail.

The witch's chest had been cut apart. Ripped open. The sternum sawn through and the ribs separated out.

The last photo displayed a close-up of the victim's opened chest. No heart. Just a gaping hole where the organ should have been.

Osorio said, "We have no idea who she was. With all the physical damage, we'll be looking at dental records. That can take time, and if this was done by a real witch and not a nutjob pretending to be a witch —"

"Definitely a real witch," Max said.

"That's why I wanted you to see it. Confirm what I suspected." Osorio crossed his arms and stared at the bloodstain. "We won't find any record of her, will we?"

"I doubt it."

Drummond said, "I've never seen anything like that. Not in all my years alive or dead. What about you, doll? This any kind of witchcraft you know?"

Sandra shook her head, her mouth held firmly closed. After she handed the last photo back, she said, "I don't know why any witch would do this. Not yet, anyway."

"Yeah," Max said for Osorio's benefit. "We've started a case that is clearly tied to this one."

Sputtering, Osorio said, "We're going to get a call about another body like this?"

"I hope not. But we have a missing witch and a spell that looks a lot like this."

"You think the dead witch is your witch?"

Max stared at the dark bloodstain and saw the crime scene photographs in his mind. For Madame Ti's sake, he hoped this had not been the end for her. He had given the idea of dying more serious thought in the last several years. Heck, the last several hours. Watching people die from curses or attempting magic, watching ghosts locked in the pain of their deaths, watching his mother suffer from a disease with no cure — it all left him wondering about his eventual death. In his line of work, the odds of that death being an appalling act of vengeance against him, Sandra, or the Porter Agency grew exponentially. But this — what was done to this witch — a truly horrendous way to go. Not even Madame Ti deserved that.

Drummond said, "We need to leave."

Locked in his own thoughts, Max barely heard the ghost. But Sandra's question brought him back.

She asked Osorio, "What about the body? Can we see it?"

"Sorry, no. This isn't like on tv." Osorio readjusted his satchel and stood quiet, but Sandra's unending stare got him to add, "The victim's body is in the morgue at Forsyth Medical. But you won't be permitted access, and it's not like you've seen on shows where you can just bribe one person and you're in. It's a small room but there's a lot of checks and double-checks going on. Nobody wants to have a body go missing."

"I'll ignore the patronizing tone and remind you that we're on the same team."

Drummond said, "Good point. We're all on the same team, and right now, this member of the team is saying to pack up and go. I'm feeling something."

With an abashed gaze downward, Osorio said, "I didn't mean to sound like that. Truly. I'm just — this place, it — it's unsettling."

Softer, Sandra said, "I forget how new this is to you."

Max said, "Since we can't go into the morgue easily, can you find out when they'll release the body?"

"And who'll pick it up? That'd be important, too."

Osorio shook his head. "I can try, but unidentified cases like this, we have nobody to contact. Unless a person shows up to say this woman was their mother or wife or such, we won't have anybody to release the body to."

"And then?"

"Cremation usually."

"This is all thrilling," Drummond said, "but I'm feeling something strange. You have to stop being idiots and go."

Max whirled towards his partner. "Look, you've been miserable since you got here, and you seem determined to go on being miserable. I don't know what happened in the Other, but—"

"He's right," Sandra said. Her eyes scanned the room as her mouth turned into a formidable line. "I can't see anything, but I feel it, too. Like pressure in the air."

"It's her," Drummond said. "She's coming back."

"Wait, wait, wait," Max said. "Why would she come back? Assuming she didn't move on, or couldn't move on, wouldn't she go after those who hurt her?"

"Look at what was done to her," Sandra said. "That's not pleasant magic. That's a curse. It has to be."

"Which means she's probably tethered to this spot."

"Tethered?" Osorio asked.

As Sandra explained, Max stepped closer to the circle. He frowned — long enough that Drummond took notice.

"Partner? What are you thinking?"

"I'm not sure." Max tapped his chin. "When I first met you, first could see you, it was because I broke the casting circle that bound you. Maybe if we break this one, we'll free the witch, too."

"Why would we want that?"

"Better than having her come here."

"No!" Sandra called out, but Max had already dragged his foot across the circle.

Nothing happened.

With a sheepish grin, he said, "Worth a try. I figured 50/50 chance that might help."

"But that's a 50/50 chance it might go bad, too. You had no right to do that without talking it over. We're all in this room. We all deserve a say."

As Sandra raised her hand to rest on her hip, as Max realized he screwed up getting lost in his thoughts and then acting on those thoughts, as Sandra tried to assess if Max's rash act had caused any problems, as Max hoped to repair any damage he had done to the inner-workings of the team, Drummond said two words that froze them all into place.

"She's here."

Chapter 7

NOBODY MOVED. Three human statues and a ghostly echo of a statue. The air stilled. Max listened for anything that would signify the arrival of a ghost witch. His heightened alertness fed into Osorio's awareness. At least, Max thought as much. He recognized that Osorio could simply be reacting off the man's police training, but Max, Sandra, and Drummond were the experts here. The detective would follow their lead should something occur.

"You sure about that feeling?" Max said, a bit too much condescension coloring his words.

Drummond kept his focus outward. "Your wife felt it, too."

"Be quiet," Sandra said. "Both of you."

"All I'm saying is that you and I feel that witch's presence, even if we can't see her. She's newly dead. Probably a bit confused considering all she's been through. We're lucky she ain't a poltergeist ripping the walls to shreds. Plus, your genius husband disrupted the circle. No telling what that did to her."

"Really?" Max said. "You're going there?"

"Breaking a circle without knowing what it'll do is not smart."

"You'd still be bound to the old office, if I didn't break your circle."

"Maybe that would have been better. Look, I can feel that witch and so can Sandra. Okay? The witch is here. Somewhere. I know it like a gut feeling."

"You don't have a gut."

Osorio pulled out his service pistol. "What's going on? What's Drummond saying that's got you being so pissy?"

"Put that away," Sandra said. "You can't shoot a ghost, and you're more likely to get one of us killed."

He considered for a moment before holstering the weapon. "Tell me what we can do, and I'll be happy to —"

The room temperature dropped. The windows frosted, the sink glistened with ice, and Max saw his breath smoking with each exhalation. The sharp change prickled his skin and froze the mucous in his nose.

"What now?" Osorio said, his voice mere mist.

In answer, Max lifted off the floor and flew back into the wall. A pinned calendar dropped loose, and the others spread out on instinct. Max hit the ground with a hard grunt.

Rubbing his back, he said, "Why am I always first to get attacked?"

"Guess you've got one of those faces." Even as Drummond spoke, he positioned towards the casting circle, his arms up and his fists ready. "Look, lady, we're here to help you. Tell us what happened and maybe we can free you from this curse. Send you on your way. You understand? Move on to a better afterlife."

Sandra hurried to the laundry room, pulling out her chalk as she peeked back at Drummond and the ghost witch. "You know what to do," she said as she passed Max.

When she lowered to her knees and started drawing her own casting circle, Osorio looked to Max. "What exactly do we know to do?"

"Stall," Max said. "Buy her as much time as we can."

Drummond tried a winning smile. "Sweetheart, you've been through a lot. If you'll stop all that hissing, maybe we can talk. That sound okay?"

A pause.

"What's Drummond saying? What's the victim saying?" Osorio's voice grew louder than necessary.

Max couldn't hear the ghost witch, either, but he could see Drummond's face. The careful smile dropped fast as the eyes widened. Drummond tried to dodge sideways, but his body contorted at the flank. Max watched as the witch appeared to tackle Drummond through the floor.

"He's gone," Max said.

"What? He left us?" Osorio clutched his satchel.

"No. She attacked him, and —" Max jumped back as Drummond raced into the kitchen, shooting upward with rocket speed until he disappeared into the ceiling. "Looks like he's fighting back."

Max needed to find something for him and Osorio to do. Not only to help the situation, but to make sure Osorio stayed focused, didn't panic. No amount of professional policework would prepare him for ghosts and witches.

Scanning the floor, looking at the symbols and lines, Max thought over all the curses they had dealt with in the past. They often had candles and ghosts and … "The tether!"

Osorio didn't startle. Good. Perhaps the old detective had found his internal footing again.

Rushing toward the circle, Max went on, "This curse, this spell, whatever this is — it should operate like a tether to this ghost. At least, that's what we call it. But it's not doing that."

"Isn't it? She's here, right?"

"Yeah, but I broke the circle, and your people took the body away. I'm hardly an expert in curses, but I've dealt with a bunch."

The dishes in the cabinets clattered as Drummond soared backwards through the wall. When he stopped, he rubbed his jaw, rolled his shoulders, and stomped back, cracking his knuckles.

"This doesn't add up." Max snapped his fingers toward the cabinets. "I could be wrong. Even Drummond remained tethered after I broke his circle, but we've got to try."

"I don't care what it is. Doing something that might help is better than doing nothing."

"It's possible she's tethered to a different object in the kitchen. Check the dishes, the utensils, glasses, everything. If it's got witch symbols on it, then it's what we want."

The two men rushed to the kitchen counter and yanked open several drawers. Even as he hastened through the task, Osorio said, "We're destroying this crime scene. Contaminating all the evidence."

"Don't worry about your kind of evidence. A case like this will never get to trial."

Max licked his frosty lips as another breath shuddered from his lungs. Tossing a serving spoon over his shoulder and a soup ladle off to the side, his brain raced to find a solution. What he knew of tethers, what he had experienced, suggested this had a slim chance of working. But the violence behind ripping that witch's heart out could not be misconstrued. Ruby was right. A war brewed, and it would certainly escalate. With all other options looking bad, Max figured best to go for the tether. It offered, at least, a slim chance. Better than nothing.

Thinking about it, maybe none of them were ready for a case like this.

Drummond strode through the outside wall, rolling his neck. "You've put up a good fight, but know when you're beat. Stay down and start talking."

Max put out his hand to stop Osorio's search. "I think we're done here. Looks like Drummond's got control."

But Drummond's tie lifted off his chest and tightened straight out. Under the control of an unseen hand, the thick end looped and twisted, curling around an unseen fist. Drummond's head rocked back from a succession of jabs. He blocked two and managed to retaliate, but a body blow sent him reeling across the kitchen floor. He smashed into the wall — not through it, into it.

Osorio jumped at the sudden dents appearing in the drywall. Drummond screamed as his body touched the corporeal world.

"How the heck did she do that?" Max said.

Struggling to free himself from the wall, Drummond said, "She's going for Sandra."

Max dashed towards his wife. Though deep in the concentration of her spell, she must have heard her name. She looked up. The dryer door swung open and clapped her across the forehead.

"Hey!" Max jabbed a finger at where he thought the witch hovered. But before he could utter anything more, stabs of ice dug into his chest and thrust him upward. He hit the ceiling, seemed to float for a second, and flailed on his return to the floor.

Smacking the linoleum, his body jinked to the side as he reflexed into a ball. Coughing spit as he tried to get a full breath of air, Max spotted Sandra sitting with her back against the washer, rubbing her bleeding forehead. Her spell — abandoned. Drummond floated in the air, but he weaved with a dazed expression. And Osorio —

From the very first case, and on a few times since, Max had suffered the horror and awe of having a ghost put its hand into his head. He watched that mixed expression form upon Osorio's face. The old cop had dropped to his knees and his eyes locked wide open. As long as the dead witch kept her hand connected to his head, Osorio would see the ghostly realm. He could see Drummond and the ghost witch. He would feel the biting chill of death — a level of bitter cold that would freeze the marrow in his bones. Witnessing it, Max recalled all the pain, the terror, the shock, and amazement that passed through his mind when he had lived through the experience.

Moving slow, wincing at the pain, Osorio's hands reached behind him. Probably going for his gun — not that it would help. Max wished he could do something, spare Osorio, but without Sandra's spell or Drummond's awareness, they were helpless. He considered tackling Osorio, but if that even worked — if it didn't kill the man from the sudden separation — the witch would only attack again.

Screaming, Osorio whipped his arm around. But he held no gun. He held nothing. All he had was his hand — ungloved.

He thrust his bare hand forward, the fingers splayed out, and his pain-drenched scream turned into a victorious roar. He stumbled to his feet, pushing his hand toward the floor. Max spotted a pale blue outline around Osorio's fingers. And when those fingers clenched into a fist, that outline flashed.

The smell of ozone infiltrated the air like the moments after a heavy thunderstorm. Osorio wobbled backwards until he hit the kitchen counter. Wiping at his sweat, he shivered. "She's gone."

"Sandra?" Max called out.

"I'm okay."

"Drummond?"

"My pride is bruised, but I'm fine, partner. No sign of that witch anymore. And I don't mean she escaped. He destroyed her. I'm not sure there's anything left of her to move on now."

Back on his feet, trying not to fall from the head rush, Max looked straight over at Osorio. "You okay?"

"I will be."

"That was incredible. I had no idea you could do that."

Osorio slipped his glove back on as he gazed around the wrecked kitchen. "Me, neither. We need to get out of here. If anybody reported the noise, the police will come. It'll be hard enough explaining what I'm doing here, but I really don't want to have to explain you." He took three steps forward and had to grab Max by the shoulder before he fell over. "And I could use a drink."

Chapter 8

WHEN THEY RETURNED TO THE PORTER HOME, they dropped into the living room like miners hitting a bar after a long, dark day. Sandra collapsed on the couch, stretching her legs across the cushions. Osorio flopped into his usual chair on the other side of the low coffee table. Max and Drummond couldn't sit, though — one because adrenaline still had him buzzing; the other because death still had him floating. Both man and ghost paced about the room, their thoughts whirring from one possible explanation to another.

"This wasn't a simple curse," Max said.

"Obviously," Sandra said. "Please get me some ice."

"And that drink," Osorio added.

When Max returned from the kitchen, he had wrapped ice in a towel for Sandra's head and sunk ice in a glass for Osorio. From the bookshelf, he pulled down Drummond's old copy of *Moby Dick,* the one hollowed out to hold the ghost detective's flask of whiskey, and filled the glass.

After downing the drink and sliding his satchel to the floor, Osorio leaned his head back. His body slumped in the chair. "I'll take another, if you don't mind."

While Max poured a second round, Osorio went on, "That was the worst thing I've ever seen. Even on that first case with the Brotherhood of the Rising and getting my hand cursed — that had a worse outcome for me, but it was nothing like this." He took the second drink and finished half of it in one gulp.

Drummond said, "At least he knows what I look like now."

Max relayed the attempt at humor. Osorio acknowledged it

with a passing grin, but his lips could not hold the amusement. The ice clinked in his unsteady hand.

"I did see our ghost, but I also saw her. I'm not ashamed to admit this — she was terrifying."

"Hey," Drummond said, crossing his arms. "I can be pretty terrifying, too. Tell him that."

"I know," Max said, topping off Osorio's glass. "I've been there before. I've felt the cold of a ghost's hand in my head and seen their world. The good news is that you held your own. Most people would have run. Even a brave police officer with years of training and more years of street experience would probably have run. But you stayed. It's proof that you belong here."

"I don't feel all that brave, but thanks for saying it."

Sandra propped her head against a couch pillow. "What did you see when you touched her?"

"A lot of light. Like sparks of energy."

Drummond said, "He's underselling it. It was a hellish fireworks display, and she shrieked through the whole thing. Did not look like a good way to die. Especially since she was dying a second time around."

Max walked a small circuit between the front door and the television. "At least we know that Madame Ti wasn't the one with her heart ripped out. It's not much, but it's more than we had when we started."

"We know more than that." Sandra sat up a little and set her laptop on her belly. "Both Ruby and this witch had similar spells written. I've never seen somebody write a spell stretching out of a casting circle like that."

"Looked like madness to me," Drummond said.

"Didn't seem right in the head," Osorio said.

Already tapping at her keyboard, Sandra went on, "For one of them, sure. Drawing symbols all over the room and on your face, that's crazy stuff. But both of them? That had purpose. Considering how odd those spells looked, I can't imagine it'll be too hard to find information about them."

Even a sniff of research perked awake Max's tired mind. "Maybe. But it could be the opposite, too. Could be very hard to find anything because it's so obscure. It's obviously not basic knowledge or even advanced knowledge. If it was, you'd already know it."

"Thanks for the pep talk."

"I don't mean it like that. I'm only saying —"

"Don't get my hopes up for an answer from a quick Google search. I understand."

Osorio pulled the case file from his satchel and flipped through the paperwork. "We have no ID on the body, and I gather we won't ever have one. We've got a house that isn't owned by anybody — in fact, the bank has been trying to unload the place for nearly two years. We've got some crazy occultists. I know they're more than that, but I can't put that into the file, and after the mess we made of the crime scene, somebody needs to put in a plausible explanation." He jotted down a note and packed up. "Thanks for the drink."

"You're going?" Max said. "I thought we'd be discussing the case and how to proceed."

"It's already tomorrow, I'm tired, and I killed a ghost witch tonight. That's enough for me. Besides, I've got to work in about five hours. If any news comes by my desk, I'll call you. Until then, I don't see how there's much I can do."

With that, he shuffled out to his car and drove off. Drummond tipped his hat back and pursed his lips. "The man ain't wrong. Not much we can get done now. You all could use some sleep, and that'll give me time to check out the Other some more. Maybe I can turn loose a stone that'll help us out."

"Right." Max checked his desire to snicker.

If Drummond noticed, he let it go. Instead, he said good night and disappeared. Sandra waved one hand yet never lifted her head from the laptop.

Not wanting to disturb her concentration, Max tried to be quiet as he cleaned up. Quiet. That word felt weird in his mouth. With only the two of them in the house, the level of quiet had compounded. All the little noises brought on by two young men living under the same roof — their music, their gaming, their video chats, or the simply sounds of them talking with each other

— all of it had gone. The void left behind filled in with quiet. So much that the ringing of glasses bumping each other as he carried them to the kitchen or the soft clatter of Sandra's keyboard — sounds that should have blended into the white noise of daily existence — amplified in the sudden emptiness.

Max shook off the thoughts he glimpsed ahead. They still had PB for a few more months, and J would be with them for another year. That gave Max plenty of time to get comfortable with the weird quiet that would grow in here. And it could be comfortable. That silence meant stability. The chaos of having teens in the house would be gone, and while he would miss the Sandwich Boys, he wouldn't mind the renewed peace.

He opened the refrigerator. His eyes rested on that bottle of wine. Not only peace, then, but also privacy. He grabbed the bottle and sauntered back toward the living room.

"My love," he said, waggling the wine in one hand. "There will be plenty of time tomorrow to do research. We should take advantage of the few hours we have here, get drunk, and enjoy being together. What do you say?"

She said nothing. With her fingers on the keyboard and her head lolling back at an awkward angle, she snored like a dog with a cold.

Max sighed. "We can't catch a break."

Chapter 9

WHEN MORNING ARRIVED, Max discovered Sandra had already brewed coffee, had already drunk a full cup, and had already set up in the living room to continue researching spells. She muttered a few good morning phrases and accepted a kiss on the cheek, but her myopic focus held little room for anybody else. Max took no offence. He did the same when speeding on the research highway.

Drummond arrived a few minutes later. Seeing Sandra at work, he waved Max to the bedroom. He had a satisfied expression, and though loathe to ask, Max couldn't help himself. "Everything work out in the Other?"

The ghost's scowl made a brief return. "Don't worry about that."

"Then what's got you acting chipper?"

"Partner, you've got to learn that each new day is a new opportunity — to right a wrong, to find the lost, and to solve a case."

"You know where Madame Ti is?"

"Not at all." He flicked the brim of his hat. "But I spent a few hours thinking over everything, and you know what I realized? We made a rookie mistake from the start. We know better than to trust Cecily Hull — or any Hull."

Max wanted to agree — would have done so most days — but he recalled Cecily's shaken appearance and attitude. She could fake a lot, but Max didn't think she could give an Oscar-winning performance like that. "You think she's lying?"

"Not directly. Madame Ti has been taken. Ruby and the dead witch show us that it's all part of something bigger. Cecily Hull making lies of omission — that would be quite possible."

"About what, though?"

"Well, that's what we've got to find out. Get dressed and we'll pay a visit to Ms. Hull. I'm sure she would appreciate a progress report, or at least buy that as a reason for showing up. We'll really be there to get some answers."

Max rubbed his face. "I'm going to need more coffee."

When he called to set up the meeting, Van Horn answered. He handled everything, agreeing to an appointment in two hours at Cecily's old office. That left Max with more questions as he drove off.

Just as the city of Winston-Salem changed over the years, so had Cecily Hull's office. The city had improved, however, whereas the Hull offices looked in decline. Though still located in the heart of downtown, the building had given up on the security measures it once boasted. The cameras remained, but they did not appear to be operating. Most notably, all the guards were gone. Drummond's continued presence spoke to a lack of wards, as well.

When they entered the lobby, they found Van Horn waiting in the center of the echoing space. Dressed in a grey suit and rocking on his fine loafers, he exuded the casual impatience of a man unaccustomed to being the greeter. Max bit back the Wal-Mart wisecracks that flooded his mind.

"Ms. Hull is expecting you. Follow me." Van Horn's deep voice rumbled each word with blatant derision.

"Oh, don't worry, I know the way. Been here before."

Van Horn glowered at Max. "You will follow me."

"Right. Then lead on."

Drummond said, "Don't screw with him. We might get more info out of this ten-foot lug than Hull."

As they stepped into the elevator and Van Horn pressed the penthouse button, Max tried to reclaim some ground. "Must be hard starting out work for Ms. Hull when everything has turned so crazy. It's not usually like this."

"These are difficult circumstance. Ms. Hull's decision to fire her entire staff could be seen as paranoia, but I think she is brave and strong-willed. She insists on continuing her work and not being afraid. Until her new office is ready and this chaos has passed, she is wise to alleviate potential threats."

"You say that like you're thinking I'm one of those threats."

Van Horn lifted an eyebrow at Max.

"Oh, come on, you can't possibly put me in the same category as all of the witches and such that your employer deals with. I'm a mosquito, a little itch, that's all."

The elevator stopped, but Van Horn held the door as he loomed over Max. "I take my job seriously. When hired, I did my research into all of Ms. Hull's business associates. You and your wife are hardly little itches. You are responsible for the Hull family's loss in stature. You are connected to the demise of several covens and a few well-respected witches. The fact that Ms. Hull used you to regain some of her family power is the only reason I am willing to deal with you in such a pleasant manner. But I'd be more than happy to break all your bones and grind them up for Ms. Hull to display in a tasteful vase."

Max reached up and patted Van Horn's arm. Firm arm. More muscle than he expected. "Good talk."

"I'm still here." Drummond emerged from the wall. "I'll freeze his head if he tries anything."

Van Horn led the way down a narrow, carpeted hall with deep red paint and several cameras covering the entire passage. Those cameras operated fine. When they reached the end, he opened a heavy wood door and gestured for Max to step inside.

The room — once an ostentatious display of wealth and power — had been gutted. It looked more like a building under construction than a well-used office space. The carpeting had been ripped out, leaving the hard concrete beneath. The walls had been stripped of every painting, molding, and lighting fixture. Wires hung loose out of rough holes. Even Cecily's desk had been removed — replaced with a wide piece of plywood set over two sawhorses.

In fact, only Cecily herself had not changed. "Welcome to the last days of this office," she said, sitting on the only chair in the room with her usual stiffness.

"Why are you even here?" Max said. "For safety and comfort, wouldn't you be better off working from your garage office?"

"That was a temporary space used for that meeting. I must keep things moving. But I refuse to let a bunch of witches bully me into anything. I have a real office being prepared, and once that new office is complete and properly warded, I'll be done here."

"Speaking of — Drummond is here with me. You've got no good wards on this property anymore."

"I'm aware."

"I don't get it. Pride, bravery, stubbornness — I can see why those might motivate you to stick it out in here, but that's not what you're doing. You've already cleared everything out."

"My presence is all that's needed to make my point."

Drummond said, "That's her problem, you know. She's always trying to make a point rather than run her business."

Max thought it best not to repeat the ghost's words. Instead, he cleared his throat. "Madame Ti is alive — at least, as far as we know." He launched into a detailed account of their investigation. Reporting to Cecily Hull did not feel good, but she did pay for the Porter Agency's services, and Max knew his obligation to do the best job possible. When he finished his summary, he said, "It's clear to us that a battle has started, and your enemies struck first by taking your witch. There's some suggestion they intend to turn this into a war."

Lacing her fingers upon her makeshift desk, Cecily tapped her thumbs against each other as she gazed off to the side. "She warned me."

"Madame Ti? She knew she would be abducted?"

"No. At least, she never said such a thing to me." With a sharp turn of her head, Cecily faced Max straight on. "Madame Ti and I had been, well, debating a lot lately."

Drummond clicked his tongue. "She means they argued. Downright screaming match, probably."

As he leaned forward to pretend concern, Max also motioned

for Drummond to back off. Hard enough to go through this verbal dance without having a ghost blathering in his ear. If Drummond had anything of value to contribute, Max wanted to hear it, but the non-stop commentary would not help this time around.

Drummond must have understood because his next words were helpful. "She wants to tell you. Just go easy."

Shifting to as a gentle a tone as he could manage, Max asked, "What were these debates about?"

"Everything. It seemed Madame Ti found fault with all my choices. I found her that secret lair below the city. She acted like I had insulted generations of her family. I provided her with nearly unlimited funds. She acted like I doled out pennies only when she came begging. But …"

"But what?"

Dispelling the thoughts wrestling across her brow, she said, "Nothing. Never mind."

"Gently now," Drummond said. "Remind her that she called the Agency in on this. She wants our help."

Max shook his head and stuck his hands in his pockets. "Then I guess we're done working for you."

"Excuse me?" Fear jittered in her eyes. "You are not done until I say so."

"You called on the Porter Agency because you wanted, you needed our help. We're staring at the brutal beginnings of a much larger conflict, and you choose now to act coy and silent about the important details. I won't work that way."

As Max turned to leave, Drummond winked. "Gutsy play, partner. I like it."

Van Horn hastened to the office door, eager to see Max out. But only two steps later, Cecily Hull uttered a defeated sigh. "Wait."

Max paused and glanced back. She gestured toward the desk. He made a performance of weighing out the moment before returning.

"What do you want to know?" she said with more ice than venom.

"Let's start again with these *debates*. It sounds like Madame Ti was unhappy."

As Cecily spoke, she continually moved the papers and folders on her desk. Reorganizing on one side, then the other. "That woman is always unhappy. I chose her to be my witch because she's powerful and ambitious — two qualities required if you intend to lead the world of magic in any area. If you're paying attention, you'll have noticed I did not say anything about her being cunning or political. She has no patience for the political side of what we are trying to achieve, and so she prefers to act like a sledgehammer when we need the precision of a gem cutter. She kept pushing for us to move faster in our growth and clamp down harder on our enemies or even those who simply want some independence."

"There is a power void. You have a lot of enemies vying to fill it."

"An argument she likes to make often. She fears the longer we delay, the greater chance for one of the others to make a move against us."

"Her abduction is clearly such a move. One designed, it seems, to provoke a witch war."

"This is why I pushed for a subtler, quieter approach. Heavy-handed power grabs ultimately fail unless you can quickly enact a dictatorship. People only follow those sorts of leaders out of fear, and to gain control through fear requires breaking the will of the people. Witches don't break so easily. So, you're all but guaranteed to have a war. But my way — though it takes longer — has the witches begging to give their power to you. I'm like a pot of water and they're the frogs. Slowly, gently I get hotter, and they never realize I've taken over until it's too late. Because it's not good enough to just gain control of magic in the state. If it was, the Hull family would never have lost that power. What's needed is political clout, too. A lot of witchcraft needs to be swept under the rug of public attention — in today's social media world, more than ever. That takes connections. Political ones. You must become the voice of reason, give them something to latch upon that promises witchcraft is fantasy. Only with both

— power and politics — can we safely rule the witches."

Drummond rushed in, his face blazing as he pointed to Max. "Show her the list."

"I want you to see something." Max pulled up a photo of the list on his phone. "We found this at Madame Ti's. Does it mean anything to you?"

Cecily needed only a second, then produced a paper from one of the piles on her desk. "I have the same list here. They're all witches — hand-picked by Madame Ti — women from all over the world we think will make great additions to the Hull organization. We invited them to come visit, see how we want to run things, and then we plan to offer them a position with us. The dates are their arrivals. With the addition of these witches, Madame Ti will gain the muscle she needs to enforce our authority while giving me the leverage to gain power through politics."

"Sounds like you were starting to see things Madame Ti's way."

"Not fast enough. We should have taken control sooner. If we had, nobody would have dared to touch Madame Ti. It would have been …" She frowned at Max's phone, then checked her own paper. "The dates are wrong."

"What's wrong with them?" Drummond said, and Max repeated.

Snapping her fingers, she waited for Van Horn to approach. "Is this the same list that you delivered to Madame Ti?"

"It is, ma'am." Van Horn showed no fear, no reaction at all.

"Then why are the dates on Madame Ti's list an entire week earlier than mine?"

Van Horn bent over the paper, then pushed his face in close to the phone. When he stood straight, he said, "The list on the phone is not the paper I handed to her. You can see that the Hull logo is not on the top of hers. I can only surmise that somebody rewrote the list with different dates."

As they talked, Drummond also inspected both documents. "Cecily's dates don't show the first witch arriving until next week."

"This is only a hypothesis," Van Horn continued, "but perhaps Madame Ti discovered this discrepancy and planned to make you aware. Perhaps she knew who was behind the alteration."

"It's plausible." Max looked over the list again. "If Madame Ti knew the truth and planned to tell you, then she might have been taken to keep her quiet. Of all the names on the revised list, only one has arrived so far — Emily Dodson. The rest come over the next few days."

"You think Emily betrayed us?" Cecily said. "Maybe she's in league with my enemies and has helped in taking Madame Ti. She could have contacted Madame Ti —"

"You know that's not what I'm saying."

She paused. "The dead witch?"

"Maybe dental records will prove otherwise, but I have my doubts. I suspect nobody will ever hear from Emily Dodson again."

Cecily's shoulders slumped. "Then I'm already too late. They've taken my witch, killed the first of my recruits, and they know when the rest are coming in. It's an ambush over time."

"Not if you warn these women. Tell them to turn back."

"But I need them." She scrunched her brow as if unable to understand how Max could doubt that most obvious fact. "I expected to have five witches to follow Madame Ti's lead, to help us with our victory. Now, I'm down to four and my head witch is gone. If I planned to cower after the first attack against me, I'd never have come this far. Those witches are going to save me. They'll find Madame Ti, probably before you do, and they'll rescue her. After that, all the witches in North Carolina will learn once again to fear the Hull name."

Drummond said, "It sure didn't take her long to go the dictator route."

"We must keep working." Cecily returned to her papers. "If my new witches prove themselves, I will inform you that your services are no longer required. Until then, you will continue your search for Madame Ti and her captors."

Using some unseen cue, Van Horn opened the office door,

cleared his throat for Max's attention, and gestured that the meeting had concluded. The man refused to speak during the short journey back to the lobby. From there, he opened the outside door and offered the slimmest of bows.

"Good day, Mr. Porter."

The words felt like an insult, but Max held off any comment. In his pocket, his phone vibrated, and he had a pretty strong sense Sandra was calling.

"I think I've got an answer," she said, when he called back from the car.

Drummond floated over the passenger seat. "Put it on speaker. I'd like to hear this, too."

Max obliged, and Sandra went on, "I've deciphered a bunch of the spells from Ruby's house, and the site of the dead witch."

"Emily Dodson," Max said.

Drummond said, "What do you mean spells?"

"I mean more than one," Sandra said.

"How many are there?"

"I don't know. This is like pulling strands from a plate of spaghetti. But I'm on my way to your favorite library, so meet me there and we'll go through it all."

She cut the call, and Max stared at the phone. Wondering how the device could pick up the sound of a ghost talking, he drove off to the Z. Smith Reynolds Library.

Chapter 10

PLENTY OF REASONS ABOUNDED for Max to love this library. For one, it's unique design — merging two older buildings together by turning the alleyway between them into an enclosed, skylit study area — made the place a delightful oddity in which floors didn't always line up correctly. It had numerous sections that did not conform to a regular library — little crannies where one of the original buildings had an unusual space and they had to use it for something. Plus, in the magical way of bookstores and libraries, this wonderful repository of thoughts and stories and history resonated its potential into every fiber of the bricks, wood, and steel that made it. Max could feel it radiate off the walls. Maybe it was a piece of North Carolina witchcraft, but he preferred to think of it as the magic of books.

When Max and Drummond met up with Sandra, she had staked out a recess near one corner of the fourth floor — a little nook surrounded by tall shelving that created a private place to talk. They pulled two chairs together, and though nobody else could be seen around, they spoke softly. Just in case.

"Why all the cloak and dagger, doll?" Drummond said, the only one not required to lower his voice.

"Our last case," Sandra said with a visible shake.

Max's nerves lit up at the thought of Sister Sadie. When she and Sandra locked in battle over the blood magic used to call Sister Sadie into being, Max witnessed a witch as powerful as Madame Ti or even the powerhouses of the past — Mother Hope and Grandma Mobley — albeit far from sane. "You think she's behind all this?"

"Maybe. But more, I'm worried about the security of our

home. When we were closing in on Sister Sadie, we were attacked with hex bags in our house. That was done for one witch. What we're investigating now — this is looking exactly like what Ruby said. A witch war. If that's true, if that's what we're facing, then it would make sense for them to take out the Porter Agency. The faster, the better, as far as they're concerned."

Drummond nodded. "Because we're the only non-witch group to ever stop any of them."

Taking Sandra's hand — more for his own comfort than hers — Max said, "But you're a witch."

"Not to all of them," she said. "Some, like the matriarchs at Haven House, have made me their pet project. Some have learned the hard way to respect me. But there are plenty of witches that I've either not met or have only seen in passing. Those witches don't fear me, don't respect me, don't see me as anything than a novice with dreams of undermining them." Sitting back, she freed her hands to rub the bruise on her forehead. "They're not exactly wrong. I am trying to be the first good witch, and if I succeed, that will pull the rug out. I mean think about it. If you're desperate enough to seek the help of a witch, would you go make a deal with one of them or me? I'll make a deal that's fair and honest. No strings attached. Their entire way of life is threatened by me."

"Then why are any of the witches on your side at all?"

"Honey, there are always people interested in making things better, people that see a new way for us to live, or simply people that want things different."

Tilting back on his floating heels, Drummond said, "And there are always people who refuse to change or profit off the conflict of change. We really are at the start of a war, then. We've got to move into a wartime mindset. I can accept that. Loose lips sink ships and all."

"Exactly. Until I can cast a few more spells at the house, until I can regularly sweep against witches, we can't trust that our home is a secure place to go over important information — or dangerous information."

Max chilled. "What did you find out?"

In a few seconds, Sandra brought out her phone to get her notes. Max knew she didn't need them — her memory had the strength of a bull stampede — but she produced her work as a sign of respect to his own research methods. Yet another reason of multitudes that he relished being married to her.

"To start," she said, and her voice grounded in the confidence of her expertise, "the castings we found at Ruby's and at Emily Dodson's were multiple spells so entangled that I couldn't decipher them all. I doubt anybody could unless they devote a few months to the work. But I was able to figure out the big ones, the key ones, that formed the spine — the purpose — of the entire thing."

"It wasn't to take her heart out?" Max said.

"That's part of it, but don't interrupt and you'll learn."

"Yeah," Drummond said, "let the lady speak."

With a warm tilt of the head toward the ghost, Sandra continued, "Three of the spells prepped the victim. One spell to confuse her mind so she could not counter the assault with any memorized spells. One spell immobilized her so they could place her in the casting circle without a fight. Last, a spell that imprisoned her in the circle — in case the other spells failed. Once they had Emily properly situated, they cast a spell giving one witch a short burst of extreme strength."

"To rip out her heart." Max's enthusiasm for research information pushed the words out of his mouth.

"But without any kind of sedative spell, Emily lived through the brutal extraction, suffering immense pain as they cracked her sternum and spread her ribs open. She would have been screaming until they pulled her heart out."

Drummond shook his head. "That kind of torturous death pretty much guarantees they would create a ghost — a tortured, insane ghost."

"Exactly. To make sure, there's another spell weaved into all that writing which tries to stop her soul from moving on."

"A spell can do that?"

"Not really. But this one reads like an attempt at it. If it had been needed, if it had even worked a little, it could have slowed her down, but even the worst curses I've come across about holding a soul in ghost form can't last infinitely. Look at yourself. Even if Max and I had never come along, even if nobody ever discovered the casting circle you were bound to, eventually, the building that spell was in would have been torn down to be replaced or maybe destroyed by accident."

"But even after Max broke the circle, I was still stuck to that office."

"Not permanently. I didn't know it back then, but I've learned that when the casting of a curse is broken, the curse will end on its own. Eventually. That could take minutes, days, decades, even centuries, depending on the spell and the skill of the witch who cast it."

Max said, "The witches that killed Emily had enough skill to pull off all these spells at once. I'm guessing they could manage to stall her moving on for a century or two."

"But it wasn't necessary. They committed enough of an atrocity against her that Emily's ghost was practically insane within in moments of her death — a full-on poltergeist. There was no way she would be moving on like that. Her mind, what had been done to her physically, doomed her to roaming as a ghost. The rest of it — well, it seems like sadism to me."

Pursing his lips, Drummond said, "Sounds like we know what that did to her — turned her into a ghost, a poltergeist, on purpose. Why, though? The level of effort gone into cursing this woman is beyond anything I've ever seen."

Sandra paused, listening close to every sound bouncing around the library floor. Taking this cue, Max also paid attention to the noises close by. A slight head motion at Drummond sent the ghost on a quick patrol of the floor. Nobody spoke until he returned to say the floor was still empty.

"This whole thing isn't only about making a ghost. In fact, it's likely the curse is intended to lock the ghost away until the witches have died — presumably of old age. Just their way of handling an ugly byproduct of their real goal."

"And that is?"

"Getting a witch's heart."

"We're not going to like this, are we?" Drummond said.

"I'm pretty confident the last spell I could figure out is keeping that heart alive."

Max said, "Definitely not liking this."

"It's worse. If you put those pieces together, ask yourself why torture this witch before taking her heart, there are only two conclusions I can see. Either the culprits really are sadists taking pleasure in this suffering or they needed to cause that suffering, push her as close as they could to being a poltergeist so that this condition would be part of the heart they tore out."

Max peeked down the aisle again. The more Sandra spoke, the more he felt the eyes of all witches watching them. "I really don't want to ask this, but I have to — what are they after?"

"Same as in any war — power. If you mean the strategy, that's much darker. There have always been scuffles over turf, that's true whenever you get differing groups in the same area. Just because they're witches doesn't mean they stop having human impulses. In some ways, these covens are no different than a street gang."

Drummond said, "I'd put them closer to the mob or, at least, a biker gang. They're organized, they have a hierarchy and sophisticated rules. Oh, and they have that pesky magic. That sets them apart."

"In that case, we should liken them to the Mafia of *The Godfather*. Organized, secretive, and ruthless. Like those crime families, there have been occasional times throughout North Carolinian history when witch wars have erupted." Sandra checked her notes. "The most recent I could find happened from 1902-1904. Before that was 1810 and before that is hard to verify, but it seems there was something of note around 1723-1728."

Max said, "Seems like once a century."

"Maybe. Or maybe the witches are excellent at hiding things they don't want others knowing about." She took a breath and placed a hand on Max's knee. "Honey, I know you get excited with the research side of all this, and I appreciate that. You're trying your best. But if you keep talking, I'm never going to finish this, the witch war will be over, and we'll be dead."

He wanted to add that more than excitement, he felt the itching fear that often accompanied their cases. Though he had come to terms with it — well, he had grown accustomed to it — he still felt those nerves rifle through him at times. Discussing the research helped him keep perspective. Perhaps it also gave him a false sense of control over matters, but he didn't want to dwell on that idea too much. Instead, he simply made a motion of zipping his lips.

"Thank you." She re-read her notes. "Okay, in the 1900s war, one of the leading covens was the Tacksaw Coven. Though they didn't use such horrible spells as the one we've found, they did use a similar tactic. They kidnapped their enemies and cursed them into ghosts. The idea was two-fold. They got rid of rival witches, of course. But by increasing the number of ghosts, cursed ghosts that would be angry and possibly confused, they made the ruling coven look ineffective, weak, unable to handle the balance between witches and the secular world. After all, if too many civilians started complaining about ghost problems, if the city got known to be a haunted place, there would be all kinds of political fallout that would make the ruling coven easy to topple. It's pretty obvious that whoever has taken Madame Ti and murdered Emily Dodson has adopted a similar strategy. Make Cecily Hull look weak, make her have to deal with secular politics, make her vulnerable, so that she can be erased from power."

Max's heart quickened. The old library walls and towering stacks of books closed in. Until this moment, all the talk about witch wars had felt small and manageable. A couple witches, maybe a couple covens fighting over leadership. Even the attack by Emily's ghost could have been discounted — Max had simply been in the wrong place, got caught in the crossfire between these warring groups. But the deeper Sandra went into the background, the more Max understood that this war might be at a devastating scale.

It only grew worse when Drummond said, "There are plenty of simple curses that would've produced plenty of angry, trapped witch ghosts. Why take out their hearts?"

"That's new," Sandra said. "Or rather, old. A witch's heart can be used in several archaic spells. Brotherhood-type stuff that often predates witchcraft itself. Those spells usually call for the heart of a corrupted soul."

"Looks like the Brotherhood conveniently updated that to mean *witch*."

"I doubt the Brotherhood is behind this. Even if Mr. Carroll has rebuilt his group this fast, the level of skill and talent required to pull off these spells — I mean he hardly succeeded at any of the spells he tried around us."

"Osorio would disagree."

"His hand is the least of what was being attempted. And you're just as bad as Max. Your interruptions are getting in the way."

"Sorry, doll. I'll try to be quiet."

"The point is that even though the spells using a heart are old, they've never been used in a witch war before. That's the new part, and the part that should concern everybody. Whatever coven has started this war, they aren't just going after a little turf. They aren't just going after Cecily Hull's desired position. This might be far more than North Carolina. This is the kind of power grab that makes civilians so afraid of witches. This is the stuff that leads to fairy tales and then adults getting scared and then witches getting burned alive and then innocent women getting burned alive."

Max raised his hand and waited for Sandra to nod at him. "You said a *coven* started this war. Not an individual or a small group but an actual coven."

"I don't see how anything less could have pulled this off. I suppose, if the witches are powerful enough, they could do it with a smaller group, but that would only work for these initial strikes. Now that the witch community is aware — and I have no doubt the community is quite aware by now — no handful of witches will succeed."

"Then there aren't that many candidates. You say the Brotherhood isn't capable. Who then? Haven House?"

"They are a full coven, though you've only met the three that manage the books. Madame Novak heads the whole coven. But it seems like if they wanted this kind of power, they would've moved on it long ago."

"Those ladies have been around for an unnaturally long time."

"There are a lot of other covens, though. More than we've ever encountered. North Carolina has attracted more and more talent over the last bunch of years. The internet has made it easier for witches to find each other, and after the Hull family fell apart, after the Mobley coven and the Magi tore each other apart, the power vacuum has gained notice all over. The more I look into it, the more obvious it seems that this war was bound to happen."

Clearing his throat until Sandra turned his way, Drummond said, "Looking at all the evidence you've dug up — what all these spells did to Emily Dodson and the potential reasons why — I think it's safe to assume that she won't be the last. This was probably a trial run."

Max's stomach dropped. "Madame Ti. They're planning to use this on her but didn't want to botch it up. If they failed the spells against such a prominent witch, they'd weaken their own case for taking over. Right?"

"Absolutely," Sandra said. "That's the most important part of it all — because the trial run isn't over. They successfully removed the witch heart, but they still plan to use it in one of those old spells."

"Which one?"

Putting away her phone, she frowned. "I don't know yet. That's my next bit of research. But if I'm right about all this, then we know the next target."

"We do?"

Drummond snapped his fingers. "We do. The list."

"You two think it's a hit list?"

"Look what happened to Emily Dodson."

Sandra said, "How hard would it be for you to find the other witches on the list?"

Giving the request serious thought, Drummond said, "The ones already here could be anywhere in the state. I'm trying to rebuild my contacts in the Other, so I can check with them, but the best we can do is see when the next one arrives and track her down."

Max said, "I'll call Cecily and get her to move on sending all their flight info."

"Good. Because somebody has dark, dark plans for Madame Ti."

In a soft whisper, Sandra added, "Dark plans for us all."

Chapter 11

THE NEXT MORNING, Van Horn knocked on the Porter's door and presented an envelope with the names, dates, and full flight information for the arriving witches. He made no attempt to hide his distaste for the delivery. Max wanted to ask why he followed Cecily Hull's questionable lead but held back. Any answer would not satisfy. Even the truth. The fact was that everybody who knew about Cecily Hull had to make a choice — be with her or be against her. Whatever the reasons, Van Horn chose to be with her.

Oddly enough, the Porters had been thrown into an unwilling alliance with Cecily — a truth that also would not satisfy the curious — but later, they had been cornered into a witch deal with Madame Ti. She asked that should she ever go against Cecily Hull, she wanted Max and Sandra to help her take over. Looked to Max like Madame Ti had been pushing Cecily for longer than he realized.

"You think it's possible Cecily had Madame Ti abducted?" Max said as they drove to Piedmont International Airport in Greensboro.

Sandra lifted her head out of an old tome of 15th century witchcraft. "Why would she do that?"

"Maybe she figured out that Madame Ti was preparing for a time without her. Maybe she thought it better to strike first. She has Madame Ti taken, puts on a whole show of trying to find her, then in the end, Madame Ti is discovered dead. In the meantime, she takes on one of these new witches as her second-in-command."

"But in the middle of a war —"

"There is no war in this scenario. Nobody has attacked the Hull power because it's Hull herself doing the attacking. Once the reality of it gets out, and Cecily would make sure it got out, then all those lining up to fight her would rethink that idea. After all, she just executed her own witch — a very powerful witch — to prove her strength."

"Show them how crazy you are so that only the craziest would dare come after you?"

"Something like that."

"I don't buy it. Cecily has never struck me as one to risk her own power out of spite. Still, it's worth keeping in mind."

They parked in a covered lot in front of the airport. It had once been a well-used airport that now struggled to keep afloat. A quiet, sparse location — perfect for bringing witches into the area with little notice. Perfect also for Max and Sandra who wanted to notice.

"You think Drummond believes he's fooling us?" Max said as they sat in the car and waited. Sung Park's flight landed in a few minutes. They had time before the witch could deplane, get her baggage, and find a ride.

"He probably is doing exactly what he said — rebuilding a contact network. But …"

"But?"

"Yeah, I'm sure he's spending some — maybe most — of his time trying to get back with Miss 1800s."

"Isn't that weird, though? The Drummond we've known for years doesn't settle on one woman."

Sandra gave Max a look he had seen often enough — one that suggested he was being obtuse. "Honey, Drummond is fiercely loyal. He plays the field not like some lothario but to find somebody worthy. Once he has her, she's all that matters."

"You think that's Miss 1800s? We don't even know her real name."

"We're not his parents. He doesn't need our approval."

"I guess. But even if you're right —"

"I am."

"— that doesn't really explain the way he's been acting. He's broken up with girlfriends before."

"Clearly, this one meant more to him than he let on. Why are you so concerned? Give the ghost some time. He'll get over it."

Max had nothing more he could say. Mostly because he didn't understand it himself. Why was he so concerned? Sandra's description of Drummond's approach to love rang true, and letting the old ghost stew in his loss until he felt ready to be himself again sounded like the right way to handle things, yet something tapped at the back of Max's brain. Something unconvinced.

However, it would have to wait. The time had come to track a witch.

Max kissed Sandra and hastened inside. He checked Van Horn's information against the arrivals board. No changes. Not surprising. The same flights ran each day, and to a smaller airport like Piedmont, there were rarely any deviations.

According to the board, Ms. Park's luggage would be delivered to baggage claim B. Max took the escalator down and waited as passengers from her flight dribbled in. Pacing the long length of baggage claim, he looked from face to face, searching for a Korean woman with a witchy countenance. But as more passengers arrived, it became clear that Ms. Park had planned to slip through unseen. Over twenty Korean women of varying ages entered the area. Whether she had paid these women to arrive with her or had simply scheduled her arrival to coincide with some Korean tourist group, she had found an excellent way to hide in plain sight.

Several of the women broke off the main group and headed for the restrooms. A few stood crowded near the opening to receive their bags the instant they became available. Others formed a small circle and chatted in their rapid-fire tongue.

As he continued observing, hoping nobody noticed him and wondered about the weirdo watching these women, his phone rang — Sandra. She said that a black Lexus had pulled into a parking space two down from her. Three women sat in the car, each wearing a black rose broach.

"If these aren't witches, I'll quit," she said.

"You won't be quitting anytime soon. Your description made this easy." Max zeroed his attention on the only woman wearing a black rose broach. "I've found Sung Park."

"One of the women is getting out of the car. She's lean, looks like a damn model, and I'd guess some Latin roots. If she's one of the witches off the list, I'd bet this is Rosita Stakson."

"I see her," Max said when the witch entered the building. Dressed in a sleek skirt, black with red buttons on the side, black rose broach and understated gold necklace, Rosita made a straight line for Sung Park. The clicking of her heels cut through the general noise of the airport. Even Ms. Park noticed. She smiled — no joy or excitement or even sisterly bonding. Rather, this smile looked ominous. Like a cheetah sizing up its next meal.

The two witches spoke, but Max could not hear them without getting close enough to be spotted. He held back, observing their tense body language that did not match their plastic grins. As they waited for her luggage, they continued to talk. He imagined the innocuous subjects barely covered the truth. Not that they spoke in thinly-veiled code, but rather the ordinary conversation — *how was the flight? how is the weather here? do you need the restroom before we go?* — could not hide the malicious vibrations flowing between them underneath. These were warriors preparing for battle.

At least, Max suspected as much. He acknowledged that if the Porter Agency had gotten it all wrong, these two might be old school chums getting ready for a class reunion.

"Except we didn't get it wrong," he muttered, garnering a questioning look from a five-year-old picking threads from her dress.

Once Park had gathered two large hardshell cases, the women headed out — Park rolling both while shoulder a handbag. Rosita led the way, never glancing back to make sure Park kept up. Max followed.

They exited the airport, and the warmth of the day swayed along a soft breeze. The black Lexus zipped toward the ladies. As Rosita settled in the backseat, the trunk popped open, and Park was left to load her bags alone.

Max pretended to peer out at the handful of cars cruising by, searching for his ride like a few other passengers, yet maintained a clear view of the targets. He thought even Drummond might be impressed. After all, the witches had not seen him, had no idea they were being followed. Max had learned a thing or two about surveillance.

As Park slammed the car trunk shut, she scanned the area. Her eyes stopped in Max's direction. He slipped behind a tall gentleman, heart hammering, brain chastising him for jinxing his success, until she entered the car.

When the Lexus drove off, Sandra pulled up to the curb. Max hopped in.

Driving down Route 73 towards 85, they kept a healthy distance from their target. Both Max and Sandra had experience in tailing a car, but after a few minutes, Max decided Sandra was better at it. He always felt the need to see the target, causing him to switch lanes more often than was natural. Watching his wife, he noticed how she maintained a steady speed and kept to one lane. If a car or truck blocked her view of the Lexus, she would catch sight of it when the road curved. She checked every exit to make sure the target didn't sneak off the highway. Should any of the witches look behind them, Sandra's driving would blend in with all the other traffic, never pulling the eye, never getting caught.

As they slowed for the curving ramp that merged with 85 South, the Lexus took a secondary exit off the ramp, one that paralleled the highway for a short distance as it ran toward the Grandover Parkway. Once there, the witches entered the Grandover Resort.

Sitting at a red light, Max stared at the resort gateway. It had been formed from long, massive stone walls and trim, manicured lawns. The word GRANDOVER in giant, gold letters had been placed on one wall. The statue of a gryphon sitting regal and ready to strike upon a stone pedestal divided the road into a two-lane entrance on one side and a two-lane exit on the other.

The light changed and the Porters slipped in. The Grandover Parkway began with housing on either side as well as signs advertising *Homes For Sale*. The road wound onward with the rolling hills of a golf course on the right and 85 South racing along the left.

Once they passed the housing area, Sandra caught up to the Lexus, so she slowed allowing the Lexus to shoot away from view. Only the hotel remained as a possible destination. Max kept expecting to reach it at the next turn, the next intersection, but signs continually pointed them onward.

When the hotel finally came into view, Max's jaw dropped. The twelve-story building, tan stone with a burgundy roof, rose amongst the carefully managed green hills like a cathedral towering over a small town. Club Road cut off to the right and became the parking lot as well as the drive up to the entrance awning.

Max waved Sandra on. "Let's go. Before they catch us."

"Relax," she said even as she turned around. "If they were going to spot us, it would already have happened."

"We need to go now."

"What's got into you? The moment you saw the place, you looked shocked. Did something happen here? Have you been here before?"

"I've seen it before. A picture of it." His stomach tightened as he looked straight at Sandra. "At Madame Ti's."

Chapter 12

MAX'S RESEARCHING GUT TOOK THE BLAME. The way he drew connections, the way he saw patterns like an instinct, these abilities raised the red flag, flashed the warning lights, sounded the alarm in his head. He didn't know why. He didn't question it. The simple fact that the same resort hotel the witches stayed in matched one he knew he saw a photo of in Madame Ti's office was enough. Meaning, reason — details that would come later. In fact, his agitation did not yield until they reached the Winston-Salem city limits.

The suspicious nature of the connection grew worse when Max called Cecily Hull asking for access to Madame Ti's office once more. Of course, first, he had to go through Van Horn.

"Your job is to find Madame Ti. You don't need to concern yourself with other matters of the witch community."

Tamping down any notes of irritation, Max said, "This is a simple request to visit the office we already visited before. There's no reason for you to stand in our way."

"Ms. Hull has many important matters to deal with. Handling your desire to be central to the situation is not one of them."

"Look, maybe the air is too thin up by your head, but think a moment about what Ms. Hull will say when she learns that I could have found Madame Ti already, but *your* desire to be central got in the way."

"Unlike you, I get paid to be central. I am the wall that protects Ms. Hull."

After silently cursing out the phone, Max flipped his middle finger at the device. In a tone barely hiding his true feelings, he said, "If you won't let me speak with her, at least pass her a note for my request."

Van Horn paused, perhaps deciding whether he should screw with Max some more, but finally put the call on hold. A few minutes went by before he clicked back on. He told Max that upon reading his note, Ms. Hull clearly refused. Too busy, she said. *Too many plates spinning* were the exact words she used.

But Van Horn's low voice dropped lower to a growl. "However, I have been ordered to deliver whatever boxes of papers I can find. That will have to suffice."

"Thank you." Max hung up before he said anything he'd regret.

A few hours later, Van Horn arrived at the Porter's home carting twenty-five boxes crammed with every paper from the sewer office. Several boxes had been taken as is from Madame Ti's personal horde. Van Horn never even opened them. Just added the boxes to the pile.

He said nothing as two burly men unloaded each box into the house. Then, before leaving, he turned to Max. "My employer wants you to succeed, or she would never have granted this request."

Max stood in the doorway, refusing to look away until he could no longer see the red dots of Van Horn's car. When he turned around to face the wall of boxes taking up most of the living room, Sandra said, "Maybe you should get us a pot of coffee going. This is going to take a long time."

"I hate the Hulls," Drummond said, throwing his hat to the floor — only to have it vanish and reappear on his head. "From the first day I ever dealt with them in life to all the times I've had to deal with them in death, they always want to complicate the simplest things." He threw his hat again. "For crying out loud, she gave us this job. She went out of her way to send Van Horn here, forced us to take the case, and now she does nothing but make it more difficult."

After several minutes filled with grumbling from all parties, Max, Sandra, and Drummond got to work. Max organized the boxes into three distinct categories: Business papers, Witchcraft papers, and Madame Ti's papers. The last category encompassed all the witch's things that Van Horn had not collected but that she had already boxed.

Meanwhile, Sandra cast several protection spells on the house. "I still need to cast a few wards, but I'm not letting anybody kick us out of our own home."

They decided to divvy up the boxes in a simple, logical way — according to expertise. Sandra, the witch, would go through the witchcraft boxes. Max, the researcher, would scour the business boxes for any useful details. And Drummond, the ghost, would risk peeking into Madame Ti's private papers. Chances were that any harmful spells she may have placed on those papers would be intended to harm the living. To go through everything meant spreading it throughout the small house.

"We really need to get some office space," Max said.

Sandra grabbed a witchcraft box and headed to their bedroom. "Let's survive this case first, okay?"

Darth Vader's breathing played on his phone — Max's latest ringtone for his mother. As he answered, he picked up a few boxes for Drummond and spread the papers through the kitchen.

"We're all doing fine," Mrs. Porter said. "Better than fine, even. They are delightful young men and have put up with my old bones slowing them down, but we've still managed to pack in quite a lot. Cavern tours, old towns, beautiful hikes. It's been wonderful."

"I'm glad to hear it," Max said. "Don't overexert yourself, though."

"No need to be a worrywart. In fact, we're doing so well, having such a good time, that I wondered if you wouldn't mind that we might take a few extra days before heading back."

"Sounds great. Enjoy yourselves."

"The boys said not to call, that you'd only worry, but I disagreed. I know what it's like being a parent. Plenty of worry."

"Should I be worried?"

With a flustered laugh, Mrs. Porter said, "Stop that nonsense. Why, I'm in the best of hands with these men. They're making sure I get all I need, and they aren't up to anything wrong and neither am I so you can quit your interrogations and we'll see you later in the week. Give my love to Sandra. Good bye."

She ended the call, and if nothing else, sending her love to Sandra set off more alarms in Max's system. "Dammit," he said, pulling out the contents of Drummond's last box. "She's a terrible liar. At least, when it comes to doing things I wouldn't approve of."

"If you want, I can go check on them," Drummond said.

From the bedroom, Sandra called out, "Don't you dare. We need you here, and we have to trust the boys. Maybe your mother, too." Holding a file folder open, she entered the kitchen. "Besides, J can see Drummond."

"I can be stealthy. I made a career of it, after all."

"You can also slip up, and if J catches you, it'll break the trust we've worked hard to build with him. Not to mention, we *do* trust him. Whatever they're doing, it'll be fine."

"Maybe," Max said. "I'm mostly worried she'll come back with a boyfriend. Some artsy widower who wants to steal what little she has left."

"So what? The woman doesn't have that much time. I hope she has found a man. Maybe getting laid will make her more pleasant to be around."

Max slammed the box onto the table. "Not another word. Nobody is to mention anything related to my mother having sex. She doesn't do that. Not at her age. Not —"

Drummond chuckled. "Sure, pal. Whatever you say."

Thrusting some papers at Sandra, Max said, "You help him. I need to be alone."

He stomped over to the living room and tried to ignore the laughter from the kitchen. After a shudder of disgust, he couldn't halt the grin that rose on his lips.

With a clear mind — well, clearer anyway — Max set to work. Sifting through the boxes, he hunted down any mention of the Grandover Resort or, more importantly, a picture of the place. Because he had seen it, and that implied some type of photo or drawing.

He leafed through electric bills, insurance bills, and other mundane matters. The address given on all of these was for an office in the building aboveground. Max had guessed all the power, plumbing, and air conditioning for Madame Ti's secret sanctuary had been siphoned off that office building. These bills appeared to confirm the idea.

He found a box detailing old bank accounts and another with tax records going back ten years. Even witches had to pay Uncle Sam. Max wondered what a witch or an occultist put down for employment. Spiritual advisor? Some, he knew, held jobs that acted as fronts. He had encountered a dentist, a museum curator, and a property owner, among others. But many witches simply lived as witches. They didn't get a W-2, didn't pay into Social Security, didn't neatly fit into the check boxes on any form.

"You've got to have one talented accountant," he said to the paperwork.

Opening the next box, he found the answer sitting atop a stack of golf magazines. An issue of Golf Pro with a picture of the Grandover Resort and the words *Top 5 Courses You've Been Missing.* Flipping through the pages, he saw aerial shots of several holes as well as charming photos of the Pro Shop and the practice green. Max read the article, searching for some clue to explain the resort's importance.

"I don't get what it means," he told the others when he showed them the magazine. "Madame Ti chose this place for the witches on that list."

"Maybe they like golf," Drummond said.

Sandra said, "We don't know that all the witches are staying at the same hotel. Only Sung Park, and possibly Rosita Stakson."

"True." Max scanned through the article for the fourth time. "I'll even say that there's a slim chance Ms. Park or Ms. Stakson is a golf enthusiast."

"I was joking." Drummond gestured to his own research pile. "Then again, I haven't found a single thing in all this, so if golf is the best we've got, we should go with it."

"There's something to this. Madame Ti spent significant time scoping out this resort. The golf magazines are only part of it. I found a printout of emails between Madame Ti and the Koury Corporation, which owns the resort. She presented herself as a tournament organizer and wanted to know the dimensions of the entire course, the path from hole-to-hole, what amenities could be provided, popular times of usage, and tons of other such questions."

Sandra frowned. "That's so odd compared to what I found. I've barely had time to dig through her papers, but she has a clear interest in transmutation — mixing people and animals."

"I've dealt with that before," Drummond said.

"I would've thought she'd be more interested in building a relationship with a zoo rather than a golf resort."

"Sounds like Max needs to hit the books on this golf angle."

Max raised an eyebrow at Drummond.

In response, the ghost said, "We each contribute our special skills. You love to remind us how you're the superhero of research. Well, here you go."

Ready with his comeback, Max never got to deliver the one-liner — his phone rang.

"I hope you've done well today," Osorio said, the police station rumbling in the background. "It would be bad if this case relied on me."

"Not a great way to start a conversation. Is this private or can I put you on speaker?"

"Oh, is Ms. Sandra there?"

"And Drummond."

An awkward pause. Then: "Yes, put me on speaker. Everyone needs to hear this." After Max tapped on his phone, Osorio continued, "The body went missing. No trace. No forged signature to claim her. We've looked into the workers and the rest of the hospital staff. Nothing. The body just vanished."

Max and Drummond both turned to Sandra, but she shook her head. "We understand what you're implying," she said, "but there were no spells written in that house to have done such a thing. None that I could recognize, anyway. Is it possible that she was stolen by non-magical means?"

"Sure. I suppose. Sorry, I'm still getting comfortable at

hearing words like *non-magical means* used in a serious sentence."

"Don't sweat it," Max said. "I've been doing this for years, and I'm still in awe at some of the words that come out of my mouth."

Drummond said, "You're the only one ever in awe over what you say."

Before the smartass comments could volley, Sandra said, "This can't be the first time a body's gone missing."

"Of course not," Osorio said. "But it is one of the strangest. I don't suppose you would have anything that might help."

"Like a spell? There are location spells, but the ones I know well, that I'd trust myself to use, require something from the person you seek. You wouldn't happen to have part of the corpse on you?"

"They hadn't even taken any samples for testing yet. Seems nobody wanted to touch her at all. We never even got the dental information to run a records check. Add this to all the other disturbing facts about the case, and the whole department is freaked out. Police can be a superstitious lot, at times, and this is pushing all the wrong buttons. Don't be surprised when my boss says that without a body, the case is pointless. He'll happily let it go cold — in the name of focusing on cases we can actually solve, of course — but nobody's going to complain."

Max said, "Does that mean what I think? You won't be allowed to do anything on the case?"

"Not officially. I won't have full police resources to use, either. I can help with some stuff, maybe, but I don't even know what I could offer since we don't have a body."

"It's okay." Sandra placed her hand on Max. "We've got some avenues to investigate on our end, and we're accustomed to working on our own. It's nice having you and sometimes the police helping us out, but we'll be fine."

Osorio let out a relieved huff. "Thank you for understanding. I hate letting you down."

As Sandra said some final words to close out the conversation, Max stepped back with his mouth agape. He had been an idiot. He suspected Drummond missed the point of the call, too. The main point, anyway. Because while Osorio did call to report the theft of the witch's corpse, only Sandra caught on that he worried the Porter's might fire him after his failure.

It never occurred to Max. Partly because failures, big and small, happened all the time in their line of work. Partly because Osorio was a volunteer. The Porter Agency didn't pay him, so Max didn't see how they could fire the man, either.

Drummond scowled as Sandra ended the call. "Can't say I'm shocked. In my day, the police held PhDs in denial of the supernatural. Lots of bizarre cases made it to their desks over the years, but if you read their reports, you'd think everything was mundane. The few times they came close to acknowledging anything, they pinned the weird parts onto an insane culprit or victim or blamed alcohol and, well, you get the idea."

"Doesn't really change much for us, though," Max said. "I've got this golf angle to investigate, Sandra has spells to find out about, and you're still working up your contacts in the Other."

"True, but we better speed up on it. There's only one name left on the list to arrive — LaShanna Mill. I suspect that once she gets here, whatever the plan is, it's going to happen."

Sandra said, "And we don't want to see Osorio dealing with another dead witch."

Smacking his hands together once, Max winked at Drummond. "Then let's get to work."

Chapter 13

NOTHING SATISFIED LIKE RESEARCH. Not for Max, anyway. Finishing a case brought a sense of closure. Surviving a case brought the rush of escaping death or a curse or worse. But research — for Max, that remained pure and true. He would start with an empty page, a hole of information, and by the end, he had answers, understandings, sometimes even more questions requiring more research. Elegant, maybe even beautiful — research had clear purpose.

Sitting at his desk stuck in the kitchen alcove, opening his laptop, he filled with a familiar, excited surge. He grinned at the screen. A lot of work ahead, but he knew where to start, he knew the goal, and he trusted his skills to get him there.

As he launched into learning about golf courses and, in particular, the Grandover Resort golf courses — he immediately discovered they had two — part of his mind jingled nervously, always aware that his beloved wife had ventured to Haven House for her own research. She would have stayed home and done the bulk of her work on her laptop; however, most dark web witch sites had been shut down. Word about Madame Ti was out. The covens were worried.

On the positive side, Sandra had not immediately returned. The Haven House witches had not rejected her. Since those old ladies ran the best library — but don't call it a library — of old texts and ancient tomes written by and for witches, Max guessed they held some of the true librarian ethos deep within. Sharing knowledge was valuable, important, virtuous. Fighting covens wouldn't stop them.

On the negative side, Sandra had not immediately returned.

Max's experiences with Madame Novak, Madame Fein, and Madame Weir nailed in the dangers simmering within those women. They adored Sandra, treated her like a granddaughter, and she had learned a tremendous amount from them. But still Max feared. He hoped they would always be fond of her, yet he knew they could turn. After all, Haven House might be the culprits behind the attack on Madame Ti. One day, Sandra might go to Haven House for research or instruction and never come home. Part of him lived like a police officer's spouse — always fretting until he saw her pull into the driveway again.

While these thoughts battered the inside of his skull, the rest of Max's brain pounced upon all the golf information he could gather. The East and West courses were highly regarded and had been used on the PGA Tour as well as other professional competitions. They once had been awarded the ranking of #5 out of the Top Ten in North Carolina. No small feat in a state known for its golf. The courses also had a strong pedigree.

Built in 1997, the courses were designed by David Graham and Gary Panks. The two men had worked together on ten courses from 1988 - 1997. A curious coincidence that the Grandover East and West courses were among the last, and Max made a note of it.

David Graham was a golf pro from Australia with a strong career including eight PGA Tour wins, three European wins, one Japan Golf Tour win, nine PGA Tour of Australasia wins, five PGA Tour of Champions wins, and more. In 1980, he made it to 5th in the Masters Tournament, and won the U.S. Open in 1981. In 2015, he was inducted into the World Golf Hall of Fame. With all that firsthand knowledge, Graham was a perfect partner to help design golf courses.

Gary Panks certainly thought so. A graduate of Michigan State University, he had been a professional course architect for years and saw a great opportunity in teaming with the Australian pro. It was a fruitful pairing. Their designs garnered awards and acclaim, and both men appeared to have enjoyed the work.

Even reading between the lines, Max could not uncover anything to suggest the use of witchcraft or the occult. These men were exactly what they looked like — enthusiastic golf lovers who turned passion into design into successful careers.

Pulling up Google Maps, Max looked over the courses from a bird's eye view. He held an unspoken thought that one look at the map would reveal the witchy truth — that the courses had been built like a pentagram or a casting circle or some other classic witch symbol. But nothing so obvious could be seen. Like giant worms, the sprawling fairways and greens, sand traps and water features, weaved amongst homes, streams, and forest with no discernable pattern. Max thought it would be strange to have people playing through right beyond his backyard, but then again, he imagined the sort of people who bought such a house considered that a feature rather than a nuisance.

In the end, he had to admit that there was nothing notably unusual about the course design or the men that created it. Nothing to suggest why Madame Ti would have picked this specific location for the visiting witches. So, Max turned his attention to the hotel itself.

He expected to discover a long, sordid history of mystery and intrigue. Instead, he found a basic bit of unused land that was bought by a major hotel-resort chain and the Grandover Resort built to make a big profit through its golf courses. Bland and boring. Not a single unsolved murder, not a whiff of witchcraft, not a bizarre moment or a haunted floor or a ghost-riddled room.

Nothing.

"There must be something, though," he said to his scrawled notes.

He had already checked the Winston-Salem Journal — the major local paper at the time of construction — and several minor sources that he relied upon. Doing research on past cases, ones that involved events from the 1800s or earlier, he often came across numerous local newspapers — small outfits that would later be swallowed by larger papers or forced out of business. Perhaps he could find smaller websites that had been swallowed up by larger media outfits. The late-1990s still marked the early days for the internet. That Wild West-Gold Rush period had not ended yet. Max figured even the defunct sites might still exist in an archive somewhere.

The internet never forgets, he thought.

A few searches brought up an enormous number of hits. Some turned out to be neighborhood gossip sites — ones he saved for future use — and others belonged in the conspiracy theory territory — also worth saving, considering the nature of their cases. But it was a little dead blog called *The Southern Weird and Wild* which had published on an erratic schedule that contained a nugget which shocked Max's heart into thumping harder.

Just a few lines, really, but they described a freak lightning strike that killed Mr. Bradley Langan — a worker helping build the East Course at Grandover Resort. The blogger provided no links, had not found any supporting evidence, and merely mentioned the story as further proof that Big Media squashed the news that locals should know. After all, if lightning struck a man at the golf course, what had attracted the lightning and what if it happened again? The blogger then launched into a fear-induced diatribe about who really benefited from the golf course and why they would hide the death of a worker.

Max ignored all the window dressing and focused on the dress — a worker on the golf course, Bradley Langan, died under strange circumstances in 1996. While Max did not subscribe to the blogger's idea that the resort might be connected to the Illuminati, his researching instincts said that something odd surrounded this man's death. Something worth looking into.

Armed with a name and a year, Max sifted through the internet like a paleontologist seeking out fossils in an entire mountain range. But for Max, there were thousands of useless false paths to follow — other people named Bradley Langan. Most he could dismiss with a cursory look. Born too early or too late for a man laboring over the construction of a golf course, living in a different region of the country in 1996, easily identified as a doctor or a teacher or any other employment, still alive, or incarcerated — plenty of reasons to strike a name off the list.

In some cases, however, confirming that he had the wrong

Langan would take nearly an hour. Each time, Max thought he had finally uncovered his target. Each time, he pushed deeper into researching the name well-beyond the point of knowing he was wrong. But eventually, the reality would overcome his denial, he would stare at the screen, his shoulders sagging, until finally, he crossed the entry off the list and went on to the next Bradley Langan.

After trudging through twenty more names and downing two cups of coffee, Max finally unearthed the winner. A local paper had published a small obituary for Bradley Langan — except it was local to his hometown in Iowa. Born in 1975, Langan grew up on a farm in Harlan, Iowa, a small town west of Des Moines. A smart kid, he graduated high school near the top of his class, snagged a spot at Wake Forest University, and took out a student loan to attend. To pay for the loan, he often spent his vacation time working — either for the university or whatever jobs he could catch in the area. The obituary read:

> *Always diligent, always dedicated, Bradley was thrilled to be helping build the new golf course at Grandover Resort. Bradley's father loved golf and spoke often of how his son worked on the course. Sadly, on August 12, 1996 our son lost his life during an unexpected storm when …*

Latching onto that specific date, Max was able to go back to his Winston-Salem sources and find the official public police report of the incident. He had looked through these databases earlier in his search and found nothing about Langan or a worker being struck by lightning. But the exact date produced results — meaning somebody had put in effort to see the information buried.

Reading over the report, Max understood why.

Bradley had a girlfriend, Lyla Yanosey, and she had an interest in — surprise — the occult. A quick search through Wake Forest records brought up a photo of Lyla. Pale skin, black hair, black makeup, black clothing, and a steady expression of disdain, she wore her interests as a statement.

Not the kind of girl Max would have pegged for Bradley. Then again, college often brought with it a sense of adventure and experimentation to students. Perhaps the boy simply wanted to try someone different from the cornfield girls back home.

According to the police report — and reading between the lines with an expert eye — Max pieced together a rough idea of what had happened. On the night of August 12, Bradley and Lyla went out to the unfinished Hole 4 on the East Course. Soon the grass would be brought in, so Lyla must have convinced him that nobody would ever know what they had done. Also a possibility — Bradley didn't believe in spells and simply went along to appease his girlfriend. Either way, the two hiked through the dirt to the modeled hill back in the woods.

With a four-foot metal pipe, Lyla carved a casting circle into the ground. From police photos of the scene, Max couldn't tell what she intended the spell to do, but he made a note to have Sandra look at it later. If Bradley ever showed concern, Lyla overcame his doubts. She must have. After all, they stayed even as a rainstorm drifted in.

Even if Lyla was a witch-in-training, Max clearly saw that she was a novice. Not only due to her youth but because she died with a stunned expression — surprised at the results of her spell. And that work? Whatever spell she had attempted, she didn't trust herself. Max discerned that from the deep grooves on the outside of the circle — Lyla pacing around and around, double- and triple- checking her work.

Max pictured it all. Bradley standing aside, holding the metal pipe, watching Lyla's serious attitude and careful consideration of all she had written in the dirt. Perhaps he felt tingling — a new energy around him. Perhaps her insistence on staying in the rain convinced him. Whatever the spark, something in him lit up. Suddenly, his girlfriend's little game became real. He urged Lyla to quit, warned her to stop playing with evil, even threatened to leave, but he never moved. Simple love compelled him. Or maybe old school chivalry. No way would Bradley leave her alone in this.

Lightning crackled out of a sky that had not threatened such a burst. Rain, yes, but not a single flash or rumble of thunder preceded the event nor was there any further activity afterward. The lightning arced down, shrieking across the dark sky, guided by forces both of and beyond physics. For while Lyla's spell may have created the bolt, it was Bradley holding the metal pipe that attracted the electrical charge.

The strike killed him instantly. Lyla appeared to have placed her hand on his shoulder at the time. Her right palm and fingers showed severe burns. She was still alive when the EMTs arrived but never made it to the hospital. Apparently, on her dying breath, she said, "I can do it."

While Max recognized there were large gaps and questions when trying to connect the tale of Bradley and Lyla with the arriving witches staying at the Grandover Resort, his gut promised the connection existed. When it came to the paranormal, sometimes he had nothing else to rely on but his gut. Besides, he felt this one particularly strong.

He called Sandra. When she answered, he could hear Madame Novak jabbering in the background. An uneasy chill crossed his spine.

"Any luck?" he asked.

"Nothing yet. I thought it would be easier, but it's turned into a bit of a needle in the haystack search at the moment."

"Well, this might help." He explained all he had learned about Bradley, Lyla, and the failed spell that killed them both.

When he finished, she said, "I don't know how that helps me figure out what spells Madame Ti's captors are using, but it does help us with one thing."

"Oh?"

"We know that whatever Sung Park and the other witches are going to do at the Grandover, it's going to happen tonight."

"And why do we know that?"

"Because the last witch on the list, LaShanna Mill, arrives at the airport tonight, and tonight is the full moon."

Chapter 14

THE PLAN FOR THAT NIGHT was simple enough, and both Max and Sandra agreed that it provided the least amount of risk. Drummond, however, disagreed. Vehemently.

"You've done some bone-headed things before," the ghost said as Max drove to the Grandover Resort, "but putting your darling wife in danger this way is the bone-headiest of them all."

"She's more than capable," Max said.

"I'm not doubting that, and doll, before you start in on my chauvinism, I'm only saying that a man shouldn't take the woman he loves for granted like this. Assuming that you'll be fine because you're a witch is, frankly, the kind of stupidity that I've come to —"

"Enough!" Sandra said. "If the two of you continue to argue about my safety, I'm going to make you worry about your own safety." She pointed at Drummond. "And you know I can cast spells at you."

Pouting as he neared the Grandover Resort exit, Max said, "Hey, I've been defending you."

"I can defend myself." To Drummond: "The fact is that Max has looked into the property, and I've looked into the magic. I've seen pictures of Lyla's spell, too. Not much there — novice is generous. But we're the two people who know all the information to make our exploration of the hotel worthwhile. We're the two who might notice the small detail that'll help us all. But we can't do that if you're not following LaShanna Mill. It's that plain, straightforward, and simple. Got it?"

Lowering his head, the ghost muttered, "Yes, ma'am."

In the end, she let him off the hook, acknowledging that his heart was in the right place — even if his mouth wasn't. For his part, Drummond apologized, admitted that Sandra had proven her strength numerous times, and that he merely worried since the plan meant he wouldn't be right by their side. Max decided to be the smartest of all. He kept quiet.

Winding through the curvy road leading to the hotel, Max pushed aside the arguments and focused on the coming moments. He and Sandra guessed they had, at most, two hours to search the hotel for any clue as to when the witches would act and what they might do. There were several witching hours throughout the night, the Big Two being midnight and three in the morning, and so far, Sandra had yet to determine the correct one.

The only factor they could count on — nothing would happen until LaShanna Mill arrived. Sandra had been the one to suggest that Drummond tail the witch. She pointed out that once the witch arrived and he confirmed the resort as her destination, he could use the Other to travel fast and meet up with them. Any deviations or concerning behaviors of the witch could be reported far faster than if Max tailed her. Max had a cell phone, but that meant making the noise of calling and talking.

Drummond put up a few more weak points of protest, but as the hotel came into view, he had run out of time. "I'm not happy about this."

"Clearly," Max said.

"You can't trust any of the witches."

"We know," Sandra said.

"The second I know Mill is coming here, I'm shooting ahead to join you."

"We expect nothing less," Max said.

"Don't make me regret this."

"Stop worrying," Sandra said. "And get going."

With a slow tip of the hat, Drummond disappeared from the car.

Max parked in the lot, and as they walked toward the hotel, passing a fountain display surrounded by red and white flowers, he held Sandra's hand. He wanted them to look casual, like a couple on vacation. He also wanted to hold her.

To their right, nestled between two trees, a spotlighted statue of an 8-point buck watched them stroll toward the entranceway. Sandra's grip tightened. At first, Max thought something about the deer had caused her reaction, but when he glanced ahead, he realized the spinning door into the hotel awaited them. She wasn't nervous. Merely asking a question. He squeezed her hand back, pulled her closer, and kissed her cheek.

They were ready.

The lobby of the Grandover Resort certainly warranted the name *Grand.* Taking old Southern architecture — large, open, with wide staircases forming an X, a small landing at the center, white with black railings, huge arched openings following the balcony above — and blending it with a modern twist — six grided skylights, contemporary furniture, lovely tiled-floor in a geometric pattern of black, tan, and white — the first taste of the resort conveyed a sense of strolling through an enclosed village, of stepping out of the mundane world and opening up to something singular, of special opportunities that awaited. Max hated to use the word, but there was a sense of the *magical* hanging in the air. Perhaps that was his knowledge of the unique guests residing somewhere inside, but he wasn't entirely convinced.

Before any of the staff could make eye contact or ask to assist them, Max and Sandra headed off to the left as if they knew exactly where they wanted to go. The entrance to a steakhouse called *1808* sat under the staircase, and the dying aroma of the night's final meals mingled with the hotel's fragrance of expensive perfumes and money. The hostess smiled from her podium, and Max offered a short nod as they continued onward. He caught the relief on her face — no last minute customers to keep everyone busy after closing.

Down a short hall, they reached a junction. The path forward looked like any hotel walkway with an abstract carpet design and quiet halls, but on their left, a long stretch of walls covered with artwork on both sides. Golden light bounced upward to a white, tiled ceiling, then rained down creating a serene, calm environment. Innocuous, easy-listening played throughout the halls. A sign on the wall read:

The Gallery at Grandover
Celebration of North Carolina Artists

The art represented a variety of styles and talent. Some focused on North Carolina landscapes while others depicted the state's people. One artist devoted all her paintings to origami swans, and another found inspiration in portraying the power of the bull.

Nothing of the occult. Nothing related to witchcraft. Max checked with Sandra to be sure, but she continued on. This wasn't what they needed.

They reached the golf club section of the hotel. The change in smell could not be mistaken. The scents of leather and new clothing now dominated. They walked up and down the length of the hall, noting a shop selling gear, a place to sign up and pay for time on the course, and off to the right, an enormous ballroom with arched wooden bracing and a stone fireplace at one end. Though empty now, Max could easily see the room abound with large, round tables, drunken men and women, and either a wedding reception or the annual meeting of the Rotary Club. Just as easily, Max could see thirteen witches gathered in a circle, chanting in forgotten tongues, writhing to the forces gathering around them.

He glanced over at Sandra. She shook her head. They headed back to take a different path.

After a short distance, they entered the convention center portion of the hotel. Conference rooms, more ballrooms, as well as two business gatherings being hosted that day — this section presented a stark change. Though the décor maintained its elegant appearance, the odor of old coffee polluted, and the rumble of distant talk mixed with hard-working air conditioners. There were small restaurants hidden in the back as well as a game room. If not for the maps on digital displays periodically, Max feared he might have gotten lost.

When they finally found their way back to the lobby, he said, "Nothing at all?"

"Not that I noticed." She jutted her chin toward the elevators. "Maybe we should check the other floors."

"There's a few more conference rooms on the second floor, but otherwise, it's all rooms for people to stay in. You want to break into those?"

She shrugged. "You got a better idea?"

"Not going to jail would be one."

"Nobody's going to call the cops. People here have too much money to call the cops. If a maid or some other staff catches us, they'll ask what we're up to, and they'll swallow whatever bull we shovel. *Oh, I'm sorry. I must've got my room number mixed up.* They'll watch us, though. Make sure we're not causing trouble. Worst thing is we get caught again, and they throw us out. They might threaten to call the cops, but as long as they can't find anything stolen on us, they'll want to quietly get us far away."

"I'm impressed." Max's face screwed up. "A bit scared, too. How do you know all this? You run a secret life of crime?"

"I don't discount everything Drummond says. I actually listen to him and learn."

"I prefer to think you're a secret master criminal."

She chuckled as they walked to the elevators. The abstract carpet design continued inside the elevator while brass railings, black paneling, and large wall-mounted mirrors completed the décor. She hovered her finger over the third-floor button. A moment of thought and she opted for the tenth floor.

"You know something I don't?" Max asked.

"I know lots of things you don't."

"Cute. But what's going on?"

She inclined her head toward the back corner. "We have a guest."

Max glanced over. "A ghost?"

"Middle-aged man. Dressed to go golfing." She stared at the corner briefly. "He says his wife poisoned him."

"Why'd she do that?" Max asked in the direction Sandra appeared to be listening.

After getting a response, she said, "According to him, she was jealous of his business success and didn't like being a housewife. He promises that the whole thing with the housekeeping woman cleaning his room was a misunderstanding."

The elevator doors slid open. As they exited, Max said, "He still with us?"

"No. I think he mostly goes up and down the elevator."

Max gazed down the long hotel corridor. Stone gray walls, wood doors, sconces spread evenly, and a window at the far end that looked over the golf courses. A library hush, too. As if staying in such a ritzy resort deserved special appreciation.

"Why are we listening to this ghost? He cheated on his wife, got caught, and she killed him. Am I missing something? I don't see how that relates to why we're here."

She halted at the first door they came across. Max reached toward the knob — not really expecting it to open but willing to try for Sandra's sake. She waved him off.

"A ghost like that is an old school, basic type of thing. He isn't malicious and he isn't causing problems. No witch cursed him. No spell binds him. Just a guy who died and can't accept it's time to move on. But before he started in on the woes of his infidelity, he specified the tenth floor. Never mentioned it again. I suspect he died of a heart attack on that elevator — that's why he stayed there. Never leaving the site of his death."

"Then why did he tell you to go to the tenth floor?"

"Exactly."

Clutching each other's hands, they pretended to stroll through the corridor, but Max thought nobody would be fooled. The tension pounding his temples had to be noticeable. At each door, they slowed and watched it closely. He didn't know what they expected to happen. Maybe something subtle like a shimmering entity would fling open the door and scream *Thar she blows!* as a monstrous witch cackled over a cauldron of boiling limbs.

Max smirked at his ridiculous thoughts.

Until they heard a murmured voice behind one door. They froze. Eyes locked on the wood, trying to pierce through it, trying not to see at the same time.

Hours seemed to pass in those few seconds, but when nothing happened, when the door remained closed, Sandra broke the charm by moving onward. Max only joined when their linked hands tugged him forward.

When they reached the window at the end of the hall, they both pressed against the glass and gazed upon the night landscape. Houses lit much of the perimeter of the golf courses giving the dark lands shape. The full moon filled in the rest of the details with its ghostly light.

Max said, "I don't get why this ghost would send us to the tenth floor when it's just another floor. You didn't see any other ghosts here, did you?"

"I would've told you."

"It doesn't make any sense. I know ghosts can be obscure sometimes, but —"

Drummond dropped through the ceiling. "Watch who you're calling obscure, pal."

Though he tried to hide it, Max had jumped at his partner's sudden appearance. He wanted to chastise Drummond, but after all these years, he knew the ghost thought it a funny thing to do. Or maybe he simply took pleasure in the few specialties of being dead.

Sandra said, "Is something wrong or is she here?"

"She's here. Room 907. Your new friend in the elevator — Carlos, by the way — he sent you here to keep you away from the witches."

Max's eyes dropped to the floor. "Are they all down there? On the ninth floor?"

"Don't know. LaShanna Mill had a ward that kept me from touching her but not from following her. No problem in the Uber that brought her here."

"Her sisters didn't bother picking her up?"

"They would have," Sandra said, pointing out the window, "but it's the full moon. That just confirms they're working a spell tonight. No time for being polite."

Drummond said, "When she got to the ninth floor, I couldn't

follow her. No ghost can get on that floor. Either the floor itself is warded, or there are enough witches staying on that floor with enough personal wards between them."

"Or both."

"Right. Both." Pursing his lips as he floated a short circle, he said, "We're out of time. What's your best guess for the spell they're going to cast tonight?"

"I don't know. I never had enough to go on. It could be one of dozens of things."

"So, no spell, and I can't spy on them because of the wards. You definitely can't spy on them because they'll see you coming easily."

Max said, "The best clue we have is Bradley Langan, but I can't connect him to the witches. Just to this hotel."

"Where in this hotel?" Sandra said, perking up. "You told me he and this girl, a witch, cast a spell and he got struck by lightning during construction, but you never said exactly where it happened."

Max slapped the wall and swore. "We were in such a rush. I can't believe I didn't mention that. I mean I'm supposed to be the expert here, the super-researcher. How could I slip up like that?"

Drummond said, "You're being a moron right now. Stop self-flagellating and tell us."

"Right. Sorry." He gazed out the window, across the dark. "Fourth hole on the East Course."

After a short burst of phone tapping, Sandra nodded. "Yeah, it'll be there. Hole 4 is tucked away from view. A little hilly, a creek, but mostly woods surround the area."

"Why wouldn't they cast their spell on the ninth floor? Drummond's right, we can't get there to stop them. They'll see us coming."

"They chose this hotel because of Bradley Langan. They chose this hotel because Hole 4 is secluded. They'll perform the spell — the rite — under the full moon on that site of magical energy because they are delving into old, old magic. The kind of thing that reverberates throughout nature. A hotel room, nine stories in the air — there's no connection to Mother Earth, up here. I'm telling you, right now, we need to get out to Hole 4. If we have any hope of stopping this, we need to get out there before they do."

Swallowing the knot in his chest, Max rushed to the elevator. The others followed.

Chapter 15

TURNING THE CORNER FROM THE ELEVATOR BLANK, Max had one simple thought. Get to that golf hole. But his adrenaline spiked as they neared the main counter in the lobby. He halted and Sandra bumped against him. He spun back.

"Michon Charee. Ten o'clock."

He turned Sandra away from the witch at the counter and headed the opposite direction. As they closed on the hallway art gallery, Drummond waved them to hurry by. Max peeked down the hall to find Sung Park taking in the North Carolina paintings.

"Shouldn't they be getting ready for their spell?" Max asked as they scurried toward the convention rooms.

Sandra checked her phone. "It's only 12:45. They've missed the first one, and they've got a couple hours until the second big witching hour. I'd guess they're killing time."

Weaving through the wide halls, evading anybody lurking around, Max and Sandra found their way to the back of the building. Drummond scouted ahead in case the other two witches had decided to explore the hotel. Without hesitation, Max pushed open the glass doors and stepped onto the manicured pathway leading to the East Course.

He wanted to pop on his phone's flashlight but held off. If any of the witches watched from the ninth floor, they would see his light traipsing toward Hole 4. Not a good way to start a spy mission.

And that was exactly how he thought of it. Keeping low, rushing over the open fairways, planning to ambush the witches before they could cause serious damage — okay, maybe not spy stuff, he admitted, but certainly more than an average stakeout.

Once they had gone far enough not to be easily spotted, Max stood, stretching his back, and took Sandra's hand again. They walked the rest of the way. Turned out to take a while. Golf courses were big.

"You ever play golf?" Max asked Drummond.

The ghost snorted a laugh. "I lived through the Great Depression. Never had the money, but even if I did, this game ain't for me. You got to have a lot of free time, too. Me — I was always working a case or trying to find a case or having a case find me. Even when work was dry, I still lived with it all."

Sandra said, "You didn't have a partner, then, did you?"

"I had people I could rely on in a pinch or when I needed information, but they had their own lives, too."

"Like Brenda and Osorio for us."

"Sort of like them. I wish the two of you could have met Leroy. A great researcher of witchcraft and the occult. You would've loved him."

"Was there anybody you could talk to? Someone to share the burden of a case or share the knowledge of what reality really is."

"Not back then. Not usually. There were some women, but they never lasted. Frankly, back in my day, men didn't talk about what bothered them. We lived through one world war, and I died during another. Talking about feelings wasn't in the cards."

Sandra let those words lift into the air, and Max refrained from a snappy comment. They let the quiet fill the spaces around them. Like soldiers closing in on an enemy position, they trudged toward Hole 4. Each slogging step weighed on Max's back. Nothing had been ordinary about this case, and his nerves jangled at the thought of what might come.

When they reached the markers for where to tee off, Max's shirt had soaked despite the cool air. The full moon bathed them, and the sound of trickling waters reached them from the nearby creek.

"Over there." Sandra indicated the tree line. "We should get a good view, and I don't think they'll be able to see us unless they're looking hard."

"Good choice," Drummond said. "Might be far enough away

from their wards that I'll be okay, too."

Max scanned the small hill they stood upon. "Are we sure it'll be here and not on the green?"

Taking a few steps, Sandra closed her eyes and put out her hands. A few more steps and she stopped. "It'll be here. There's an energy push on this hill. If I had to, I'd bet Bradley Langan died right here."

"Isn't he around to ask?"

"Must've moved on."

Drummond added, "No ghosts around here, at all. A bit surprising, really. Considering the advanced age of most golfers — all those heart attacks and strokes — a course like this can often have as many ghosts as a small graveyard."

Leading the way, Sandra brought the trio to the tree line. "Makes me think this is the right place when even the ghosts are afraid to hang around here."

Several feet into the thick of trees, Max and Sandra found a vantage point from where they could observe anybody who came by. Not too uncomfortable, either. Once settled, the soft roll of the night pushed forward — the drone of cars on the nearby highway, the trill of one family's noise blending with another, the press of silence within the gaps. They waited.

Not long after, Drummond thrust back his shoulders. "It'll be a while before the witching hour. Think I'll go check the Other, see if there's any news that might be helpful."

"You kidding?" The words whipping out before Max could stop his mouth.

"What's wrong with that?"

"We're on a stakeout. You love stakeouts. I've never known you to blow off this kind of opportunity. And don't tell me you're going to the Other for our benefit. We're here for you, you know. We're family. Why don't you stop being a stubborn prick and tell us what's going on over there?"

Drummond glowered back. The top of his lip curled enough to be noticed. His eyes cut through the air. The combination caused Max's insides to chill.

"I'll return later," the ghost said in a cold monotone. Then he vanished.

Sandra slapped Max's thigh. "Why'd you do that?"

"What? He's been weird for days, and now, when things might get dangerous, he's abandoning us to go play with his girlfriend or ex-girlfriend or whatever she is."

"We don't know what he's going to do, and you of all people should trust him."

"I do trust him." Max's voice rose enough that the sound blared around the stillness of the trees. He immediately dropped to a stern whisper. "I do trust him."

Matching his intensity, she said, "Then why did you yell at him? You want to know what's upsetting him, but something's upsetting you, too. How about you tell me that?"

"Me? I'm not upset." The words threatened to rise again. She cocked her head to the side, gazing at him until he snickered at his absurdity. Then: "I care about him, that's all."

"I do, too, but —"

"PB and J are pretty much gone. Once school starts up, PB will drive away, and once the year's done, J will graduate and go on to college or wherever. My mother is dying. There's no stopping that, and we're all just trying to make her comfortable and maybe find a few moments of joy in what time she has left. Soon, it'll be us again."

"You're worried Drummond's going to leave, too?"

"Not like that. Not like I'm an empty-nester or something. It's more like — it's that if he holds everything inside, bottles it up like his generation is prone to do, then whatever's going on in the Other will eat away at him. The Sandwich Boys and my mother — their presence has helped loosen Drummond, helped him open up. He's become a real friend. I'd hate to lose that."

Sandra thread her arm around his and rested her head on his shoulder. "Honey, he's not going anywhere. He loves working these cases. He loves us."

"You and I are both old enough to know better. Most friendships are like tides — they come in for a time and then go away. And they're rarely as deep as we think."

"Getting poetic on me?"

"I'm serious. Think back to when we were in college. I had a whole bunch of friends. Now? I haven't spoken to any of them in years. Over a decade. My life is us and the boys, my mother and Drummond. That's it."

"You also have Brenda and Osorio. They're new, but they are with us."

"They work with us. At best, they're acquaintances."

"That's how friendships often start. You work with someone, stop a few witches with them, have a few near-death experiences together, and *voila*, you've bonded into something more. At least, that's how it can happen in our business." When he didn't laugh, she kissed his shoulder. "Look, honey, I know you're worried about all of it, but if you can't trust him, you can trust me. I'm not going anywhere, and I'm confident that Drummond isn't, either. Maybe someday he'll take a different path, but I suspect he's going to stay with us until we're ghosts ourselves."

"You mean we've got to spend eternity with him, too?"

They both chuckled. Soft but sincere.

"The dead can be like that," she said. "When they find a connection to the living — and we're a very strong connection for Drummond — they don't want to give it up. It's like a cozy campfire on a winter night."

"Now you're getting poetic."

She stood and inhaled the woodsy scents. The moonlight cast an ethereal glow around her, and Max wished they weren't on stakeout. But that always seemed to be the situation.

When not on a case, they stayed at home and watched something on Netflix. It took abducted witches and ancient spells to get them out here, together in the woods, talking honest and plain. Then again, Max figured if some off night he suggested they go into the woods to fool around under the moonlight, she would laugh. For that matter, he had plenty of opportunities to make such offers, yet he never took them.

"I had only a few friends growing up," she said, whirling him out of his spiraling thoughts. "Hard to make friends when you see all the ghosts around. As a kid, I would tell people — early on, I assumed everybody saw them — so you can imagine my popularity. I was the weird kid. Spooky kid. But somehow, I always had at least one person in my life, and that's always been enough. I think it is for everyone. Some people want more, think they need more, but if you've got one person you can rely on, you'll be okay. And you know that I'm not going anywhere. You can always count on me. So, even if Drummond were to take on a new personality and drop all his well-earned loyalty and go off with Miss 1800s to Cancun, you're stuck with me never leaving your side."

Max rose next to her. He placed a finger under her chin, tilting her head up gently, and he kissed her. Slow. Soft. She nuzzled her head against his chest, and they held each other under the moonlight. They listened to each other breathe, they felt the thump of each other's heart. Max would have been content to spend hours without moving, and indeed, he lost track of how long they held each other in those woods.

Until the witches arrived.

Chapter 16

DRUMMOND APPEARED SECONDS AFTER the first witch reached the hill. "That's LaShanna Mill. She's much taller than the rest."

All four witches wore hooded cloaks that brushed the grass with their bordered edges. Though Max couldn't be sure of the color — probably black — the moonlight made the cloaks' designs quite clear. Witch symbols created wide pinstripes, painting each cloak — thus, each witch — with ancient words and blessings.

The tall woman, LaShanna, moved to an assigned point with silent grace. Another carried a large canvas bag that she set to the side before cueing her position off LaShanna. One by one the witches took their spots, each in clear relation to the next, until they formed a large circle. Max had no doubt they stood on the direct compass points.

"Any idea what they're casting yet?" Max whispered.

Sandra said, "I don't think I'll know until it's done."

"You want to let them cast it? That can't be a good idea."

"What could we do right now that wouldn't get us killed?"

Drummond clicked his tongue. "Sandra's right. There are four of them and only two of you. They're all warded. This is as far as I can go toward them. Best thing tonight is to consider this information gathering."

Watching as the witches bowed their heads — a flock of red splashing out of one hood marked Rosita Stakson — Max ground his teeth. The urge to disrupt this spell flushed through him like pulsating heat, but he pushed that aside. Sandra and Drummond were being smart, and he had to be smart, too.

They simply didn't know enough. Madame Ti was still missing. Emily Dodson was still dead. And they still had no idea who perpetrated either crime. All they knew for sure — the entire witch community had heard about it and prepared for war. It'd be a good thing for the Porters to know who all the players were before this got started.

Except it's already started. Well, Max could keep those defeatist thoughts to himself.

"My dear sisters from around the world," LaShanna said, opening her arms in welcome. "A call was put out, and you answered. I thank you. We face perilous times as many of our ancestors have faced before, but if we four perish, we can do so knowing that we acted. When history knocked upon our doors, we answered."

Not the usual mystical blathering of witches, but not that far off, either. Max half-listened as he scanned the area for any other witches to arrive. Part of him wanted to pay closer attention, treat this as an unusual event, but he had seen group castings before. Numerous times. A lot of posturing went on before the actual spellwork began.

Sandra had explained to him that the speeches were an important part of the process. Not because they imbued any magical energy to the spell, but rather, in a group casting, they worked much like a coach giving a pep talk. They served to unite the group, build their excitement, jostle them out of their daily lives, and fill them with a sense of importance — at least, importance surrounding this moment, this spell.

For Max, however, it amounted to little more than jabbering. He didn't see the need to listen. Besides, he knew Sandra would be examining and dissecting every millisecond of the casting in her search to understand what they hoped to achieve. That included the pre-game pep talk.

But as Max's attention wandered, all sense of the usual slipped away. LaShanna did not crescendo her speech until reaching a moment that she would gather the witches' hands and begin the spell in earnest. Instead, she stopped speaking. That sudden quiet caught his attention. Ratcheted up his pulse, too.

"What's going on?" He cringed at the shiver in his voice.

"I have no idea."

No other answer could have struck harder. The rustling leaves on the night's gentle wind sounded like a torrential downpour, the croaking frogs and chirping crickets transformed into an off-key chorus, and Max's beating heart became a thrash-metal metronome. His mouth dried. His fingers jittered.

With one hand, LaShanna picked the witch opposite her. That witch — Max guessed Sung Park based on height — bowed deep before turning away from the circle. With graceful steps, she slid across the grass and headed straight towards the tree line.

Max clutched Sandra's hand — partly for strength, partly to yank her away from danger should they be discovered. For her part, Sandra pushed off her knees into a crouch — ready to run.

"Don't worry." Drummond drifted closer to the forest edge. "If she tries anything, I'll slam into her ward. Worst thing that'll happen is it'll distract her for a few seconds. Long enough for you to get away. Best thing is I knock her back a step or two and really draw her attention."

Either way, it would hurt their ghost partner terribly. Max appreciated that despite Drummond's recent grumpiness, he remained loyal to the team. While the sacrifice deserved some acknowledgement, Max couldn't risk speaking. The trees blocked most of the moonlight, and the ghost's pale glow did not provide any real light of its own — nothing that allowed Max to make eye contact.

If not for Sandra's fingers tightening around his, Max would have felt isolated amongst those dark trees. Instead, he held still, lungs tight, muscles locked, ready to explode, but not alone. They could do nothing more than remain motionless, be statues — rocks — and watch as Park approached.

Each step closer thumped through the ground and up Max's spine. She moved steady yet slow. So damn slow. He fought the urge to launch to his feet, to scream as he blitzed out of the trees and tackled her to the ground. He would yell for Sandra to run and trust that Drummond would help deflect the other witches. Then he would sprint off and hope that he survived.

But he held still. And she stepped closer.

"What the heck?" Drummond said.

Max heard somebody walking from deeper in the woods. He glanced back even as he caught Sung Park halting before reaching the tree line. A large, shadowed shape moved in the distance.

"You may enter," Park said, her voice as quiet as the wind yet as clear as if her mouth pressed against Max's ear.

Walking by close enough that Max could have brushed his hand against them, a man broke from the forest. He held leather reins that stretched back into the woods. With a firm tug, a deer trundled forth. A buck carrying a rack of horns that would have made a hunter salivate. The animal huffed and snorted but did not resist.

The man — young, broad shoulders, wearing jeans and a plaid shirt — knelt before Park. "I offer this gift to you all and pray I will receive your good favor." Mixing the words of formal ritual with a strong North Carolinian accent brought images of the Old South, but Max knew something far more sinister occurred.

Placing the reins into Park's outstretched hand, the man lowered his head further and scuttled backwards. As he retreated into the woods, he stood yet never turned his back on these women. Even in the shadows of the forest, Max could see the blending of fear and respect on the man's face. When he could no longer be seen, they all heard his running feet crunching the forest floor.

Sandra never stopped watching the witches. "That deer must be charmed, but I've never seen an animal charm work like that. Never seen one actually work at all."

"I have," Drummond said but did not elaborate.

"We've seen spells that can control human minds," Max said. "Why not animals?"

Sandra said, "Their fight or flight is a lot stronger."

She waved off further talk as Park led the deer into the circle of witches. Placing her hand on the animal's snout, Park arched her head back towards the moon. The deer snorted. Then it lowered to the ground, its eyes wide, its breathing shallow and fast.

It knows something's off, Max thought. It probably knew it had been compelled to obey yet sensed the wrongness.

LaShanna raised her hands wide once more. This time, she chanted one of many ancient, dead languages — secret languages — that the witches often employed. Michon, the witch Max identified by process of elimination, moved to the canvas bag while the others crowded close to the buck. When she rejoined the group, she made sure that each witch received a wooden bowl and an ornate dagger.

No sooner had she taken her position, then LaShanna bellowed a final word, and the witches moved as if the lightning that had killed Bradley Langan unleashed within them. Three witches stabbed the animal while LaShanna slit its neck with merciful speed. It managed a short sound — not quite bleating, not quite moaning, not quite surprise. Perhaps a deer's version of mortal acceptance. Max suspected no deer had ever made that sound before. Then again, Sandra had said the spell was an ancient one, so probably quite a few deer had made that sound. Long ago.

Holding the animal firmly under the chin, forcing its eyes toward the night sky, LaShanna smiled at the moon while the other witches filled their bowls with the blood spewing from its open throat. Once all four bowls had been topped off, they released the deer. It slapped the ground like meat on a wood cutting board. The witches moved back to their compass points, each holding a bowl with solemn care. Steam rose from the dead animal's neck as well as the blood-filled bowls. The stench of death grew stronger, pushing away the heavy musk of the deer and the earthy notes of the forest.

From the canvas bag, Michon brought out a large paintbrush. Horsehair, Max guessed. Or maybe even human. Certainly real hair from a once living creature. She dipped the brush in the bowl of blood and slashed it against the ground. Max didn't need to ask — the witch painted a casting circle. This spell had more to come.

As Michon continued her work, tracing over her original lines to strengthen them while also adding new symbols to the spell, the other witches repeated a single phrase. Max peeked at Sandra, but she shook her head.

"If we're lucky," she said, "we can take a picture of the casting circle when they leave."

Michon set the paintbrush aside. Instead of returning to her spot, however, she stepped behind LaShanna and removed the woman's cloak. Standing tall, holding out a bowl of blood with both hands, LaShanna wore nothing underneath. Michon continued around the circle, removing the cloaks of each witch and revealing their full nudity to the moon. When she finished, she stripped her own cloak and finally took her position on the circle.

"Very old school," Sandra said.

LaShanna raised her bowl straight above and the others followed. "To Mother Earth, to all the energies that surround and define, to the North, the South, the East, and the West, to the divine within and without, we four come together tonight to serve, to strengthen, and above all else, to claim that which is too often denied."

The word *power* flashed in Max's head as all four women tipped their bowls, drenching their naked bodies in the deer's blood. It flowed down them like warm syrup — cutting lines through their hair, forming dark tears on their faces, and painting dribbles from their shoulders. Tossing the bowls away, each woman smeared the blood straight from the shoulders, over the breasts, to circle on the belly. They swirled the blood as if caressing a pregnancy. Soon, however, Max noticed that all four made the same swirling motion — exactly the same and in exact time together.

Continuing to move in unison like a dance troupe staging a macabre performance, they joined their bloody hands and chanted for a third time. Their heads rolled from side to side, yet their focus never wavered from the deer's corpse. Max rested his arm on a low tree branch as his attention dropped to the steaming fur.

It moved.

Not as if alive. Instead, it quivered. The more intense the witches grew in their chanting, the faster the deer's muscles rippled until it appeared to be having a seizure.

Without warning, the women stiffened. So did the deer. The women thrust their heads back. The deer's ribs cracked open. A loud noise like splitting lumber. A wide hole ripped through the skin and a gust of steam billowed from the animal.

LaShanna eased to her knees. She rested a hand on the deer's fur, petting it as if to soothe, before plunging her hand into the gaping hole. Twisting her arm, she dug deeper. A breath, then she pulled her arm free, coated in more blood. With a triumphant smile, she lifted the animal's heart for the other witches to see.

That was when the branch Max leaned upon gave out. A loud snap carried through the air.

Chapter 17

WITH THE PRECISION OF A WELL-HONED MILITARY UNIT, the four witches jumped into action. LaShanna's eyes pierced into the tree line as she stood tall. In one swift motion, she handed the deer heart to Park who swaddled it in a blanket before placing it inside the canvas bag. Michon and Rosita took positions on either side of LaShanna, blocking a clear view of Park.

"Don't run," Drummond said. "Don't move at all. I don't think they can see you."

Indeed, as Max arrested all movement, the three witches waited. They listened. They leaned to peer in, but they didn't react. He and Sandra were merely shadows amongst the trees.

Park was gone. That had been the point of their maneuvers. Protect Park and the deer heart. Let them escape.

Not that Max had any intention of stopping them. Earlier, Drummond had made a good case for the Porter's weakened position, and nothing had changed. Max could hear Sandra in his head, too, pointing out that they did not know these witches, did not know their strengths or weaknesses, had no idea of their skill or accomplishments. Picking fights with unknown witches was the pinnacle of stupidity. Max could admit that he had been dumb at times, but never that kind of dumb. Well, not often, anyway.

LaShanna twitched her left hand, and the other two witches stepped forward. They craned their necks, trying to glimpse what had made that sound. Max listened to his heartbeat growing louder in his ears. He labored to breathe.

LaShanna's mouth made little movements. Silently. That could only mean one thing — she was casting a spell.

Without moving his head, Max tried to peek toward his side. Had Sandra started casting a spell, too? He thought he saw movement — perhaps she mouthed the proper words to create some form of defense — but the same shadows that protected them made it difficult to discern such specifics in his peripheral vision. Still, he knew of only a couple spells she could pull off without a proper casting circle and the time to prepare. Though they weren't overly powerful, any would be better than nothing.

Drummond said, "This'll hurt, so be ready to move."

He swished off to the left, sliding through the tree line toward the creek that led up to the green surrounding the golf hole. He hissed, bellowed, and loud cracking branches followed in the distance.

The witches flinched. A wordless conversation passed between them. Michon broke off along the fairway toward the sound. But Rosita remained. Drummond's distraction wouldn't be enough.

Rosita managed a few more tentative steps toward the trees. Worry circled her eyes. Anger, too. She expected to be attacked. He could see that. Of course, she would. The witches had gone to war. Whoever snatched Madame Ti and killed Emily Dodson probably targeted the other witches on the list. Certainly, Rosita Stakson knew that.

But whatever spell Sandra closed in on casting, it would not harm the witch. Even if she could cast such a spell under these circumstances, Sandra sought to be a different kind of witch. Harming another did not factor in. Yet her spell would do something, and Max realized what the logical choice would be. His muscles tensed as he attempted to clear his mind. When Sandra gave the command, he had to be ready. Be ready, listen, and wait.

Rosita's eyes locked on Max. Her brow scrunched, trying to comprehend the shape of a man in the woods. Not a witch. But then her focus narrowed to his side — to Sandra. As some form of comprehension struck, as Rosita's eyes widened with realization, she discovered she had been too slow. Sandra yelled one word, and Max shut his eyes like prison doors slamming closed. Yet even through his clenched lids, he saw the forest brighten with sunlight.

"Run!"

The word jolted through him, whirling his body around. He squinted against the shining light that blinded in all directions. The shocked hisses of the witches told him that Sandra's light burst caused more problems for them. She grabbed his hand and yanked him into motion.

"Go, go," LaShanna said, but she might as well have been urging Max, too. He ran faster.

Dodging limbs and leaping over rocks, they weaved through the forest. He heard Rosita stumbling behind, growling at her inability to see clearly. Michon tore in, coming in from the side, and able to see better having missed the direct attack.

Already the light dimmed like a burst of fireworks fading in the night sky. After-images of trees formed glowing skeletal shapes in Max's eyes. A limb smacked his cheek, and he sensed trunks brushing by the side. Each time he tried to slow, to get his bearings, Sandra tugged on his arm. Kept him moving.

"This way." Drummond appeared in front of them before dashing toward the left.

Too dark to run now, they stuttered through the forest. Rosita and Michon followed but also had to move cautiously. Anybody daring to run would end up with a broken leg or worse.

"Just up ahead." Drummond glanced back and winked. "We should be stepping out near the first hole. Right by the hotel."

But when they emerged from the trees, they stood directly in front of LaShanna — still on Hole 4.

"Now wait a minute." Drummond pointed back at the woods and then at the fairway.

Max's own confusion washed away under the cocky grin of the witch. "Your spell?"

LaShanna said, "A simple matter of directional misguidance." She lowered her head toward Sandra. "Nice bit of blinding light on your part."

Max forced a laugh and a casual demeanor. "Look, ladies, my wife and I thought it would be neat to come out here under the full moon and cast a little magic. It's her thing she's into. Me, I'm the golfer, but she's always liked the dark stuff. We had no idea anybody else was going to be doing the same. Especially this late at night. When we saw you, frankly, we were impressed. I mean she can make her little dazzling lights and all, but what you did was amazing. We're just amateurs at all of this. Didn't mean to intrude. So, we thank you for the show, but I think we should go home now and let you get on with whatever you're getting on with."

"She ain't buying it." Drummond cracked his knuckles and hunched forward.

With a sharp but hopefully subtle motion of his hand, Max stopped his partner from barreling into the witch's ward. Drummond had to know he couldn't break through on the first try, and Max guessed these witches wouldn't allow a second. But beyond that, Max watched their behavior, their expressions. All the witches were new to the area. If they had heard of the Porter Agency, they certainly didn't know what the Porters looked like. In fact, the one slice of information they would have heard — if they heard anything at all — was that these locally-known paranormal investigators had a ghost partner. If Drummond slammed into LaShanna's ghost ward, these witches would fast realize the catch they had made.

At the same time, Max knew Drummond was right — she wasn't buying the story. LaShanna inspected the two before her as if inspecting troops for any mistake in their uniforms. To Sandra, she said, "You made that light without a casting circle."

Sandra held her ground, not even flinching. "You spun us in a loop without a casting circle."

"I've been a witch for a long time. Your husband says you're an amateur, but I've never met somebody starting out who can do that. Are you the most gifted beginner I've come across, or are you lying about your experience?"

"Lying? I haven't claimed anything. Those were his words."

LaShanna's lips pulled back with true amusement. "Spoken like a true witch." She gazed at her peers, and her joy vanished. "Did you come here to kill the rest of us?"

Max said, "Hold on. Don't you accuse her of anything. We didn't kill Emily or anybody."

Stomping forward, Michon backhanded Max across the cheek. Hard. As the night sparkled with a private light show, he tried to refocus on LaShanna. But with an expert motion, Michon swept Max's leg out from under him, dropping him to the short grass. As he attempted to sit up, she rushed in and pressed her knee against his head.

Again, Drummond readied to attack. Again, Max waved him off.

"I can't just float here and wait for her to kill you."

"Please, stop," Sandra said, so calmly and in control that Drummond and the witches responded the same — they stopped. With the carefulness of a seasoned witch, one that used the honorific of Madame, Sandra gestured towards Michon. She said nothing more, yet the knee lifted off Max's head. He saw Michon look at LaShanna before standing and joining her leader's side.

LaShanna said, "You have more presence than I gave you credit, but —"

Sandra put out her hand and waited until she had all three witches' undivided attention. "You have come here during a stressful period, and it's understandable that you would be cautious, even skeptical, but those are the same reasons we are here tonight. Strangers to our town, witches no less, make us cautious and skeptical. Let me assure you that we are not assassins sent by one of the many groups vying for power. That's your place, I suspect. You already know I am a witch — more than an amateur — but I had no intention of harming you tonight. I only wanted to observe, wanted to know who had come to North Carolina and why."

LaShanna weighed these words. Then she nodded toward Max. "And him?"

"Dragged along tonight and probably not going to let me forget it for a few years."

The lie was delivered so smoothly, Max could have believed it, too. Sandra offered her hand, and he managed to stand without groaning.

Backing away, she said, "We're leaving now. I suggest you do the same."

"You suggest?" LaShanna's eyes flared with a fire Max had failed to notice before. "I think you're misreading your predicament. You will not leave here to go report what we have done. You will not be allowed to speak of this night ever."

Rosita and Michon spread to either side of the Porters. Max clenched his fists, but the ache throbbing along his flank promised he would not fare well in a physical confrontation.

"That's it," Drummond said. "I've heard enough threats made against you tonight."

Despite Max's urgent motions that he tried to hide, Drummond blitzed forward, shouting as he flew overhead, and slammed into the barrier formed from three witches all wearing ghost wards. He ricocheted upward and off to the left like a pinball hitting a bumper. As his limbs flailed and his body tumbled, his unmistakable roar attested to the pain he suffered.

Though unable to hear or see any of it, the witches certainly felt the hit. All three paused and gazed off in the direction Drummond hovered. While staring at this empty space, LaShanna's brow crinkled. Max thought she might be putting it together — married couple, one a witch, and now a ghost attempting to interfere.

If the women on this list had been brought in to bolster Cecily Hull's power, then surely she would have informed them of the Porters. Unless Max overestimated the value of the Agency — value and threat. After all, several high-profile witches no longer existed because of the Porters.

Whatever LaShanna's thoughts, however, she turned back to Max and Sandra with a dismissive shrug and an angry eye. She stood over Max, savoring his impending pain. Gazing up at her, he hoped he projected either calm acceptance or stiff defiance but figured he gave off a more terrified sensation. His throat dried up.

But her face flashed with red light as the whine of a siren grew in the distance.

"Hell," Rosita said, her attention pulled to the resort parking lot. A fire engine rolled in.

"Why are they here?" Michon said.

LaShanna shifted toward Sandra. "Her. That spell was seen. Nearby houses or people in the hotel — they saw the flash of light and called the fire department or 9-1-1. Probably thought something exploded."

Finding his voice again, Max said, "If you kill us, there won't be time to get away, let alone dispose of our bodies. As it is, they'll find the dead deer."

Crouching down but maintaining her focus on Sandra, LaShanna said, "This isn't your town anymore, witch. Move away. Find some small village to call home. Maybe in another state. Pretty soon, North Carolina will belong to us. If I find you're still here, then, well — I'll show you some spells you'll never forget."

She flashed her teeth and made a biting motion. As she stood, she slapped Max across the face. Without another word, she and her witches gathered all their things and strolled off — heading further north, away from the hotel.

More sirens. A quick peek revealed several fire engines, an ambulance, and some police cruisers flooding the parking lot with their multi-colored lights.

Sandra said, "We better go, too."

"Definitely." To Drummond: "You going to be okay?"

Rubbing the side of his head, the ghost nodded. "Go home. Take the woods until you can get out on one of the neighborhood streets, but yeah, go home. Get some rest. I'll see you in the morning to figure all this out."

With sunrise was only a few hours off, Max hoped Drummond's definition of *the morning* included part of the afternoon. Holding Sandra's hand, leaning against her shoulder, they stumbled back through the tree line.

Chapter 18

WHEN THEY FINALLY ARRIVED HOME — after traipsing through the woods, slinking into their car, and evading the chaos of the police and fire departments — Max and Sandra were exhausted. Sandra allowed one minute to discard her clothing and throw on some sweats before collapsing onto the bed. Max tried to do the same, but sleep eluded him.

Too many thoughts battled for his attention, and his heightened nerves refused to relax. Tomorrow night, sleep would come. He had no doubt of that. A body could only withstand so much. But there would be no rest for now.

Shuffling into the kitchen, he turned on the coffee maker and stared out the window. The tiny backyard needed mowing. That had been PB's job for the last few years. But PB would be gone soon, and though handing the job off to J would be easy enough, that young man would be heading off to college in a year. Max wondered what other jobs would soon revert to him. He had come to rely on the Sandwich Boys.

Hot coffee steamed from his *#1 Dad* mug as Max drifted from one room to the next. He kept seeing LaShanna's face — looming over him, savoring the control she wielded, anticipating the pain she planned to inflict. Not all witches murdered people, of course. Not all delighted in it, either. No matter what else, they were still human beings. But just as murderers could be found in the general population of the world, they existed within the witch community, too. And when words such as *war* were thrown about, the sadistic and bloodthirsty discovered their societal leash removed.

Despite drinking more coffee, Max's mouth dried out. His

pulse increased. If he now faced these types of witches, then the old way of doing things might no longer work. After all, he relied on a witch's desire to remain anonymous, to avoid public scrutiny. Centuries of being burned at the stake had taught them that secrecy held great benefits. In the past, no matter what trouble he had fallen into, only the worst of witches truly consider killing him. Often, other witches prevented it. Murders tended to get noticed, and the police could only ignore so much.

But now — a war. Already one witch had been abducted and another slaughtered. The public would have to be kept out of the way as much as possible, but Max didn't think LaShanna fretted over a little collateral damage. Even a few *Occultists on the Rise* news pieces wouldn't upset her. She might want the publicity — make her more mysterious, give her more power through fear.

In the living room, he saw a pale blue light sweep by the driveway window. Drummond. Though only a short time until dawn, the ghost had chosen to patrol the house like he did on many nights.

Max strolled back through the kitchen and out the side door. The crisp air filled his lungs, waking him as much as the coffee. He sat on the concrete block that acted as a stoop to the kitchen entrance and waved as Drummond came around again.

"What are you doing up?" Drummond's concern mixed with a slight annoyance. "I figured you and Sandra would be out until noon."

"Not sure I'm ever going to sleep again."

"Oh? What's got you? Not the first time you've almost died."

Max set his coffee mug aside and stretched his legs. Leaning back on his elbows, his head thumped against the kitchen door. "You didn't think this was different?"

"The deer heart thing was new, but blood magic is like that — bloody. Otherwise, just your average crazy witches doing crazy things."

"Seemed different to me. In fact, from the moment Cecily Hull called us into this case, everything's felt different. There's a strange vibe about all this."

"Yeah, well, you've been caught between warring factions of

witches before, but if this is a true witch war, it'll be the first time with the entire witch community. That's going to bring out some big spells. Things nobody's seen in ages."

"I'm concerned what effect that might have on our business — on Sandra. Everything has been up in the air for so long, and every time I think we've found some kind of equilibrium, it all gets blown out of whack. I finally saw a path ahead that led to — I don't know — maybe some predictability. You know? A way where our days would be somewhat reliable, routine, even in the madness of what we do. But now —"

Drummond laughed. He brought his hat down to his chest, shook his head, and laughed. "Not possible, my friend. Not possible."

"Of course, it is."

"Go through your entire life. Not just the time in North Carolina after you met me, not just the Porter Agency stuff, but your entire life. Can you name one point that lasted more than a few days in which life was stable? Maybe it seemed so when you were a kid, but that's only because you didn't know what really went on around you. You were too focused on playing baseball or videogames or whatever your generation was into. I guarantee that if you even found one such stable time before, no way did that exist after you discovered sex. Trust me on this. You've got to embrace the instability of life. Don't go trying to fix it all because you can't. It's inherently off-kilter."

The combination of caffeine, adrenaline, and near-death made Max a little punchy. Or perhaps he had simply had enough. "If that's true, then why do you keep trying to patch things up with Miss 1800s? You been running off to the Other every chance you get and come back grumpier every time. Only wanting to focus on work, never willing to talk about anything."

"I'm no grumpier than usual."

"Don't do that. Don't try to laugh it off or shut it down. Something's going on, and we have enough problems outside of the agency. I don't need to worry about you, too."

"Nobody's asking you to worry about me."

"You're my partner and my friend. Of course, I'm going to

worry."

Drummond muttered a curse under his breath as he set his hat back on. He floated out to the edge of the driveway and checked up and down the street. Max waited in quiet.

When the ghost returned, he released several huffs before finally saying, "You folks love to chatter about your feelings and thoughts and nonsense. I'll do it your way this once."

"Thank you for your sacrifice," Max said, inserting as much friendly humor as he could manage.

Drummond lowered next to Max, hovering an inch above the concrete block. Max felt the dead cold coming off his partner but did not move. If this was what Drummond needed to open up, then Max would give it to him. And he thought he understood — seated this way, Drummond could speak without having to look at Max directly. They were two men watching the dim light on the horizon, having a morning cup of joe, and shooting the breeze.

Clearing his throat, Drummond said, "It is about Miss 1800s, you're right about that. But it's not what you think. Not exactly. See, at first, it started with me not being able to find her. I checked all the usual spots — our usual spots as well as places I knew she liked to hang out when I wasn't around. But I came up empty. That was unusual. And I know what you and Sandra were thinking — you're not as quiet as you want to be sometimes."

Max almost responded to that, but out of respect for his friend, he kept his mouth shut. Also, he didn't want Drummond to elaborate on that statement.

"I know you thought she dumped me and was keeping her distance until I got the message. But that's not how ghosts are. I told you this before, but you don't listen very well sometimes. Truth about ghosts is they tend to be a little bit more open in their relationships. A little more promiscuous. After all, there are a lot of us, and we don't have relationships the way you do. Pairing off with a gal in the Other doesn't result in a child. We're not looking for a home, a career, or any kind of lifelong commitment like that. Lifelong is over, and deathlong is forever. For most ghosts, it's all a little fun to pass the time. In fact, our friendships tend to last far longer than our love interests. So, you're wrong to think that she broke up with me. There was never any relationship to break up. We just liked to spend time together when the opportunity arose."

"Okay. If she wanted to stop having romantic encounters with you, then she simply would stop."

"Now you're getting it. We could still talk to each other. Neither one of us would've been upset or offended or anything. Heck, even if her personality made her feel awkward about a ghost's kind of relationships, I've known her for a long time. I guarantee she is not the type to cut off all communication like that. Too rude. Too impersonal. Frankly, too cowardly. If she never wanted to see me again for any reason, she would've told me to my face."

"I want to ask if you suspect foul play, but she's already dead."

"I know the feeling. It only got worse after we learned that Madame Ti was abducted. Because then I started thinking that maybe somebody had taken Miss 1800s in the only way you can take a ghost."

Max started to see it now — the grumpiness, the constant trips to the Other, the attitude. Drummond feared for his friend. Max's eyes widened because it was more. "You think a witch took her? Summoned her soul, maybe? Has control over her?"

"With everything we've seen, the thought crossed my mind. But that's not what happened. See, it took some tracking down of the few confidantes she had — they were also mostly unfindable — but I finally caught up with Lydia Beth Silverton. Lady Lydia. She told me the truth plain and simple. My friend had moved on."

It took tremendous willpower for Max to stare forward and not look at Drummond with concern. "I'm confused," he managed to say in a firm tone. "Isn't that a good thing?"

"Yeah, it's good. It's wonderful. She finally worked out whatever demons kept her stuck here and found her way to a better beyond. I'm thrilled for her. But she never said a word. Never gave any indication that she was getting close to moving on or even trying."

"Maybe she didn't know. We've helped plenty of ghosts move on, and before they met us, they had no idea anything was going to happen."

"I know that. I do. It's not the sudden loss of her that had me upset. That part stinks, no doubt about it, but really, if I'm honest about it all, it's losing her. She was a friend, and I don't have many."

"You got me."

"Don't make this worse than it has to be." Drummond snickered for a second. Then he sobered and said, "I spoke with Lady Lydia right before joining you all on the golf course. She was pretty upset, too. Because all those confidantes I couldn't find — they all had moved on. She's the only one of that group left behind. She said something that cut into me — she said that losing her whole group of friends was a reminder that even after death nothing remained settled or peaceful. She saw it all better than I ever did. She understands. The moment you start thinking your life is set, the world will shift under your feet."

He lifted higher in the air and straightened. He adjusted his hat and reset his coat. Peering at the horizon, he put his hands in his pockets.

This being Max's first early-morning version of a 1940s man-to-man chat, he waited a few moments before deciding the conversation had ended. Snatching his coffee mug, he stepped next to the ghost. They remained silent, watching dawn paint its lovely hues onto the sky, and Max pondered all that Drummond had said. Let it stew in his thoughts as the sun's warmth woke him better than the caffeine.

An old Ford Escort — well-kept and practical — pulled into the driveway. Brenda stepped out, taking several final drags on a cigarette, and waved as she approached. She wore a simple blouse with African colors, dark jeans, and a brightness entirely too cheery for Max's state of mind.

"Good morning," she said, her thick drawl adding a smile to the words.

"What are you doing here?" Max didn't intend to sound rude and hoped she interpreted his abruptness as morning-grumpy.

"Your wonderful wife called me in. Said she needs some help researching a spell today. From the looks of you and how she sounded on the phone, I take it you two had a bit of an adventure last night."

"You could say that."

"I did." She laughed harder than the quip deserved as she entered the house.

Max heard Sandra utter a greeting in the kitchen. He downed the last of his coffee and watched the sun a bit longer. It felt good. Calming. Tranquil. Even meditative.

He peeked up at Drummond. Maybe all those old-timers had it right. A bit of silence had its place in a friendship. A real therapeutic place.

"Good talk," he said.

Drummond gave a sharp warning glare. "Don't ruin it."

Then again, maybe they were all cranky bastards who wanted to hide from emotions by pretending to value nature. Max chuckled. Probably both.

He entered the house with the ghost behind him, and they found Sandra and Brenda taking books into the living room. Sandra kissed Max, and though she smiled a *good morning*, he knew she needed to sleep for hours more. They both did. That's why she phoned Brenda, of course. With proper sleep and a clear mind, Sandra could do the research herself — had been doing it all along. But in her current state, she made the right call in bringing in backup. Plus, Brenda volunteered for the Agency in exchange for learning to be a good witch from Sandra, so this work satisfied both needs.

"Osorio will be here soon, too." Sandra set her own coffee mug next to a book simply titled *Rites*. She sat on the couch while Brenda curled in her usual chair.

Drummond slipped through the wall. "Osorio? Book work isn't really his sort of thing."

Addressing Max so as not to make Brenda uncomfortable, Sandra said, "After last night, we need all the help we can get. You and Osorio need to go back to the Grandover. Maybe search the witches' rooms while they're out today."

"And if they're not out?"

"Osorio's got a brain like Drummond. He'll think of something."

Drummond said, "Hold on. You're making it sound like I won't be there."

Turning towards him, she said, "How could our ghost friend provide his usual aid when the witches have wards against him?"

"Oh. Right. Still, couldn't I —"

"The best thing for him to do is either go back to the Other and work with his contacts there or stay here and help us figure out what spells are being used and being planned. His choice."

Drummond looked into Sandra's firm eyes and firmer stance before drooping like a scolded grade schooler. "Guess I'll go to the Other."

Max said, "Don't worry. I'll be fine."

"Yeah? You warn Osorio that if anything happens to you, I'm blaming him. I'll haunt him until the day he dies." To Sandra: "You sure you don't want me shadowing them?"

She gave Max a hug and both men knew that she did so as a way of hugging the ghost, too. "We're not going to succeed unless we strike on all fronts. The Other is the hardest front for us to work. We only have one way in. Luckily, he's most capable."

"Okay, okay. No need to butter me up."

After Drummond left, Sandra dove straight into her books. Max took a quick shower, and by the time he had dressed for the day, Osorio arrived. Wishing they headed anywhere but the Grandover Resort, Max got in the detective's car and tried hard to banish LaShanna's terrible grin from his mind.

Chapter 19

WHILE OSORIO NAVIGATED THE SNAKING ROADS to the Grandover Resort, Max marveled at how normal everything appeared. The police were gone. Fire Department, too. In fact, all signs that anything out of the ordinary had occurred only hours before had been wiped away as if it had never happened. Max figured that the resort guests continued to play Hole 4, as well. Not one of them would have a clue that they teed off the spot of a ritual involving an animal sacrifice — even those few awake during the commotion would have been kept in the dark.

Entering the lobby, Osorio dug out his police badge. "Which floor?" he asked Max.

"We think they're on the ninth."

Marching straight to the front desk, Osorio flashed his badge, instantly causing the desk receptionist to stiffen her posture. "I'm following up on last night's incident."

"Yes, sir. How can we be of assistance?" She had a pleasant voice though her eyes darted to Max with suspicion.

"It's okay. He's with me. A consultant."

"For what? We were told it was some university students pulling a prank."

"It might be a little more than that. If you want, I can explain it all in plenty of detail that I'm sure your guests would find interesting."

Her gentle tone hardened. "No need for that. I was simply curious. My apologies. What can the Grandover Resort do to help?"

"Right now, I need to know the room numbers of four women and if you know where they are at the moment.

LaShanna Mill, Sung Park, Rosita Stakson, and …"

Max said, "Michon Charee."

"Yeah, her too."

The desk receptionist clacked away at her keyboard for a moment. Then: "All four checked out this morning at six. I have no way to know where they went, but they are not here anymore."

"Room numbers?" Osorio said.

Clack clack. "920, 921, 922, and 923." Clack clack clack. "All on one card and prepaid."

"By?"

Clack clack clackity clack. "The Hull Group."

At least that much of the story checked out. No reason for Cecily Hull to pay the bill if she hadn't planned on the witches coming to visit. But why didn't Cecily tell these witches about the Porters?

Osorio stayed on point. "Have the rooms already been cleaned?"

"Not according to this, but some of the staff are not as prompt as we would like when reporting that information."

"Is it alright if we go take a look?"

"Of course." She prepared a keycard for him. "We only ask that you be discrete. There are still guests on that floor, and we wouldn't want them worried."

"Thank you, ma'am." Osorio placed the keycard in his satchel and headed for the elevators.

Following close behind, Max said, "Sure is handy having you around. Before, I would have had to sneak onto the floor and break into the rooms."

"Glad to be of service, but don't get too reliant on me. I don't like putting my neck out unless I absolutely must. For one thing, I'm not even assigned to this case, so if that lady at the desk calls the police to check or the actual detectives on this case show up, we're going to have some problems. For a second thing —" He raised his gloved hand. "— not exactly thrilled to have more of my body cursed."

When they stepped into the dark, mirrored elevator car and

Osorio pressed the button for the ninth floor, Max felt his nerves rise. The lady at the front desk said the witches had checked out, that they were gone, but perhaps they doubled-back for some reason. He pictured the elevator door sliding open and LaShanna staring at them with a malicious grin as she plunged a knife into his chest. He shuddered.

"You okay?" Osorio asked.

"Just running on no sleep."

"Oh, I get that. I once was part of a week-long stakeout. You don't know tired until you've spent thirty-six hours stuck inside an old Chevy with a broken heater in the middle of winter."

Wrapping his arms around his waist, Max braced for the sensation of cold to strike his body. That would be the only warning the elevator ghost could give. If he felt that, he would press the next available floor and call Sandra. He might have to explain it all to Osorio, but the detective accepted the presence of Drummond. A ghost in the elevator warning of witches on the ninth floor wouldn't be that much further to leap.

Except no chill of a ghost hit and the elevator stopped on the ninth floor. The door slid open. Max winced and his muscles strained and — nothing.

They walked into the small waiting area, paused as Osorio readjusted the straps of his satchel, and then followed the signs pointing to the hall with rooms 920 - 923. The ninth floor resembled the tenth exactly. No surprise, most of a hotel's guest floors looked the same, yet Max felt an odd twinge in his head. The swirling carpet design, the evenly spaced sconces, the wood doors — all as expected. Maybe the witches left something in the air. A spell to confuse, perhaps.

Or maybe I'm extra-nervous.

Osorio used the keycard on Room 290. They found a basic room with two queen beds, marble entrance and bathroom, wood flooring elsewhere, and brightly lit. The sheets and comforter lay in a pile at the foot of one bed.

"Let's get started." Osorio pulled open each drawer one by one.

Max stayed in the doorway. That odd sensation grew

stronger. It warned him to be alert despite the mundane sameness of every room, every hallway, every color, every light, everything.

He could be picking up on the witches' wake. Sandra taught him that magic — particularly strong magic — often lingered in a location. Eventually, it would dissipate, but it could hold out after a witch left. Considering the strength of these four witches, Max figured he should be sensing leftover energy.

Please, let it be leftover energy.

Osorio cocked his head toward Max. "I'm not doing this all by myself."

"Sorry." Max hastened in.

Searching an empty hotel room turned out to be easy. The closet, bathroom, and dresser — empty. If the witch had bothered to unpack at all, she made sure to leave nothing behind. Osorio used a pen to poke around the trashcans but found nothing beyond some used tissues. The only object left behind of significance was a teacup with a lipstick imprint on it.

"Can you get DNA from that?" Max asked.

"Probably. But we're not in a position to call in Forensics on something like that. I mean think about it — what are the chances that your witch's DNA is on file in this state? Some of them flew in from overseas, so we won't have their info at all. And while I have favors in Forensics, and I might even admit I have some favors at the federal level, too, I don't have the pull to see this thing into international territory."

"So, that would be a *no?*"

"Here's the real question you should ask — since the witch drank from this Grandover Resort teacup, where's the saucer? I doubt a place as ritzy as this would offer room service without the saucer to go with the cup."

They redoubled their search. While Osorio checked the drawers and closet once more, Max went to the beds. He had rifled through the pillows, sheets, and comforter, but only on the used bed. Turning his attention to the bed not slept in, he flipped the pillows over. Under the middle one, he found the saucer. Dried tea stained the white porcelain, and a tiny shred of napkin sat in the center.

"Over here," he said.

Osorio rushed the few steps to the bedside. He peered at the saucer before digging through his satchel. Max thought the detective might pull out an old magnifying glass, but instead, Osorio produced tweezers. He reached down and clamped them onto the darkened corner of napkin. When he lifted it, when the sunlight hit it, the object no longer looked like a napkin.

"Is that paper?" Max said.

"Looks like it. Burned, too."

"Set it flat on the table."

As Osorio walked the paper to the small writing desk, Max fished out his phone. Using the zoom function on the camera, he inspected the paper. Snapped a few photos, too.

"Some writing," Osorio said. "Yeah, there's definitely writing that was burned."

"I can't make out anything more than the one letter — *D*. You see anything clearly?"

As they crowded closer to the tiny piece of paper, Max felt relief from that tightness, that twinge, in his head. Like having a humming in the ear suddenly cease, it was gone in an instant. He stood straight and listened to the room. He closed his eyes, trying to sense the strange vibrations of energy that had caused the discomfort in the first place.

He looked down at the scrap of burnt paper. They had moved the paper from the saucer on the bed to the writing table. If breaking a casting circle disrupted a spell, could this have done the same? Could a burnt piece of paper even be a spell?

Max guessed the answer to both was *yes*, and though he would confirm it later with Sandra, for now, he decided to operate on the assumption that he was correct. One other way to confirm his suspicion flashed in his head.

"We need to check the other rooms." He bolted across the hall.

When Osorio unlocked the room, Max rushed right for the unused bed. He threw back the center pillow and found another saucer with another burnt piece of paper. This one had nothing legible on it, so they moved to the third room. There, they found the expected paper, this time with more letters on it — *YN*. Finally, in the fourth room, the hit upon the letters — *PAY*. The burn marks on this paper, however, gouged out the middle and left one letter at the end — *R* — before destroying the corner.

Max photographed all four saucers and papers. They checked through each room again, but only found empty drawers, closets, and bathrooms. Osorio said he had to go — he had a late-night shift to get ready for. No matter. Max thought they had certainly found what they came for. Now, he only had to figure out what it meant.

Chapter 20

OSORIO DROPPED MAX OFF AT THE HOUSE, wished him luck, and drove away. Standing outside, Max could hear Sandra and Brenda discussing witchcraft and spells, bouncing ideas off each other with vigor and enthusiasm. Their zeal turned their volume up, and he saw no possibility of being able to concentrate in that small space.

As fast as he could without being rude, he swept through the house, gathered his research materials — laptop, notebooks, extra pens — kissed his wife, waved at Brenda, told them he would be at the library, and left. From the car, he sent the photos to Sandra's phone, texting what he had found, and asking that she look it over when she finished with Brenda or, at least, took a break from their reverie. Then he headed into downtown Winston-Salem and the public library.

By the time he found a decent parking space, walked to the library, located a good worktable that gave him enough privacy, and wrote down the letters he had found on the burnt papers — D, YN, R, PAY — Sandra had texted him back with a load of information. Apparently, despite their energy, she and Brenda had not found much success. *We're stumped,* Sandra wrote. So, they both eagerly jumped into the burnt paper puzzle as a diversion and to let their subconscious do some of the work on the larger problem.

The use of teacups, probably simultaneous usage, as well as the burning of paper led Sandra to believe the witches performed another ancient ritual that pre-dated formalized witchcraft. It certainly would fit their M.O. Best guess was that they used the spell to ask for a specific communication from the dead. Sort of how regular people use a medium, except the spell forced the ghost to answer.

— *Could it be our elevator ghost?* Max texted back.

— *Maybe. But it really could be almost any ghost.*

Basically, the witches all wrote the same question upon their papers, and at a specific time, usually one of the witching hours, they all chanted the spell aloud. When they finished the incantation, they sipped the tea, then repeated. They had to all be synched in rhythm and pace. Eventually, the answer would appear on the bottom of the page. At that point, they burned the paper and left it hidden as an offering of thanks.

— *That's the general idea, anyway. There are variations from different cultures.*

Max offered his own thanks to his wife. She had provided great help.

— *Happy to hear it because we're not doing so well on this end. Too many spell possibilities with what we have. Lots of animal sacrifices in the ancient spells.*

— *Hang in there.*

— *One thing is for sure. All the spells we're giving a serious look at have to do with power grabs. None of them look good for Madame Ti. I think she's probably dead.*

Max had been having similar thoughts for too long. He dreaded reporting that to Cecily Hull. Though she often reacted in strange ways. She might surprise him, might have concluded and accepted as much already, might even have plans to shove LaShanna Mill into the position, sell it as a job opportunity. The idea that he could end up stuck dealing with LaShanna on a regular basis sickened him. Especially the flash of that smile.

Focus on the letters from the burnt papers. Figure that out. Push the rest aside.

He could do that. Taking a sharp inhale, he held his breath for a moment, then exhaled slowly — letting all thoughts of LaShanna nearly killing him release upon the air in his lungs.

The letters could be anything, and he had to remember that

he only had partials of the answer. Plus, he had no guarantee the answer had been delivered in English. But he had no way to succeed otherwise, so he had to make a go of it with the assumption that he knew the language and that the letters provided enough clues.

First thing he spotted — the two single letters formed DR. Perhaps the witches sought who had taken Madame Ti, who had killed Emily Dodson. If that proved true, then the answer may have been a doctor of some kind or the initials of the killer. But the other letters did little to provide a name. YN might be a compound name or part of an Eastern name, but those possibilities didn't feel right.

"And what do I really have here besides my gut?" he asked the paper.

There was also the longest portion — PAY. Did the witches seek money from someone? Or did they owe somebody? The doctor, perhaps. Or maybe the ghost answering the questions wrote under strain.

Thinking on it further, Max had to assume the ghost suffered. The spell forced the answer, so the ghost was under duress, and writing into the corporeal world would have caused a ghost great pain. Under those conditions, the ghost would provide the answer as fast as possible. The word PAYD could be a misspelling.

Max saw the YN again and wondered if the ghost had asked a question back. Was that even allowed with the spell? But if the ghost sought a Yes/No answer — old grade-school note passing flashed in his head: *Do you like me? Circle one Yes No* — then the other letters made no sense. That didn't even factor in that there could be other letters that had been burned away.

He rubbed his face. Only a few minutes in and his brain whirled in circles.

"This isn't going to work," he said. Not knowing the language, the letters involved, the question, or even the number of total letters meant too many variables. He closed his notebook and sat back. When researching a topic, if he hit a wall, he often found changing the angle of attack solved the problem. It opened new ways to see, to think, and that opened new ideas.

Sounded good in his head, but he had to find that new angle first. He looked around the library. The place felt like a heavy blanket on a winter morning. Cozy and quiet like a library should be. His eyes grew heavy. Maybe if he rested a few minutes, cleared his mind. His head lolled forward, and the sudden drop jolted him awake.

Scooting to the front edge of his chair, Max widened his eyes. Maybe he should have grabbed those few hours that morning when he had the chance.

Focus. That's what he needed to do. And research. Forget solving letter puzzles — not enough givens to make that work. Forget the spells — Sandra and Brenda worked on that and were far more qualified. Forget Madame Ti and the war — for now, those things hung far out of reach.

The witches.

Those four ladies did not appear out of nowhere. If he could find out who they are, where they came from, their histories, then maybe he could find something helpful to the case. At worst, he would know his enemies a little better, and that might help predict their future actions.

Yeah. This felt right. His researching brain kicked him fully awake.

Though many witches tried to hide their information — and Max guessed these witches would be no different — there were limits unless they chose to live a hermit's life. These four — they were not hermits.

His initial searching proved easy enough. All four women had flown in from other countries. The flight information from the list with their names revealed that much. LaShanna came from the UK, Rosita from South America, Michon from France, and Sung Park from South Korea. International travel meant tickets, passports, and other identification. A lot of that could be counterfeited, but fake IDs were best for short-term use. If Cecily Hull told the truth, these women were being recruited. The intention would have been for them to stay in North Carolina for a long time. Possibly move here permanently. Fake

IDs would be a bad idea with that goal in mind. Plus, living in the modern age, better for a witch to hide in plain sight. Max dug in and spent the next few hours investigating each witch.

Rosita Stakson proved easy to find. She kept rather active on social media. Born and raised in Argentina, her father was an American businessman who turned out to be married to an American housewife. Rosita's Argentinian mother, a devout Catholic, only learned of the father's last crucial detail when she got pregnant. She gave her daughter the father's name, anyway — perhaps in hopes that an American surname would help. It didn't. At least, Max didn't think it helped based on her bouncing from one school to another, as well as ending up in jail several times as a teenager.

From her angry postings regarding nuns and the Catholic Church, Max guessed she turned to witchcraft in further defiance. Somewhere through the years, her exploration of magic changed. No longer simple rebellion, she joined an online organization that led her to meeting real witches. From there, her true tutelage began, and like witches had done for centuries, she made a living by selling her skills to the desperate with one sketchy witch deal after another.

Sung Park was a more difficult search. Most of her information could only be found on Korean websites, and free translation software still promised more than it could deliver. In another decade, he expected these difficulties to have vanished, but he didn't have a decade to wait. Yet despite that issue — and the added problem that the name Park was as common in Korea as Smith in America — Max narrowed his choices down to three women, all from Seoul, and all involved either in the occult or something equally dark. In fact, the more he looked at the Sung Park with an arrest that made the newspapers, he decided her version of dark was criminal, not magic.

The other two had done an admirable job of keeping off the internet. At least, off the sites he had easy access to. Max figured birth records, tax records, and other government records abounded for both women, but he was poking around through an American internet provider and using translations to navigate his way. The Korean government sites were not user-friendly to him.

He made a note to ask Sandra to search for Sung Park on the dark web witch sites. Perhaps they would get lucky.

Turning his attention to Michon Charee sent him to France and far more fruitful results. She grew up in a small town composed of farms, wineries, and not much else. A rural life, but Max thought it looked lovely. He used Google Maps to view her childhood house, one of several small homes along the street leading into town, and that produced more answers — from the street view he saw that a pentagram hung over the front door.

Of several of the homes.

With that clue, he had little trouble finding that the Felzin coven had been accepted as a religious group in the town. They openly practiced witchcraft with no problems, started their own elementary school in 2003, and now had plans for a high school program, if they could overcome a few regulatory hurdles. Max even found an old article about Michon winning first place in a school history-bee. The accompanying picture showed little Michon smiling for the camera while holding the medal around her neck — the symbols on the medal eerily familiar.

So far, Max had one woman who sought witchcraft to rebel and escape, one who he couldn't find much about, and one who had been raised as a witch. He saw no commonalities amongst the women, nothing that tied them to North Carolina, nothing at all. That left LaShanna Mill, and Max had to admit he had been putting her off until last because he didn't want to find pictures of her smiling for the camera.

Not surprisingly, of all four women, LaShanna turned out to be the easiest to find and the most disturbing. Born and raised in London, LaShanna showed early promise in life. She excelled at the piano, aced all her classes, and received early-admission into Oxford. Nothing in the newspaper articles — of which there were several — nor in her official records indicated any problematic behavior. Not so much as an official caution for a loud party. Certainly nothing pointing to witchcraft.

Yet in all those articles, he noticed that she never smiled in her pictures. At first, he felt thankful. But the more photos he viewed, the stranger it became. Here was a bright, accomplished young woman getting praise and acknowledgement for her achievements, something many women never received, yet she looked miserable. Maybe even lonely.

Max searched police records for any indication that LaShanna had been abused or suspected of being abused. Not so much as a visit from Child Services. No mention anywhere of seeing a therapist, either. Maybe he had the wrong woman.

But as an adult, her career was easily tracked, and there Max found the evidence that he had the correct LaShanna Mill. She became an educator, a history professor at her alma mater, doing research in myths, legends, and the occult. Her most recent book on the subject — *The Enlightened Dark Ages: When Witch Hunts Found Real Witches.* Clunky, yet catchy.

Drummond appeared across the worktable, his face beaming. "Put your stuff away. You've got a short trip to make."

"Hello to you, too."

"Trust me here. I'll explain on the way, but I met a ghost in the Other, and why aren't you packing up?"

"Give me a second. I'm saving the info I found on the witches from the golf course."

Drummond swished through the table to look at Max's computer. "Her. The ghost I met — his mother grew up in the UK and went to school with her, LaShanna Mill."

Max looked at the photo of LaShanna, then at Drummond. He slammed his computer shut and swept his papers together as he stood. "What are you jabbering on for? Let's get in the car. You can explain more on the way."

Chapter 21

IT WAS MORE COMPLICATED. A twenty-minute drive across town gave Drummond ample time to explain. Apparently, while combing the Other for anybody who knew anything about Madame Ti or the four witches, one of Drummond's contacts mentioned a young man, Mitchell Wharton, that might have some information.

"He knew the kid came from somewhere in England," Drummond said, floating higher than usual in his seat. "Said the kid was stuck in the Other because of a curse. The name LaShanna Mill isn't exactly everyday, so my contact remembered it."

Drummond tracked down the young man, and it turned out that his mother went to Oxford with LaShanna. They were friends for a time until LaShanna's darker interests pulled her away from normal relationships. Years after graduation, the two women met on rare occasions to catch up and pretend they still had a strong friendship.

"The kid didn't understand it, but he supposed his mother lacked anybody else. He figured even an ex-friend willing to chat for a few hours once or twice a year was better than nothing."

During one of these reunions, LaShanna and Mitchell's mother stumbled in from a lengthy night at the local pub, and both passed out downstairs. Mitchell sat in his room reading comic books instead of studying. He thought nothing of it. His mother had been drunk before, but she never was violent. Really just meant that he'd be fixing his own breakfast in the morning.

Until he heard the creak of the stairs. LaShanna opened his

door and entered his bedroom, sauntering as if she owned everything including the air and time itself. Mitchell watched, confused, unsure, heart pounding, on edge.

Max took the on-ramp for Business 40 and headed East towards Kernersville. He pictured the scene Drummond described and though the ghost made no mention of it, Max knew LaShanna wore a special smile on her lips. A prowling, devouring smile.

"This next part," Drummond said, shifting his gaze outside, "well, I'd never say any of this in front of Sandra or any lady, but you need to know the full story."

According to Mitchell, this woman commanding his room sat on the edge of his bed and unbuttoned her blouse. She never said a word. Mitchell didn't ask a question. His voice would have cracked seven times if he had tried. Hormones drove away any concerns when she revealed her bare breasts. He was fifteen.

"Of course, the kid thought he'd hit the jackpot. Greatest night of his life, he told me."

But LaShanna was a witch and one who specialized in the occult and ancient rites. Sex magic was some of the oldest magic in existence. At that point in her career, LaShanna may have been using Mitchell as a learning tool or she may have targeted him for a specific spell and purpose. Mitchell didn't care at the time, and since his death and cursing, he's never been able to find out.

"I told him that if we can't break his curse, we'd do our best to figure out that answer. But I sort of promised him there was a good chance we could break the curse."

As Max took the exit for Kernersville, he said, "Wait, we're going to this house to break a curse? I mean I'm happy to help a ghost out, but we're in the middle of a dangerous case. Don't you think that's a steep price for a little information?"

"Rein it in, partner. Give ol' Drummond some credit."

About a year after Mitchell lost his virginity to LaShanna, his mother met and fell in love with Tyler Wharton. He worked for Duke University and had been sent to England for some conference. At least, that was how Mitchell remembered it.

"Those details don't really matter. The important part is that pretty soon, Mitchell's mom becomes Mrs. Wharton, and they move to America. Shortly after that, Tyler changes jobs to work at Wake Forest University, and that has them move to Kernersville."

Only a few months later, LaShanna arrived for a surprise visit. Mitchell said he knew something was off by the way LaShanna overtly came on to him. He was older now and saw the signs much clearer, but his mother missed it all.

That night, when LaShanna came to his bed, he welcomed her, even as the back of his brain warned him. Drummond tried to tell the young man not to blame himself — after all, what straight teenage boy would turn down a beautiful, willing woman? — but as she removed her nightgown and climbed atop him, he saw her mouth open. Not a smile, but the pleasure of a hungry animal close to bagging its prey.

Max's skin prickled. "I don't think I need the dirty details here."

"Not entirely, but the key thing happened near the end."

As their moments of passion reached its heights, LaShanna pulled out a large dagger and plunged it into Mitchell's neck. He wanted to scream, but the blade left nothing to scream with. She stabbed him in the chest twice. Never climbing off him, never releasing their physical connection.

"Mixing blood magic with sex magic," Max said. "Sandra's going to have her work cut out adding this into the research."

Mitchell further told Drummond that LaShanna cursed him that night. He wasn't sure how — shock had locked his eyes on the ceiling — but he's stuck as a ghost now. He can't move on.

"He's not traumatized by the whole thing," Drummond said. "Seems like a well-adjusted kid who accepts that he's dead and while sad about it, he isn't trying to stay here with the living. Everything that kid said to me, every way he said it, I'm telling you — he should have moved on. LaShanna definitely cursed him to be a ghost."

"What's the plan, then? We free his ghost and let him move on, and then what?"

"Mitchell's parents knew LaShanna killed their son. Not

entirely clear on how she got away, but this is going back quite a few decades."

"Social media didn't exist back then."

"Right. It would've been a lot easier for her to hide from scrutiny — especially with a few well-placed threats. The parents divorced, and Mitchell doesn't know what became of Mr. Wharton. The kid's ghost is bound to his bedroom, and the mother kept the house. Way I see it, when she realizes that her son is still suffering because of that witch, when we fix that problem for her, I think she'll open up to us, no problem. Tell us all she ever knew about her old friend from across the pond."

Max parked the car on a small-town street lined with nice homes and decent yards. "Guess that's what we're doing because we're here. At least we got Mitchell to help us."

"Not quite."

Turning off the car, Max raised an eyebrow at Drummond. "You piss him off or something?"

"He died young and confused by the betrayal. Spent much of the time since convinced he couldn't leave that bedroom."

"He can't. You said he's bound."

"He is. But the strength of that binding depends on the witch, and at the time, LaShanna was not nearly as strong or knowledgeable as she seems to be now. Eventually, the kid met another ghost and learned of the Other. He can't leave that bedroom for other places on Earth, but he can go to the Other. Once he did that, he never went back to that house. Refuses to. I tried, but he won't budge. Says if he's got to be stuck, he'd rather be stuck in the Other. Frankly, the kid's suffered enough anyway."

"Yeah, but what if we need him?"

"We won't. This is a curse done by a novice witch at the time. We'll be fine to break it ourselves. If I have to, I can jump into the Other and track him down, but more likely we'll need to call on Sandra before we need to bother Mitchell."

"I guess. I just —"

"You're stalling. I know you like to have the full lay of the land before we jump in, but today ain't one of those days. So, get out of this car and go smooth talk that old lady."

Heading down the sidewalk, Max tried to clear his head. He needed a good way to approach this, some way not to scare Mrs. Wharton yet still convince her of the seriousness of the situation. He also needed for her to believe in ghosts, witches, and curses.

Sure. No problem.

Chapter 22

MRS. WHARTON STOOPED OVER HER CANE as she answered the door. She wore a powder blue housecoat, stained tan slippers, and tortoiseshell glasses with a chain around the neck. Squinting, her wrinkles like a withered frog, she gazed up.

"Max Porter," she said, her British accent as strong as if she had arrived in the States hours ago.

Stunned, he said, "You know me?"

"I watch the news, don't I? I've seen your contributions from time to time. Can't say I ever expected you on my doorstep, but I really don't think complaining is the proper reaction. Please, please, come in. I'll put the kettle on."

Max knew better than to deny tea from an Englishwoman. The house had been built in the 1970s and retained much of the original architecture — wood-paneled walls and an odd flow to the floorplan chief among them. Mrs. Wharton indicated for Max to sit in the living room. Photographs of her family covered every inch of the walls, particularly photos of Mitchell, while still more photographs lined the fireplace mantel and several side tables. Though consisting of a couch, two chairs, a coffee table and little else, the living room was large yet felt claustrophobic.

Drummond soared ahead, sliding through the walls as he inspected the layout of the house and searched for any dangers. He returned a few minutes later, reporting that the house looked much like the living room — sparse furnishings, tons of photographs — except for Mitchell's bedroom.

"That you've got to see for yourself."

Before he could explain further, Mrs. Wharton wheeled a tray in from the kitchen. A teapot and two cups had been placed on the tray along with several dry-looking cookies. She took slow, painful steps, but when Max stood to help, she waved him back down.

Over the next several minutes, they spoke about his experiences on television and her experiences living in a foreign country. Max had done this enough that he knew patience would win out. She needed time to come around.

He thought it would take longer, yet after their short conversation, Mrs. Wharton jumped right in. "I'm not ignorant. You did not come out here to natter away the day with an old lady. But I have not had any problems with a haunting or such. What brings you here?"

"Your son."

She nodded, and her entire body rose and fell with the motion. "I guessed as much." She sniffled. Max thought she might start crying, reliving the most tragic night of her life. Instead, she summoned some inner-strength, most likely the same inner-strength that saw her through every traumatic day since losing her son, and in a calm voice, she said, "Truly, I have never had anything ghostly happen in this house. Nothing paranormal of any kind. No noises or moving objects or any of the matter. I should think that if my son were haunting this house, I would know about it."

"It's not a haunting."

"Oh? Can ghosts do something else?"

After a short primer on ghosts and binding curses, Max said, "I'm here to help free your son. Let him move on to the afterlife he should have."

For a woman who had learned that her lovely son had spent the decades since his death suffering under a witch's curse, she took it quite well. Her chin quivered and her face paled. In a weak, lost tone, she said, "I suppose you'll want to see his room."

She led the way, taking small, shuffling steps. They climbed the stairs and approached a closed door on the right. The closer they came to the door, the slower Mrs. Wharton moved. Her hands shook, and Max caught a choked gasp.

Floating nearby, Drummond said, "The door is going to tell

you the whole story."

Max saw right away. Two posters had been taped to the door. One featured four skinny, long-haired men barely above eighteen, uncomfortable in front of the camera, and trying to look angry and mean — the band *Metallica* in their youngest years. The other poster showed four more young, long-haired men. These were smiling, laughing, looking ready to party — *Van Halen*. Both posters were from the early-1980s.

The tape holding them to the door had browned and the edges of the posters had curled. Otherwise, they looked in good condition for forty-plus-year-old paper. Considering the state of Mitchell's bedroom door, Max knew that Drummond was right. This door set up the expectation, and when Mrs. Wharton opened the door, that expectation was fulfilled — apparently, nothing in the room had been touched in four decades. All remained the same as it had the night LaShanna Mill murdered Mitchell.

A single bed took up one corner of the room with a bedside table next to it. The bed had a basic metal frame, and the table had been made of two plastic milk crates with a cloth hung over it. One window with black curtains and more posters of rock bands decorated the walls. Across the bare wood floor, a dresser stood with clothes shoved in the drawers by a teenager who couldn't be bothered to fold his laundry, while next to the window, Mitchell had a small desk with a small black and white television. A Commodore 64 had been set up in front — one of the earliest home computers. Max guessed that a modern, empty Word file would cause the thing to crash.

"Look around," Mrs. Wharton said, "and call for me when you're done. I … I don't go in there. Not often."

She shuffled down the hall, muttering to herself. Max knew his visit would cause the woman painful memories, but it had to be done.

Once she closed her bedroom door, Drummond clapped his hands a single time and gestured to the entire room. "You see this? Nothing has been changed. Nothing's been moved. The irony is rich. By preserving every last detail, she's only helped the binding maintain its hold on her son."

Max ran a finger along the dresser top. "She's kept the room clean. No dust. She had to move things to do that."

"I'm not saying that moving things would break the curse — only that it weakens the binding. Like with me. It wasn't until you moved my office desk that we formed the connection so you could see me and hear me. Binding spells are tricky, and they can create strange side effects. In fact, I'm willing to bet that her cleaning in here is what allowed Mitchell such freedom in the Other. Without that, he would've had to use a lot of energy to stay in the Other. He'd be stuck in this room for the majority of his time."

"Where does that get us? Do we move everything around until he can break free?"

"You know it doesn't work like that."

"I'm not the witch in this outfit. We should call Sandra, show her what we're dealing with."

"No argument from me, but I recommend you take some photos and search around. That way you have some answers to the obvious questions she'll ask."

With a despondent groan, Max said, "Yeah."

He began with several shots of the room in its frozen state. Feeling like a sleazy motel owner trying to get the best angle for a website, he did what he could to encompass the entire room. Then, after photos of all the surrounding furniture, he focused on the bed.

The first shots were easy enough, but he knew he would have to pull back the blankets and photograph the sheets. After all, LaShanna stabbed Mitchell to death. Without a body, the bloodstains might be all that remains for Sandra to work with — assuming he could find bloodstains. Mrs. Wharton had cleaned the rest of the room. She probably washed those sheets, too. But to do so would entail touching those sheets, seeing her son's blood, reliving what had happened. Considering the lengths she had gone to preserve the room, Max thought the odds were even that he would find bloodstains.

"We're on the clock," Drummond said, making a nudging

motion with his elbow but carefully avoiding contact.

Mustering his courage, Max pulled back the blanket. Nothing. No blood. Not even a wrinkle.

Drummond said, "Guess you'll have to check under the bed."

"Why can't you do it? Stick your head through there and —"

"You want me, a ghost, to poke my head into what might be part of a binding curse? The very thing that cursed me? You want to hear the choice words I have for you?"

"Fine. I'll do it."

But when Max reached toward the bed, the air chilled as Drummond shot out a hand. "Hold it. Mitchell just showed up."

Max followed Drummond's gaze toward the empty back corner of the room. "What's he saying? What does he want?"

"Be quiet a moment, and I'll let you know." Drummond kept his attention on the young man that only he could see. He tipped back his hat. "Look, kid, I know this is a lot to take in. You've been through the wringer, but now's not the time for cold feet. You didn't deserve what happened to you, and you don't deserve to be kept locked up because of it. Let us free you."

"What's the problem?" Max said. "Why doesn't he want us to break the curse?"

"He's scared, that's all." To Mitchell: "Kid, I'm telling you, I know all about it." Drummond flinched, and Max pictured the young man yelling something like *Nobody knows what I've been through!* or perhaps *Really? You weren't murdered in your teens, were you?* But Drummond pulled his composure back in line. "I didn't mean it like that. You're right. But I do know all about being a ghost and being one for a long, long time — longer than you've been dead. It develops a rhythm to it, a pattern far more consistent than living ever could. It becomes a morning cup of coffee or a favorite shirt — it gets comfortable. The idea of losing that, of facing what awaits beyond, can be frightening." Drummond's head swiveled as Mitchell darted to the corner by the door. "When you're alive, the idea of an afterlife is academic for some, religious for others, but it's always abstract. Here, for us — well, we know that there's an afterlife. We're in it. And we know that moving on is real, that there is a next step. Maybe a final step." Drummond leaned forward. "Listen up, kid, because I've got a secret to share. I've been there. It's true. When I first met Max, he and his wife freed me, and I got to move on. I chose to come back so I could help others, ghosts like you, so you can trust me — it's beautiful out there. Nothing to be afraid of."

Max waited as Drummond hovered in silence. The ghost didn't seem to be listening, only watching. Max pictured Mitchell trying to decide, tormented by the tug-o-war Drummond had described. On one end — staying in a ghost's comforting by numbing routine; on the other — moving on to an unknown but possibly brighter future.

At length, Drummond pulled the front of his hat down and turned back to Max. "Okay. He's nervous, but he won't get in our way. Go ahead, now. Let's see what's underneath that bed."

Though tentative in his movements, Max turned toward the metal frame. His breathing tightened. Part of him braced for a bullet of cold through his back when Mitchell changed attitudes. Part of him cringed at what lay ahead when he shifted that bed to the side.

One last peek over his shoulder — Drummond offering an encouraging nod — and Max reached for the edge of the bedframe. He pulled it out from the wall, the metal feet making a terrible racket against the wood floor. Underneath, a casting circle had been painted in black ink. A second later, Max realized it wasn't ink. Blood. Mitchell's blood stained the floor, turning black over the decades.

"That's weird," Max said, looking closer at the floor.

"I kind of thought that's what we were expecting."

"Not the casting circle. The dust bunnies."

"Dust bunnies?" Drummond swished over Max's shoulder. "I don't see anything. Looks pretty clean."

"Exactly. Mrs. Wharton cleaned in here, cleaned under the bed."

Drummond drifted backward. "She would have seen the casting circle."

"Yet she left it here."

"She knew about it yet didn't touch it. That would mean she

knew not to touch it. LaShanna couldn't have warned her to leave it alone because she had just killed the woman's son. She would have to run."

"Unless Mrs. Wharton knew. Unless it was planned out."

"But that would mean —"

Locking eyes and thoughts, they both said, "She's a witch."

Chapter 23

SNAPPING HIS FINGERS and pointed at the casting circle, Drummond said, "You break that thing open. I'll take care of the witch." He jerked his head towards Mitchell. "Don't worry. We can handle this."

As Drummond rushed through the walls, Max inspected the casting circle. He didn't share the ghost's confidence. Not when the circle had been made in blood, old blood, blood that had seeped into the wood, become part of the house.

He dragged his heel across the lines of the circle. Nothing. Not the slightest alteration. He didn't really think it would work, but it would've been nice.

Scanning the room for anything to pry loose one of the planks, he shook his head. Why would a teenager have a crowbar leaning against the wall? But Max had one in the car.

"Lady, I don't want to hurt you." Drummond's urgency rippled down the hall and into Mitchell's bedroom tomb.

Max stepped out of the room. The door to the master bedroom stood ajar, and he saw Mrs. Wharton's back as she knelt on the floor. Drummond flew circles over her head which suggested she had a casting circle with a thin ward protecting her — anything stronger would have tossed the ghost out or worse. Drummond could break through the ward easily enough, but it would hurt.

When Max caught his partner's attention, he mouthed the words *Stall her*. Never made an actual sound, but Mrs. Wharton's head perked up. She slanted an ear toward him.

Max held his breath, afraid to make any noise.

No good. She swept around, rising to her feet in a motion too fast and too smooth for the aged woman he had met downstairs. Her eyes had become solid gray balls and her veins popped out as black lines. With a rasping grate, she said, "In the name of Mother Earth and the Infinite, I set upon thee —"

Max didn't wait for her to announce the horrors she hoped to inflict. He dashed down the hall and took the stairs two at a time. Banging into the front door at the bottom, he fumbled for the knob. It wouldn't turn.

The lights in the living room flashed on and off as the blinds on the windows all dropped down and closed. Deeper in the house, a radio blared away, flipping through stations, only allowing two seconds snippets of music or talk. Desk drawers, side table drawers, and cabinet doors of every piece of furniture slammed open and closed.

Max flipped the deadbolt and twisted the knob again — still wouldn't budge. The chairs and couch in the living room rushed across the floor, scraping the wood and bunching the rugs, until they blocked the entrance. He could climb over them, but nothing would stop them from moving again. He didn't want to know what they would do to him.

Whirling around, he faced the dining room. In the far corner, Max saw the way into the kitchen. Next to it, an enormous China cabinet had all its glass doors open like a gunfighter facing off. The dishes and teacups jittered, ready to fire. Slow and careful, two drawers slid open — the silver cutlery. Forks and knives clinked as they itched to hurl at a target. Max had experienced a lot of bizarre things in his career, but he couldn't recall being threatened by furniture before. This house would not let him leave and seemed willing to kill him if necessary.

He considered sprinting to the kitchen. He'd take a hit or two, but if he crouched low, he might make it. After all, his adversary had no arms. Sure, it would vault the dishes across the room, but he doubted it could aim. Only problem — he would then be in the kitchen. With all the cooking utensils, knives, pans, glasses, dishes, things that heated up, and things that made ice — the entire room was a nightmare of ballistic weapons.

In the chaos, only the staircase remained calm. It beckoned

him to return.

"Open the door," he whispered. "I'll come right back. I promise."

The lights stopped flashing. The drawers ceased opening. The China and cutlery no longer danced their desire to maim. The entire floor ceased all its activity.

"I can't believe that worked."

An enraged cry echoed from above. Max understood right away — his plea had not worked. Drummond had. The ghost must have plunged through the ward and attacked the witch. Breaking her concentration broke the spell that controlled the house. Max didn't have long, but he had a chance.

He threw open the front door and bolted toward his car. Tripping on the lawn, he banged his knees on the hard ground. Stumbling back up, he pushed on as he fished out his key fob.

"Open, open, open," he said, stabbing the button to pop the trunk.

The glorious chunk sound of the lock unlatching filled Max with a grin. Stuttering to a stop, he whipped open the trunk and took in the contents — the tire changing kit, the plastic bin of spellcasting paraphernalia, and the crowbar. Reaching forward, his eyes shifted and he pulled back. There was one more key piece of equipment. An axe.

Racing back to the house, axe in hand, Max shoved down the whirlwind of thoughts clogging up his brain. Time for that later. Drummond and Mitchell needed help now.

When he re-entered the house, he expected to fend off attacking furniture while dodging plates shooting through the air. But everything had returned to its original place. He paused to listen. No sounds to cause concern. That was concerning.

His head lifted as he watched the staircase. He had climbed several old, wooden stairs during tense moments. It never got easier. Nor safer. But he had an idea how to avoid the slow, terrifying climb.

Taking a deep breath, he darted forward. If anything lunged at him, at least he would be moving fast. Skipping steps, he blasted up the stairs and leaped into the hallway. He gasped for air — having held that one breath the entire flight up — and spots danced in his vision. But he made it intact and unharmed.

With a lurching gait, he thumped toward Mitchell's room. The mother's door at the end had been closed, and Max kept his attention there, gripping the axe, ready to act should she come out. But the knob did not turn; the door did not open.

He didn't hear anything, either. No sounds of struggle. No sounds of an anguished ghost. Whatever happened in there, however, Max could not change it. He had a job to do, and when he accomplished that, then he could allow worry for Drummond. And if that witch did anything to his partner, she would learn why witches treated the Porters with respect.

Licking his lips, he entered Mitchell's room. He regripped the axe, his sweating hands making it more difficult to hold. With his foot, he shoved the bed further aside so that he had a clear path to strike.

"Not yet, boy." The witch swept into the room with unnatural speed. She held a jewel-encrusted dagger that had to be centuries old. Jabbing the blade in his direction, salivating as she sneered, she said, "First, you've got to bleed."

Max dodged out of her way. He should have clocked her in the head with the axe handle, but he found it hard to overcome the idea that he shouldn't be assaulting old ladies. Maybe a good push would knock her down and he could swing that axe to finish this.

"Shut up," she snapped at the corner. Apparently, she could see and hear Mitchell. "I know what you did, bringing this boy and his ghost into my house. I know what you thought would happen. Mum is no fool." She swiped the dagger at Max, but he evaded the attack. To Mitchell: "After I'm done spilling this boy's blood, Mum's going to set you right. We are not going to have this nonsense again and again."

Max lifted the axe and chopped it into the circle in the floor. As he yanked it free, the witch came at him. He had to let go of the handle or get cut. Backing off, he settled into a fighting stance. Not the way he wanted to do this, but knocking out this granny was better than get cut to ribbons.

"I'm too strong," he said. Maybe some common sense would get through to her. "You're not going to stop me."

Rising behind her, Drummond appeared. "She's not trying to stop you."

Her eyes widened. She spun to face the detective, but he thrust his hand into her head. Her body vibrated as if electrified. She dropped.

"Hurry," Drummond said. "Crack that floor open before she wakes."

Max wrenched the axe free and chopped away. Three strong hits did the trick. The wood around part of the casting circle split, breaking the circle open.

"Now what?" he asked. "Why did you say she didn't want to stop me?"

"Cut her. Take the knife and slice across her arm or hand or wherever. This curse used blood magic to make it." Drummond glowered in Mitchell's direction. "Only the blood of witch can break it."

Max followed the gaze, though he couldn't see the young man. An idea of what had happened started to form. He picked up the dagger and opened a line on Mrs. Wharton's arm. He then let her blood seep into the split wood, into the casting circle. The wood drank her blood, soaking it through every symbol, every line. The circle glowed bright and disappeared. Pulling a bedsheet free, Max bundled it around the witch's arm.

"Not a nice trick," Drummond said to Mitchell. He listened a bit longer, finally nodded, and turned away. "He's gone. Moved on."

"It was a set up?" Max asked.

"Not exactly. The curse could only be broken with a witch's blood, and it prevented Mitchell from revealing that fact. Thing is that any other blood strengthened the curse, made it harder for him to be in the Other."

"So, he had to send us in blind and hope I didn't get cut up by his mom?"

"Worse still, the mother was behind the whole thing. She had LaShanna take the boy's virginity back in England as part of a spell to bring her a new man."

"Mr. Wharton?"

"That didn't turn out quite how she wanted, and the idea of being alone without her boy was unthinkable. Rather than deal with an empty nest —"

"She had LaShanna curse her son. She could see him as a ghost, and he could never get away." Resting the axe over his shoulder, Max glanced down at Mrs. Wharton. "I'm glad we were able to free him, but I doubt we'll get her to tell us anything about LaShanna. She won't betray the woman who helped her curse her own son. For that matter, she's nutty enough to curse her own son in the first place."

"Not a problem. Parting words from Mitchell — check her bedroom bookshelf."

Max and Drummond hurried into the master bedroom. Ignoring the casting circle and all the hoarded clutter boxed up against the walls, Max zeroed in on the bookshelf standing near the bathroom door. He kept peeking at the walls, doors, and furniture, waiting for the house to attack again. He rushed through the titles on the bookshelf, unsure of what he sought but guessing it would stand out. Indeed, he saw it right away. Three books — all by LaShanna Mill.

Chapter 24

NOT WANTING TO BE IN THE HOUSE when Mrs. Wharton woke up, Max snatched the three books and hurried to his car. With his heart hammering, he tossed the axe in the backseat and sped off. He ran a stop sign, swerved around a delivery truck turning into a bakery, and slammed the brakes before plugging through a busy intersection.

He could feel Drummond's eyes. Wiping sweat off his brow, he finally said, "What?"

Drummond laced his fingers over his belly. "Just trying to figure out why you're so on edge."

"Maybe because a crazy witch tried to kill me with her entire house."

"Nah. You've had crazy witches try to kill you before. Heck, LaShanna Mill tried to do it."

Max pulled over to the curb, shut the car off, and got out. They bordered an office park on one side and a winding road into a development on the other. A scant few cars whisked by.

"This isn't going to stop."

"Witches? Yeah, but that's always been the case. I had to deal with them when I was alive, and so did others stretching back centuries."

Pacing the length of his car, Max said, "Not like that. I'm talking about how everything was going along fine — even with the occasional witch gunning for us — but now, one stolen witch and this whole war breaks out. Since then, in only a few days, we've nearly died twice. Twice. A leash has been taken off the witch community's neck, and I think they're going to go wild."

"Maybe. But if we can stop LaShanna, if we can find Madame

Ti or at least find out what happened to her, things will calm."

"That won't stop a war."

"It'll cool the boil. The war is going to happen no matter what we do, but it doesn't have to raze the city."

Max clutched his stomach and clenched his eyes against his welling tears. "I heard what you said about stability in the world and such, and that was fine when we're talking about the Sandwich Boys or my mother. Sure, things won't ever be in balance exactly. I get it. But c'mon — all of this has to happen at once?"

"I wish I had a magic answer for you, but that's not the way life works. You know that."

Max nodded. "I'm venting, that's all."

"That's not all. This has been bothering you for a while. Not the war or the witches — I'm talking about the boys and your mother. You've got to get a handle on that."

"Suddenly you're a psychologist? Where's my partner that doesn't like to open up about anything?"

"This is you we're talking about, not me. My problems like to stay buried. You're the one who likes to vent, to spew it all out, to talk it through. So, I'm trying to be a good friend here since you can't talk to your wife right now."

"Sandra. If these witches are jumping at the chance to kill me, then she's not safe, either." Max dug out his phone.

"Put the phone away." Drummond pushed closer until Max stopped tapping the screen. "If you call her now, you're going to babble and make no sense and upset her."

"I need to make sure she's okay."

"That's why I'm going over to the house, and I'll check on her. I'll explain what happened, and I'll do it calmly. She'll call you later. In the meantime, you sit in your car and go through those books. Find out what we got from all of this. Okay? Do some research — it'll make you feel better, and it'll get you thinking right again."

As the adrenaline rush died, Max's tension eased. He nodded to Drummond. The ghost floated for a moment, watching close, before he flicked the brim of his hat and vanished.

Blowing out a long breath, puffing his cheeks, Max arched back and chuckled. He must have sounded like a panicked fool. Sounded like? He was a fool.

He settled in his car and grabbed the three books by LaShanna Mill. Focus on the case, push on through, and like always, they would emerge on the other side of it all. Things would work out. Maybe not exactly as he wanted, but they would work out.

And if they didn't? Well, that meant he would be dead. Nothing he could do about it, then. A bit fatalistic, perhaps, but it was a philosophy that had helped him face all these ghastly challenges without suffering massive PTSD.

"Okay, Max. Enough of this bellyaching. Get to work."

LaShanna's most recent book rested on the top of the pile — *The Enlightened Dark Ages: When Witch Hunts Found Real Witches.* Scanning through the table of contents and skimming a few random pages, Max found a dry, academic text. The kind of thing a professor wrote as part of her bid towards tenure.

Despite his disgust at the witch, he had to admit the book might be a good reference for his personal library. Her view of historical events — even if he didn't agree with her interpretations — could help with other research someday. Or the bookaholic in him might be justifying another addition to his collection. Either way, he intended to keep it.

The second book on the pile — *Haunted America: Ten Terrifying Homes in the United States.* This turned out to be more of a pop culture look into some famous hauntings. The Amityville home, the Lizzie Borden house, and the Winchester mansion stood out among the listings. Max checked the copyright information. The book had been published by a small press out of London in 2014. Not the kind of thing her Oxford peers would approve of and not something she could make much money from, but clearly a desire to share her knowledge beyond her witch peers.

The final book stopped him cold — *Payne Road: The Most Haunted Road in North Carolina.* He swiped through his phone to bring up the pictures of those burned letter fragments. Since all four papers would have the same answer written from the spell,

Max felt safe assuming the letter Y in both the PAY fragment and the YN fragment might be the same. The other two fragments — R and D. PAYN, R, D. Fill in one missing letter and he had PAYNE RD. Max didn't doubt the answer. The idea that these letter fragments could accidentally name the most haunted road in all of North Carolina was absurd. Especially in the absurd world of witches.

"Okay, LaShanna," he said as he picked up the book. "Tell me about where you're going."

Chapter 25

KNOCKING AGAINST GLASS. Rubbing his eyes then his temples then his cheeks, Max started to see the fuzzy world around him. A window? A car window. Max's car window. A police officer tapped his window. Police? Suddenly, he was wide awake. He bolted upright, turned on the car to lower the window.

"You okay in there?" the officer said, her mouth stern, her brow concerned as she leaned over for a closer look.

"Sorry." Max fumbled for an explanation. He settled on a partial truth. "I haven't slept in over a day and thought I'd better pull over. Didn't want to cause an accident." He flipped the book in his lap onto the pile in the passenger seat, making sure the title went face down and covered the others. His phone had the websites of his research into Payne Road, but thankfully, the screen had gone blank.

She watched his actions but didn't push further. He guessed she looked for signs of drugs or alcohol or some other illegal activity. At length, she settled for, "License and registration."

With an appreciative grin, Drummond appeared next to the officer. "I always enjoyed a woman in a waitress or a nurse's outfit, but if we had enough lady police back in my day, I may never have quit the force."

The officer paused to scan behind her. She may have been performing a routine search of her surroundings, making sure she was safe, but she had the look of somebody who sensed things. He wanted to ask her about it but held back. Not the time or place. Besides, what could he say? *Gee, officer, I happen to know that you're being checked out by a long-dead ghost with a penchant for ladies in uniform. I wondered if you had noticed?*

When she walked back to her car to look up Max's information on her computer, Drummond drifted to the passenger seat. "Sandra's doing fine, and I explained everything to her. She's worried about you."

Max glanced at the clock. "It's been hours."

He checked the rearview mirror. The officer looked to be talking on her radio while typing. He assumed she kept an eye on him as well, but hopefully, if he kept his head forward, she wouldn't see his lips moving. If she caught him talking to an empty car, she might have him carted off for a psych-evaluation.

"I did come back earlier, but you didn't even notice me. Too buried in your research. I told Sandra about that, too. She asked that I keep an eye on you and let you work. Once you passed out, we decided to let you rest. You've been going hard for over a day now."

Max's stiff back and neck agreed. "You can tell her I'll be on my way home once I'm done here."

"I think I better stick with you. An hour of sleep after all that research ain't going to be enough."

The officer strutted back to the car. She peered over at the backseat as she handed back his license and papers. "Is that an axe?"

Max forced a smile. "Yes, ma'am. I was helping a friend chop up some old wood."

"Uh-huh." She weighed all the scraps of data coming her way. Some odd bits, but hopefully not enough worth her trouble. At length, she tapped the car's roof. "You can't sleep here."

"I'm really sorry. I just thought —"

"You look awake now. You go straight home, get some rest, and I'll let you off with a warning."

"Yes, ma'am. I understand. I'm really sorry."

When Max pulled into his driveway, he had to admit Drummond had been right to stay. Only minutes back on the road, and Max's eyes weighed heavy. The ghost chatted away about the police officer and how he wished he were young and alive. Max didn't hear much of it, didn't want to, but the rambling voice kept him conscious long enough to reach home in one piece.

As he gathered the books and headed for the side door, Sandra rushed out. She hugged him, slapped his chest, admonished him for taking fool risks, and finally sat him at the kitchen table. "We have a lot to discuss," she said, setting a pan on the stove and grabbing some eggs and butter from the fridge.

"I'm not that hungry," Max said.

"Good, because the food's for me. I'm starving. You want me to put some eggs in for you, too?"

Drummond floated to the table. "I'll take mine over-easy with a side of toast."

She chuckled. "If you could eat, I'd love to cook for you. I have a feeling you were a man who would appreciate a well-made meal."

"Indeed, I was."

"Where's Brenda?" Max asked.

"When we hit one hundred possible spells, I sent her home."

"One hundred?"

"Those are just the recorded ones. There could be another hundred or more that have only been passed down by being taught one witch to the next. Spells are a lot like chocolate chip cookie recipes that way. You can find tons of them in cookbooks, but there are special ones that grandmothers hold in their heads to only give to the next generation when she feels it's the right time."

"Speaking of," Max said, "I wouldn't object to you making your grandma's cookies sometime soon."

Sandra turned figure-8s with a spatula. "Do you want to talk cookies, or do you want to hear what we found?"

"Cookies, please. At least, those morsels of tastiness aren't actively trying to kill me."

Drummond said, "If you uncovered one hundred spells that all could be the spell these witches are trying to pull off, then what good is it to us?"

"That's a smart question, and I wondered the same thing once we hit twenty spells. But Brenda already started noticing commonalities. By the end, we identified that many spells using an animal heart — and *all* the spells using a deer heart — require at least three consecutive nights to properly cast. The first night must be done under the full moon, and its primary purpose is to safely remove the heart without losing its lifeforce energy."

As Sandra plated her eggs and sat, Max said, "That would be last night's adventure?"

"Definitely. The killing of Emily Dodson might be a separate spell to be used in conjunction on the third night. It gets muddy, but tonight is the second night, and the witches will gather again to prepare the heart's energy for the final spell. The rules for the second night are more varied as are the preparations. We spent hours trying to find something that would clue us into where they could end up or what they might need, but the work they have to do could be in the basement of a house or in a ruined church or any number of other locations."

Drummond said, "Meaning we can't stop them from taking tonight's step forward."

"Afraid not. But, tomorrow night, the third night, is the big one. The heart is ready, and at the witching hour, the witches must come together like they did the first time — not in the same place, but in the same type of place. So, if they were conducting a spell that required the heart to be removed by a body of water the first night, then on the third night, the main spell would also have to be by a body of water."

"We got a find another golf course?"

Max said, "No. We need another place where a tragedy related to misusing magic occurred."

"That's right," Sandra said. "The problem is that there are hundreds, maybe thousands, of places that could fall into the category. I don't see how we can narrow it down to a manageable amount."

"We won't have to. I know where they're going to be tomorrow night, and I might even know why." To the curious looks, he said, "Payne Road. The stories about this place — well, buckle up."

Chapter 26

DESPITE EXHAUSTION FILLING every pore in his body, Max lifted higher in his chair. The chance to share research would never lose its appeal.

Drummond groaned. "Can't you just tell us where —"

"It's not that simple."

"Never is."

Sandra said, "Don't we already know now? Payne Road."

"It's a long, twisting road with a long, twisted history, and the location for casting this spell could be a number of places. I'll give everything I know about it all, and either you'll agree with my conclusion or you'll have a better idea." Max waited for further objections. When none came, he said, "There are a lot of Payne Roads in North Carolina, and a few too many claim to be *the* Payne Road. But after digging into it, the truth is that only the one Payne Road north of Winston-Salem in Rural Hall is the real one. Lots of reasons for this to be true — you don't need to hear it all, and I'm sure Drummond doesn't care — but one important factor is that so many teenagers were going out to the various spooky parts of the road and causing problems that the town eventually renamed part of the road to Edwards Road. They hoped to make it harder for kids to find."

"That worked?" Sandra said.

"Before the internet, yeah. Not so much now. Anyway, one of the biggest legends is about a guy name Edward Payne. Sometime during the 1930s, Payne ran a farm in the area. It's common for roads to be named after the farm, so not surprising that the road around his farm was Payne Road. The story is that he went crazy. One evening he took his wife into the living room of their small house and tied her to a chair. Then, one by one, he brought each of his four children into the living room and forced them to kiss their mother good night. After the kiss, he killed them. One by one. Now, there was also an infant. This caused his poisoned mind to hesitate, and as he argued with himself, his wife managed to break free. She grabbed the infant and ran out the back door. In a furious rage, Edward chased after her. She put everything she had into getting away, ran onto the infamous road and over the covered bridge that crossed a small stream. More on that bridge to come. Now, not far from there, Edward Payne caught up to her. With an axe, he lopped off her head and tossed the infant down a well on his property. By this point, he started to realize what he had done. Distraught, confused, insane — he went back to that bridge and killed himself. Some stories say he hung himself off the bridge. Others claim he hung himself from a tree next to the bridge."

Drummond frowned. "I was alive then. I don't remember any wild story about this guy. It does sound a bit like the Charlie Lawson murders, though."

"I thought so, too. I pulled out my notes from our old case that dealt with the Lawson murders, and I checked the census data all around that period. I couldn't find any records of an Edward Payne or a Payne family living in the area or owning that specific property. It seems clear that the Payne legend grew out of the Lawson murders, especially since the Lawson home wasn't that far away from Payne Road. In fact, I found online an old documentary from 2006 about the Lawson murders that said when Charlie Lawson went down to his creek to wash the blood from his hands, that bloody water ran under the Payne Road bridge. This legend suggests that it was the blood of the dead Lawson family washing under the Payne Road bridge that is the source of all the disturbances surrounding that bridge."

"Such as?" Sandra said.

"Strange hand prints appearing on your car after driving across. People claim to have heard a crying infant, a screaming woman, and some say they saw the shadow of a man hung in a tree. But by far, the most prevalent story is that if you take your car to that bridge, turn off the engine, whistle *Dixie*, and then try to start your car again, it won't start. You'll have to get out and push the car off the bridge before it'll start again."

Drummond clearly didn't like that last part. "What does Edward Payne or Charlie Lawson have to do with a car?"

"Nothing. I doubt any of that is true, but it is an urban legend about the bridge, and we know many of those can be traced back to an actual event. So, I wanted to mention it."

Finishing her eggs, Sandra said, "If the Payne story is true, or if Lawson put enough blood into the water, then perhaps there is a lot of angry energy surrounding that bridge. It doesn't have to be about the cars. Could simply be the way a car's electronics get screwed up around ghostly energy."

Max got up from the table, cleared Sandra's empty dish, and started handwashing it as he spoke. He needed the movement, some way to dissipate his own non-ghostly energy. "There might be more to it, but I did this research mostly from LaShanna's book and from what I could get on my phone from my car. One piece that stood out, and may account for a lot of the myths about that road, concerned Milus Frank Edwards. He owned a lot of land in the area, including the cemetery."

"Wait," Drummond said. "There's a cemetery?"

"Oak Grove Methodist Church. Very old one. Small. People have checked it out and there are no graves for the supposedly murdered Payne family, but there are some graves that are old enough to be illegible now. Those could be for the family. Others looked burned, but that's for a bit later."

"Who is this Milus fellow?"

"Milus Edwards was born in 1885 and went by his middle name, Frank. He suffered from some undiagnosed mental illness, spending much of his life misunderstood. On October 5, 1955, after making several threats on his own life over the years, he finally followed through. After a series of financial setbacks, he drove his truck to a shed on the other side of Payne Road, opposite his house, and then — well, this part is a bit hard to believe but I found his obituary in the Winston-Salem Journal which confirmed it — he killed himself by resting a stick of dynamite under his head. Lit the thing and blew himself to smithereens."

"Now, that's a statement."

Sandra said, "A horrible one."

"Not the only one, either," Max said. "Turns out he had a whole bunch of siblings. Three of them also committed suicide at different times."

"Was the family cursed?"

"It's something to consider. I didn't see any evidence of witchcraft, and even LaShanna points that out in her book. It does appear that a lot of his life served as starting points for many of the urban legends, though. It must have been a hard death for the little town to handle. Wouldn't be the first time people took these real events and mixed them up with fictions or other real events to help them cope."

Drummond tapped his chin as he floated near the ceiling. "We got the bridge and this shed as possible locations for the witches to cast their spell. Also, the old house where Payne murdered his family — if that happened at all. Any others?"

"The cemetery," Sandra said. "It's a classic location to cast any spell. Lots of dead energy there."

"Right. There's also the well where Payne supposedly threw his baby down."

Max said, "It gets worse."

"There's more?"

Leaning against the counter, he dried his hands. "Oh yeah, there's more. This one is difficult because I can prove some of it is false, but given the nature of what we do, other parts of it ring very true. Apparently, there was a Mr. Robert Payne who owned a plantation on the land and around thirty slaves. He was a loving husband and father, and according to LaShanna's book, he treated his slaves with decency and respect."

"Other than owning them," Sandra said.

"I think she meant that he wasn't a sadistic bastard who reveled in causing them to suffer. He was also a stern man, though. With four daughters, he always had his eye out for men who came sniffing around. Possible suitors or dangerous threats, he knew any man could be either. Maybe even both. But like other Payne's in these stories, he had an unstable mind, and one day, certain events tilted it. The story is that he discovered one of his daughters had fooled around with one of his slaves resulting in a pregnancy. Rage fired out of him, and he order the slave killed. But then, not too long after, another one of his daughters became pregnant by another one of his slaves. Here, his madness took over completely. He rampaged through his house and his slave quarters, killing his family, all the slaves, and burning the entire plantation to the ground. People claim that this unholy act is why so many of the trees on Payne Road are young and many of the Oak Grove Cemetery stones are charred."

"Doesn't seem likely." Drummond lowered to the table, his attention on the surface as if he stared at a map of the Payne farm. "I can believe that old Mr. Payne might lose his mind and kill his family. Tragic, of course, but his daughters and wife would be so shocked by his actions, they might not react fast enough to save themselves. Even if they tried to run, it'd be near-impossible to get away when you're wearing several layers of dress and pants and everything they had to put on back then. But the slaves — these are hardened folks, young and strong. Hard to believe that when Mr. Payne started slaughtering them, they did nothing."

"It's not easy to go against ideas beaten into you, ideas you may have been born into," Sandra said. "Many of those slaves would be terrified to strike a white man, especially their owner, no matter what crazy things he was doing."

"Still, there were thirty of them. Surely, some of them would have run. Self-preservation can overcome a lot of mental obstacles."

"Hold those thoughts," Max said, taking a seat again. As he neared the end, his weary bones tried to reacquaint his body with how tired he actually was. "A little diving around found that the Payne house was on land that is right now held in trust by Robert Payne's descendants. He lived in Stokes County but held land all over the area, including the Payne Road property. I'd have to go to the library to confirm the slave count in the Heritage Book of Stokes County registry, but I did find online reference to him having ten children including six girls — Delia, Mitilda, Paulina, Lavinia Jane, Mary Anne, and Ruth. All born between 1811 and 1837. Robert died in 1873, and now a lot of old wills are getting digitized, so I found that, too. In his will, he split his slave holdings amongst many of his children."

Sandra crossed her arms. "Stop showing off, honey. You wouldn't have told us this whole story just to debunk it at the end. What part of your brilliant research haven't you shared yet that's going to amaze us and have us thinking how fabulous you are?"

Snickering, Drummond said, "She's got you pegged there."

"I'm not — I mean — I didn't —" Max held his tongue a moment. Some people would never be able to appreciate the value of a dramatic presentation. Deflated but determined to push on in the way he wanted, he folded his hands on the table and lifted his head. "While I was busy finding out that Robert Payne could not have done the things said in the legend, I discovered another story that pointed me back to that very legend. This one sounds like a typical teenager story starting with the lack of dates and details, but hear me out. The story goes that a young man was driving late one night, and being young, he drove too fast. Payne Road has a lot of curves, and one very sharp curve surprised the young driver. He swerved but it was too late. He crashed right next to where a chapel once stood. His car caught fire, he couldn't get out, and he died — a slow, painful, burning death. People gathered around the fire, but nobody moved to help. They watched him die and did nothing about it. It's said that if you drive down Payne Road late at night during the witching hour, you might see headlights following you. But when you pass that specific curve, the lights will vanish, and no car will be found."

"I'm not seeing much here besides campfire stories. What about you, doll?"

Though Sandra carried an amused smile, Max detected a hint of interest. "You see it?" he asked, more hopeful than he cared to admit.

"You did mention the witching hour," she said.

Max clapped his hands and pointed at her. "Bingo. That caught my eye, too. Plus, this little chapel that was mentioned. I thought it an odd detail, so I checked it out. The reason it pops up is that supposedly, Edward Payne performed occult rites there. People thought he was a devil-worshipper. Once I found that tidbit, all kinds of weird fragments of stories started showing up — all of them dealing with old artifacts and magic spells and witchcraft. More and more, I'm convinced that one of these particular sites on Payne Road is where LaShanna and her witches are going to be tomorrow night."

Drummond said, "I thought Edward Payne wasn't real. Just a blend of the Charlie Lawson murders and other superstition."

"I can only confirm for certain that Milus Edwards was real — he's the one that killed himself with a stick of dynamite. I know that happened because I read his obituary. The Payne family that owned slaves and still owns land there, well, they're real, too but Robert Payne was hardly the mass murdering psychopath in the stories. But Edward Payne — I can't prove he existed, I do think much of his story has been taken from the Lawson murders, yet there's something real behind all of it. And that brings me to my final thing."

"You said the last story was the last one."

"This isn't a story. In LaShanna's book on Payne Road, there's a sentence, a throw away at the end where she mentions that she even came across stories of Edward Payne having wrote his madness down, creating a book of his demented soul."

"A grimoire?"

Standing again, his legs shaking, he said, "I think there was an Edward Payne, but he was no family man. I think he discovered the truth of witches and magic, and he tried to learn it. There was a little chapel near the road, and he probably practiced witchcraft there. The neighbors would not have approved. My best guess — maybe he was insane, or maybe screwing up enough spells had destroyed his mind. Either way, I think he messed with blood magic. Maybe some animals or even a few people went missing. The town got upset, the neighbors mentioned that devil-worshipper Edward Payne, and one night, a group of people, maybe the whole town at the time, headed down Payne Road and killed Edward. Burned his house to the ground. Ended his witchcraft. Something horrible like that would resonate through a town, and they would have to come up with these myths to protect themselves from what they had done."

Sandra said, "Something along those lines is entirely plausible. It's happened before to witches."

"If some version of that is true, then it's not hard to fathom that Edward Payne wrote down all that he did. Made his version of a grimoire."

"A grimoire made from madness and buried under the ashes of the town's shameful act — that would create very powerful energy."

"The kind of thing a group of witches getting into a war might want?"

"Definitely."

Drummond clapped his hands once. "Sounds like we're going to Payne Road tomorrow night and try to stop these witches from escalating this war."

Chapter 27

THEY DISCUSSED THE SITUATION for another ten minutes until Drummond smacked his fist into his palm. "I've got to go back to the Other tonight."

"What's wrong?" Sandra asked.

"Mitchell."

"The cursed boy? You freed him. Didn't he move on?"

"Yeah, but he set us up. There is no way that Mitchell accidentally found me. That'd be like bumping into an old pal from high school while walking the streets of New York City — highly unlikely. But if he sought me out —"

"How?" Max said. "He couldn't have known about you."

"Unless his mother told him. The woman who once was close friends with —"

"LaShanna Mill."

"I think LaShanna tried to get Max out of the way by using Mitchell, and to do that, she had to use his mother."

Sandra said, "Or connect with the Other. Not an easy thing for a witch. If she can pull that off, then she'll try to use that to her advantage. The ghosts in the Other are going to get dragged into this war if they're not careful."

"I've got to warn them."

Max said, "If you can, see if any of the Paynes are still around. Maybe we can get a clearer idea of what's true and what isn't. Any information is going to help us because Payne Road stretches a lot of acreage. It would take us more than a single night to cover it all."

Sandra said, "I've got a few spells to help us with that."

After Drummond left, Max finished cleaning up while Sandra

went to the living room and combed through the compiled list of one hundred spells. She had fresh eyes now and searched for spells involving grimoires or the power associated with such an object. Calling out the various pieces she found, Max listened from the kitchen.

He wanted to hit the books again, but his body refused. He opened the refrigerator, thinking a last-minute boost from some soda would be a good idea, and he saw the unopened wine bottle.

"I thought about it, too," Sandra said, standing in the hallway. "But I can barely keep my eyes open. Let's curl up together and get some sleep."

Max followed her to the bedroom. Half-awake, half-zombie, they dressed for bed and got under the covers. Sandra nestled against Max's chest. He closed his eyes, squeezed her arm, and she nuzzled in closer — a familiar, warm, wonderful place. He kissed the top of her head.

He considered a few things to say about possible spells, LaShanna, and even Payne Road. But those words never left his lips. Sleep took hold, and neither of them tried to stop it.

Morning came too fast. When Max opened his eyes, his groggy head noticed that Sandra had already awoken. He found her in the living room going over possible spells one more time.

She said that the answer had to be there. If she could only find it, then she could determine the specific witching hour the spell needed to be properly cast. They would also be able to learn if a counter-spell existed and what such a spell required.

"We're going into battle tonight." Her grim eyes had a faraway gaze. "We need the best intel we can get, and I'm the one set up to provide it."

The unspoken truth — they had hours of the day to eat up before facing those witches. Any work, no matter how useful or futile, consumed those hours and kept their minds off the dangers ahead.

Max tried to do the same. He sat in the kitchen alcove office and dug deeper into the various Payne Road legends. But his efforts proved more futile than useful. He found a Facebook Group devoted to the road and its many stories. Over three thousand people had joined. There he read first-hand accounts of growing up near Payne Road. People that claimed to have lived in the 1940s, -50s, and -60s, who took the bus to school over that road. They talked about the eerie quiet that came upon the students when the bus turned on Payne Road. They spoke of Halloween dates where they dared to drive over the covered bridge, getting thrills regardless of what happened. Some described strange sensations and bizarre experiences while others promised nothing had ever occurred there.

Futile indeed.

Sandra would have skipped lunch, but Max insisted. At the kitchen table, they ate reheated chili with gobs of cheese. Both kept their heads buried in laptops.

An hour later, Max had to admit that he had gone as far as the research could take him. He closed his laptop and stretched. While his wife scoured through each spell on her list, searching for any morsel of doubt to cross it off, he paced the house, imagining one horror after the other, playing out all the doom scenarios of what they might face that night. Lunch curdled in his stomach.

Stepping outside for some fresh air, he tapped on his phone and called J. "Everything's fine," he assured J after their greetings. "Last I heard, you were extending your vacation. I wanted to see when you might be coming back."

"Oh." J paused. Max got the distinct impression that PB or his mother or both stood nearby. "Not much longer. The others thought it would be fun to go check out the Biltmore Estates in Ashville. Kind of take the long way around coming back."

"Isn't that place supposed to be haunted?"

"Yeah, but that's okay."

"I know you've gotten comfortable seeing ghosts, but I think the Biltmore is a bit like a cemetery or hospital — a lot of ghosts."

"I've got to learn to deal with it, don't I? It's not like I can avoid going into places with lots of ghosts for the rest of my life.

Besides, Sandra's been helping me with that."

It shouldn't have surprised him, yet Max wondered when Sandra and J had discussed such things. He knew they had talked about ghosts and living with the Sight, but other than a couple times early on, Max couldn't recall seeing them dive deep into it all.

Misunderstanding Max's pause, J said, "I know you want to see PB as much as possible before he leaves, but so do I. If we can talk honest, well, we all know Grandma Porter doesn't have a lot of time left. When she asked for us to join her on this trip, PB and I both understood what this was about."

"That's sort of true, but she could live for many years, still."

"Not with a great quality of life."

Max stared at the phone in shock. Nothing about his boys remained boys anymore.

"The way I see it," J went on, "as long as I get back before school starts, the more time we spend with Grandma Porter, the better."

When the call ended, Max felt the relief of knowing the boys and his mother would remain away from whatever the night would bring. He marveled at the maturity of his children yet struggled at that nagging idea that his mother might infect their minds. He had spent years overcoming the guilt she had laid at his feet. With her death — yes, he could acknowledge that inevitability — with her death nearing, he could believe that she might throw all decorum away, speak her mind with a freedom she never had before, and ruin the Sandwich Boys just when they were starting to excel.

But perhaps that wasn't fair to her. He had grown. Perhaps she could, too. Perhaps she had. Some grandparents see their grandchildren as a second chance, an opportunity to right the wrongs they had done to their own children.

And the boys did love her. They were smart, young men, too. He should give them more credit. No matter what weird things she might say, they had their brains, they could think for themselves, they could parse out the good from the bad in her words.

His phone rang, and he jumped. Pleased to have something intrude on his spiraling thoughts, he glanced at the screen — Van Horn. Not too pleased, then.

The moment Max accepted the call, Van Horn said, "I am texting you an address. Ms. Hull expects to see you. You have an hour to comply." Without another word, he cut the call and sent the text.

When Max informed Sandra, she threw down the book in her hand. "I'm tired of that woman," she said, before insisting on coming along.

Forty minutes later, Max and Sandra once again took the exit for the Grandover Resort. When Max first saw the address, he assumed Cecily Hull had chosen to meet on the golf course. She must have heard what happened — all the witch community must have heard — and wanted to remind Max of his place while upsetting him with the memory of nearly dying. Yet it turned out that the address wasn't for the resort itself but rather one of the homes on the resort property.

He parked in the driveway of a beautiful house, well-cared for, and far beyond anything they could afford. Van Horn towered on the small porch, waiting for them with the perturbed glare of a father wondering where his teenage daughter had been all night.

"You ought to smile," Sandra said as they entered the house. "It'll make you so much prettier."

Max covered his mouth to hide his grin. A peek at Van Horn's unamused frown, and Max snorted a sharp laugh. Stepping in the house, he rubbed his wife's back so she knew he appreciated what she had done. It was more than a joke. It broke the tension consuming him — even if only for a moment.

That moment vanished at the sight of the house interior. Lacking all decoration and most furniture, the house echoed Cecily Hull's voice off its bland, impersonal walls. Van Horn led the way to the living room — a cavernous space with wood floors and a stone fireplace. Another makeshift desk had been erected for Cecily's use. She paced behind it while holding a cell phone to her ear.

With an impatient wave, she directed them to two folding chairs. She limped on her right leg — that was new. Behind her, a cane leaned against the stone fireplace — that was very new. When she finished her call and settled in the one nice office chair, Max caught the wince flashing across her face.

He said, "Three offices in three days — things aren't looking too good."

A dismissive cock of the head. Then: "They can't hit what they can't find."

"Looks like somebody found your leg."

Cecily's forehead wrinkled and her chin pulled in. A fraction of a second and it was gone, but Max knew he had seen it.

"Do you know who did it?" he asked, hoping directness would bypass any denials. "Chances are good whoever hurt you is connected to our case."

Halfway through ignoring him, she stopped, reconsidered, and finally said, "You weren't the only ones in danger last night. After closing the downtown office, I went to the first temporary site — where we met in Lexington." She snuck a peek at Van Horn. "There was a fire. The official investigation is still going on, of course, but I know they won't find anything. They'll say it was faulty wiring or something. There won't be evidence of arson."

"But you know."

"I saw a burning pentagram floating before me as the floor gave out beneath. Mr. Van Horn helped me escape, and the pentagram followed us. When we crossed the threshold to the outside, that's when it vanished. That is all I know about it. Never saw anybody running away, and nobody contacted me to further the threat."

"Then why did you make a new office here?" Sandra said. "The witches already know about the Grandover Resort, obviously. They'll have no trouble finding you."

"I think they'll be more like lightning — never strike the same place twice." Cecily tented her fingers on her desk. They trembled enough to make the move awkward until each finger settled in position. "Now, let us focus on what's important — results. What do you have for me? Where is Madame Ti?"

While Max debated how much of the truth to tell, Sandra blustered on forward. "Most likely, she's dead. Somebody wanted to start this war, was fed up with how you were running things — intending to run them — and they struck. You haven't mentioned any ransom call or demands of any kind, so it seems pretty likely they killed Madame Ti right from the beginning."

Cecily digested the information in a long silence. At length, she spoke with strict control and a clear lack of emotion. "I appreciate your candor, if not your tact. But you are wrong to question my leadership when I have yet the actual opportunity to do so, to lead. We have come close to full control of the state, but our enemies launched this attack before Madame Ti and I could finish our work."

"No, no." Sandra wagged her finger. "You have had years to pull this thing together. We supported that. I supported that. There are countless witches I've spoken to during that time, trying to convince them that you would bring about a peaceful period for us. One where we weren't being burned at the stake or hunted down, one where we could practice our spells in private. As long as we did not use them for harm, we would be free. That was the Hull promise, and that was what we told others. Yet year after year — nothing."

Max did his best not to betray the shock running through him. Sandra could be brash at times, but she held nothing in check now. Taken aback, Cecily looked as if she had been slapped.

"If you feel so strongly that I have failed, why are you here now? Why aren't you teaming up with those that are against me?"

"Because war has never been a solution to anything. I'm now wondering if you're a solution to anything, either."

Putting a hand on his wife's bouncing knee, Max said, "Ms. Cecily, with all due respect —"

"I don't think you've shown me any due respect."

"We came here when you called. That's a lot of respect. But we've got a busy day. So, please, what is it that you want?"

Sandra said, "She wants assurances. She wants to know whose side we're taking."

"Is that right?"

Cecily's mouth twisted through several thoughts. "In part, yes. After all, money has never truly bought loyalty."

Max looked at her as if she had admitted she didn't understand how numbers worked. "Why would you ever think you had our loyalty? You've done nothing but force us to side with you over the years. You've put us in life-threatening situations, and you've directly threatened our lives."

She shrugged. "I would have thought you could put that behind us when you realized that we have a common interest."

"What is that?"

"My success. If I don't win the leadership of magic in North Carolina, then look at who will. Do you really want to live in a world where Sister Sadie is in charge? Do you honestly believe you would be better off? Or the Brotherhood? That is a horrible thought."

"You're missing the whole point. I don't want anybody running magic in North Carolina. I don't want it to be a concern. A perfect life would be all witches only practicing magic that is beneficial. No murders. No power struggles. None of it. In a perfect world, the Porter Agency would spend most of our time helping ghosts move on. But that can't be because all of you cannot handle this power without letting it corrupt you."

"Your wife is a witch. From what I've heard and what I've seen, she has considerable power."

"A responsibility we take quite seriously."

As if scoring a point, Cecily said, "Yes, that's right. You're the good witch."

Sandra pounced to her feet. In response, Van Horn took one step forward, but Max put his arm around his wife to hold her back. To Cecily, he said, "You wanted to know our progress regarding Madame Ti, and we told you. You wanted to know whose side we're on, and we told you. If there's nothing else, we have to get going."

He held still a moment, and when no answer came, he nudged

Sandra to turn around. As they walked out of the room, Cecily chuckled. It was a bitter sound, one that betrayed her uneasy state of mind. Yet the sound echoed around them.

"You know the classic saying — nobody gets to be neutral on a moving train. Well, the world of magic is a bullet train, and it's only getting faster."

Chapter 28

DURING THE FINAL HOURS BEFORE DUSK, Max and Sandra meandered through their tiny home like lost ghosts unable to find their bodies. They spoke little. They filled the time with minor chores — dusting this, wiping down that. For the coming battle, they were prepared, and they had nothing left to do but wait.

And think.

That part troubled Max because his brain wanted to mull over every word, every twitch, every wince, every single detail from their conversation with Cecily Hull. She had been panicked and erratic the last few days. Understandable at first, but what had happened to the brutally tough woman he knew? Years ago, when she had been denied the opportunity to lead the Hull family, she didn't back down. She fought when she could and hid in the shadows when necessary. It took over a decade, but she succeeded. She won control of the family and its businesses. While this current situation was dangerous and tense and larger than any conflict she had experienced, Max could not see why any of that daunted her. Even the fire set to harm her, maybe kill her — why should that scare her? Why should it shake her confidence?

That was it, he thought. It wasn't that she had lost control, so much as lost confidence. That mattered. With a power like the government, it had the police to enforce its laws. But a community — a niche like the witch community — only had self-imposed rules. For the witches, they enjoyed peace when they had a leader that they feared and respected. That fear came from the power the leader wielded. That respect came from the leader's confidence. Cecily Hull had lost both.

Only a power vacuum remained.

"We're going to be okay," Sandra said, but she let the last word drift up in pitch, turning it into a possible question.

Max had wandered into their bedroom and found her scrunched up against the pillows. With her legs held in tight and her chin resting on her knees, she had become his emotional mirror. All his anxiety reflected through her eyes. It bounced off her in the rocking of her body and odd tone in her words.

He sat next to her, his shoulder brushing hers. "You're feeling it, too?"

"This one is different."

"Why? We've faced very experienced, very tough witches before. I'm not sure that's what we're dealing with this time."

"You're not?"

"Oh, they're plenty tough, but it seems like we're making them out to be tougher than they are. They got the better of us last night, and that scared us. We weren't ready for them. We got cocky, even a little lazy."

Gesturing toward the living room and the list of one hundred spells, Sandra said, "I am hardly lazy."

"You know what I mean. Don't you?"

"Yeah, I do. Now that we're talking about it, I think you know what I'm going to say."

Max thought about it a moment and laughed. "Nothing for us to do but push on through."

"Absolutely right."

The drive out to Payne Road went quietly. Plenty of nervous energy bounced between Max and Sandra, but neither wanted to talk. Max guessed his wife continued to go over the spells in her head, cutting out any that gave the slimmest excuse for not being what they sought. He wished he had that big a task to occupy his mind. Instead, he thought about his gun.

The Glock 9mm sat in the trunk along with all their usual

supplies. Still unloaded, still unfired, he had considered selling it on several occasions. After all, he had avoided training with it. Part of him clearly did not want to carry the weapon. But Sandra insisted he bring it along tonight.

"The dead don't care about guns," he had said.

"The living do. And I'm not some superwoman. You think I can stop four witches by myself? I'm not that good at magic, yet."

"That's not the impression I get. Seems like every witch we come across has respect for what you can do."

"Don't believe the hype. I've got a long way to go."

In the end, he agreed to bring the firearm along, but only to ease her mind. He figured if Sandra's concentration was clouded because she worried about failing and the fallout, and if having the Glock sitting in the trunk helped her think there were alternatives, then that was the best way to go. Neither of them wanted to use the gun — ever — but he understood that they reached a firmer footing with it nearby.

Drummond joined them ten minutes before they arrived. Like a racehorse standing in the gates, he shuffled in the confines of the backseat, itching for the chance to run. In that moment, as Max entered the town limits of Rural Hall, he saw his ghost partner differently.

Being dead, time changed for a ghost. With no need to sleep or eat or anything but exist, there would be endless hours of boredom. No wonder most hauntings occurred late at night. During the day, people were awake, were doing things. Life happened, and a ghost could partake in some of it. But the nights — they would drag on and on. Even for a ghost like Drummond, one that had the Porter Agency to bring interesting and strange experiences into his afterlife, he still had to endure the long silent nights.

The town drifted into the rearview mirror. Up ahead, the trees grew over, some locking together to form a foliage tunnel. As his research had suggested, things became quieter. He didn't notice an eerie feeling, nor did Payne Road appear more haunted than any other road, yet he could not deny some shift in the air. The trees knew. The insects and animals knew. This was a dark place. An ancient place. One brimming with ominous energy.

The road meandered like an old river, and the homes poked through the forested sections like large boulders breaking up the water's path. Sandra had suggested they drive the entire road first, so they headed by the tiny cemetery on the right and continued along as the trees thickened. Seeing the headstones in uneven rows, pointing in different directions, chilled Max. He had seen many cemeteries before, but this little one cut deep. That feeling worsened the further they drove.

"That's one of the properties people think may have been the Edwards house," he said, pointing off to the left — a modern house with a clean lawn. "Don't know who owns it now."

Drummond said, "That's the one who used dynamite on himself?"

"Yeah."

"I found a guy in the Other who knew him. Kept saying what a terrible shock the whole thing had been. That at least supports the story. I asked him if he thought it had anything to do with Payne Road. He didn't want to say, but he mentioned that he didn't believe in most of those hauntings because after he died, he came out here and couldn't find any ghosts in the forest."

"None?" Max looked to Sandra.

"I don't see anything. Drummond?"

"Not a peep."

Further on, Max slowed so that they could observe the thick woods to the left. "Somewhere in there is the remains of the Payne homestead. In 1991, it burned to the ground leaving some of the foundation and a chimney standing. A few people have gone out to find it and those that were successful said the chimney has since fallen over. But standing or not, it's there. I've seen pictures."

"Even if it is there," Drummond said, "I'm not seeing any ghosts. At least, not from here."

As the road curved about, Max again slowed at a new section. The road continued straight with warning signs of an embankment. "That used to be the covered bridge and all this road was gravel and dirt. The town eventually paved the whole thing. When they did that, they tore down the bridge and put in a culvert to keep the water flowing. They claimed that the bridge was in danger of collapsing, and that may have been partially true, but I think the real hazard was all the annoying teens who wanted to find the haunted bridge."

They drove for a few minutes longer until they reached the point where Payne Road officially became Edwards Road. Max turned around and went to the Oak Grove Cemetery. He parked on the side of the road.

A starter home could have fit on the cemetery's plot of land — not much more — and with forest lining the back and one side, the place felt secluded. Walking along one of the short rows — only ten graves — Max wondered how there was room for anyone but the Paynes to be buried here. Yet on the grave markers, he found plenty of others — Smithson, Driver, Brewer. Further in, he came across gravestones that no longer bore legible writing, that had a charred look as if actual flames had raged against the stone. If any graves in this cemetery belonged to the Payne family, it would be these.

Sandra approached from behind. Her footsteps crunching the grass amplified in the uneasy stillness. Every swish of clothing, every breath, every leaf pattering against the old stones — all these sounds exploded compared to the unnatural quiet tension.

"I'll set up over there," Sandra said, choosing a small section devoid of graves backed by the woods.

As she set down her bag and planned out the exact area to cast her spell, Max watched from a distance. He did not want to disturb her. The less distractions, the faster this would be done.

With a click of his tongue, Drummond said, "This is not your usual graveyard."

"It's not exactly attached to the most usual road."

"True, but it's not only that. Your wife is focused on casting her spell, she may not have even noticed."

"Noticed what?"

"The ghosts."

Max hadn't noticed, either. Not that he could see other

ghosts, but he knew what they felt like. Small pockets of cold that could chill the skin in an instant. Some could be strong enough to send an unwelcome shake straight to the bone. The worst struck even deeper.

Yet Max felt none of this. A graveyard should be teeming with cold spots. "They couldn't have all moved on."

"Oh, plenty of them are still here. But in most graveyards, they hang out near their markers or float around in little groups like cliques of high schoolers during lunch."

"Using metaphor. You started reading, finally?"

"I'll put my education up against yours any day."

"Am I about to get a tale of woe and the hard knock life of Marshall Drummond?"

"You're about to get a knuckle sandwich that'll freeze your brain. Joking aside, the ghosts are here, but they're all in one big cluster in the back. And they ain't moving. They're standing there, staring out."

"At us? At Sandra?"

"Doesn't look like they're watching anybody in particular."

Sandra paused her preparations. "It's the energy here. You've got to be feeling it, too."

Drummond rubbed the back of his neck as he gazed across the cemetery. "Things are certainly odd here. How long is this spell going to take?"

Setting out a green candle and a white one, she said, "There's no telling. I can't simply cast a location spell for a grimoire that I don't even know exists. Even if we did know that for sure, I have nothing from the book — not a scrap of paper or a piece of the cover — nothing that could be used to help the spell narrow its focus."

Max said, "So what do you focus it on?"

"The energy. Every part of the road we drove on, I could feel the unique energy humming in the background. If an object like this grimoire had been here, surrounded by hateful, angry energy for a long time, my spell will see that as an uneven break in the general hum. That's what we're looking for."

She resumed her work with a finality that stopped the men

from asking further questions. Not wanting to disturb her by staring and not wanting to get closer to the congregating ghosts, Max sauntered back to the car and leaned against the trunk. Drummond joined him.

"Maybe you can go ask your ghost friends where we can find this grimoire. Save Sandra the trouble."

"Would if I could. But this weird energy your wife is talking about, I'm guessing that a big part of it comes from those ghosts. From the crap they've endured. They're lost souls."

"You can't get through to them? Help them, I don't know, find themselves?"

Drummond shrugged. "I can try."

At a non-threatening pace, he floated off toward the back of the cemetery. Max watched his partner gesturing and murmuring in the distance like an actor pantomiming conversation. He thought that when people saw him talking to Drummond, this is what they saw. To Max, it looked amusing, but he could understand why others found it creepy.

When Drummond returned, he looked disappointed. "No go. It's like talking to a drunk. Not a happy drunk, either, but one of those guys who can't get a complete sentence together. They're not talking any sense."

"What are they saying exactly? Maybe I can —"

"Nothing but a slur of half-words and mumbling nonsense."

With the last of dusk turning into night, Max dug out a jacket and a high-powered flashlight from the car. The amber flickers of Sandra's candles popped like sun flares against the dark. The bright moonlight would help, but the thick woods fought against it. If they were lucky, the grimoire would be buried in somebody's front yard, and they wouldn't have to go traipsing through the darkened forest.

There is no way we'll be that lucky.

Standing in a field of the dead, Max's mind wandered towards his mother. Because of her illness, her eventual death was guaranteed to be unpleasant and far from peaceful. The idea that she might end up a ghost no longer sounded farfetched. She would have a seasoned team to help her move on, but if this witch war truly broke out, the Porters had enemies who would gladly use his mother's death against them — curse her ghost or detach her from her body, or in some other way, shred her chances of finding rest.

"How are things in the Other?" he asked, more to break his own thoughts than to seek an actual answer.

Drummond let out a soft whistle. "Not good. I sent out a warning and it spread fast. I knew it would — the ghost network can be quite efficient — but I only intended to make them wary. Be cautious. Vigilant. They need to recognize if a witch tries to cast her way into the Other."

"I take it your fellow ghosts didn't react that way."

"All I got was a lot of tension, a lot of worry, a lot of fear. After you're dead, things are supposed to get easier. Even the cursed dead are mostly just stuck. Or take these folks in this cemetery, all huddled up back there together. It ain't paradise, but it ain't hell, either. This witch war could change all of that."

"Y'know, we keep acting like it's all a done deal, but there's no guarantee, yet, that we're interpreting everything right."

"That's some nice, wishful thinking. War or no war — LaShanna and these other new witches only mean trouble. Very big trouble."

"Then I'm sorry you don't have Miss 1800s anymore. I'm sure she would've been quite appreciative of your protective arms."

Drummond barked a short laugh. "That she would. But I'm not entirely alone."

"Oh?"

"Spent some time chatting with Lady Lydia."

"Miss 1800s close friend?"

"Turns out we get along. Nothing romantic — not yet — but she's easy to talk with and smarter than she lets on."

"You really do live in a different world."

"Because she's Miss 1800s old friend? Ghosts don't have the luxury of being picky. I once thought we did, but clearly you never know when somebody's going to move on. We're opportunists and pragmatic. For me — for a lot of us — we seek companionship in the cold and lonely. You see? We're not going to be choosy when one of those rare chances arrive."

Putting up his hands, Max said, "I'm not judging. Just trying to understand."

Before Drummond could snap a reply, Sandra called out, "I think I've got something."

Chapter 29

DRUMMOND ZIPPED ACROSS THE CEMETERY. Max jogged along a row of graves, and when he reached his wife, her casting circle glowed the deep orange-red of embers. She watched the pulse of color, mesmerized and full of awe.

Max thought of Cecily Hull's warning — that Sandra danced with the same corruptible power as all witches. He and Sandra had considered it numerous times. But being aware of the dangers of a thing did not prevent those dangers. He trusted Sandra to tell him if she felt the warping pull of magic upon her; however, seeing her face fill with hypnotized joy, watching the lust for power all people harbor rise to the surface of her lips, he had to wonder how far gone she would have to be before she dared cry out for help.

A single, glowing ember lifted into the air. It hovered over the center of the casting circle, and its light bathed Sandra with its warmth. She lifted one finger as if offering a perch to a butterfly, but before she could touch the summoned energy, it shot off toward the road.

"Follow it," Sandra said, hurrying after the ember.

Max and Drummond hustled up behind. When they reached the road, the ember jumped ahead fifty feet and waited. They rushed to catch it, only to have it dash further along. In this way, they continued to follow its jerky movements until it crossed the street and darted into the forest.

Turning on his flashlight, Max said, "Be careful in there. Go slow. Following that spark of light won't do us any good if we twist our ankles."

"Then make sure you light my way," Sandra said. "That magic

won't last long."

She blasted into the woods chasing the ember. Max chased after her like a police officer following a hound dog running down a fugitive. He swore under his breath. Trying to keep the flashlight on his wife's feet while at the same time not trip on the tangled earth beneath him resulted in numerous stumbles.

"I'll stay with her." Drummond soared forward.

Max's foot hit a loose rock, and he battered into a tree.

"I saw that," Drummond said over his shoulder.

Max wanted to yell for Sandra, get her to slow down, have her turn back and help him, but bellowing her name would only alert the witches if they were near. In fact, as these thoughts weaved in his mind, he worried his flashlight might give them away. He flicked it off, but the total darkness overwhelmed him. Max didn't care. He raced through the woods in the dark.

And where was the moonlight? He gazed up. The moon was there, nearly full and lighting up the night sky. Yet little of the pale glow reached the forest floor. A result of the dense forest or the dark energies that cursed this land? Or perhaps a witch's spell.

Sweat — his old friend — trickled down his sides and back. He trudged on. Even with the sounds of snapping twigs, kicked rocks, and crunching leaves, the woods clung to that unsettling quiet — an absence of sound Max thought he might forever associate with Payne Road. Stranger still — the smell of the forest had changed. The sweet, vibrant, earthy aroma common to most woods never materialized here. There was an odor, though — only hints, barely a full scent. Max shuddered when he finally recognized the off-putting smell. Stale death.

Up ahead, Sandra, Drummond, and the ember had all stopped.

As he trundled over a fallen log, Max marveled that his wife had navigated the dark woods without injury. When he reached them, the hovering ember sputtered out. Sandra put a finger to her lips to keep Max quiet, then gestured for him to turn off the flashlight. He hadn't realized it was back on. When he pressed the off switch, when his eyes adjusted to the dark, he discovered a clearing in the forest ceiling that allowed the bright moonlight to shine down.

A few feet ahead, a mound of grasping vines, thorny bushes, and creeping weeds had swallowed most of the remnants of the Payne household. Warped and rotting floorboards outlined where the house had stood, and a rubble pile of brick and stones marked the last stand of the chimney. Shards of glass twinkled the moonlight back through the overgrowth.

A lump lodged in Max's throat. The weight of Payne Road, all its stories, all its horrors, pressed against his chest. Though he knew half of the stories could not be true — nothing more than urban myths developed over decades of embellishments blended with a horrid whisper down the lane — that still left the rest of the stories to be quite true. Or, at least, based in truth. Enough real tragedy had occurred in these woods to create the unwelcome energy Sandra's spell had discovered.

A dim echo of laughter sifted through the trees. Max and Sandra crouched low, both hyperaware of every sound. Neither one needed to get an answer from the other. They both knew. That laugh — it had to be one of the witches.

"I'd offer to go check it out," Drummond said as he stared into the trees, "but those witches will still have their ghost wards."

Max gestured to a small opening between two trees that looked like a pass. "Stay as close with us as you can. If it gets too strong, let us know."

Proceeding with cautious steps, Max and Sandra squatted low to the ground. As they worked their way toward the sounds hidden amongst the trees, Max's thighs burned. Still, he kept low. Each footfall crinkled leaves on the ground. His muscles clenched. At any moment, he expected one of the four witches to appear with a cackling laugh and a sociopathic glare.

The ground sloped upward. Nothing too steep, but navigating the uneven surface while crouching, at best, sent throbs of pain along his spine, the back of his neck, and into his shoulders. When they reached a point that leveled-off, Max couldn't tell where one sore spot ended and another began.

Sandra appeared fine, but he didn't ask, once again for fear of drawing unwanted attention.

Several feet ahead, Drummond said, "Stop here."

Wiping her face, Sandra whispered, "Are the wards hurting you?"

"Not yet. But join me and you'll see all you need."

Max and Sandra approached the ghost and discovered the ground dropping off at a sharp angle. About ten feet below this ledge, the four witches stood around a small fire made of four torches leaning into each other. A large casting circle of white powder encompassed them all. Each woman held her arms out. Wearing only long cloaks, their bare bodies flickered in the firelight. Each had columns of symbols painted on their faces.

LaShanna uttered a series of sounds that the other witches repeated. Max and Drummond looked to Sandra.

"Hard to tell. I know the words for the spells I want to cast, but I'm not fluent in any of these forgotten languages. I couldn't even hold a basic conversation."

"It doesn't matter," Max said. "They've already started casting something. Let's get down there and disrupt things."

"Hold on, there, partner." Drummond dropped off the ledge until he was at eye-level. "We need to take our time. You don't know what's going on here."

"Last time, we waited and it nearly cost our lives."

"And when you finally tried to run, look what happened. These witches are strong. Much stronger than we gave them credit for at the golf course. We go running in there without a plan, they'll destroy us."

Sandra placed her hand on Max's shoulder. "He's right. Until we know what that spell is, we won't be able to break it — not safely."

Grinding his teeth, Max inched closer to the ledge and watched the witches. With no way to help Sandra and no immediate action to take, he fidgeted with the surrounding stones and leaves while never taking his eyes off the spellcasting witches. His thoughts drifted to Emily Dodson.

Had she been here, they would have had too many to stand

at the compass points. Somebody would have had to sit out. Unless they had never intended for her to be part of this group. He should have dug deeper into her life. If she lacked the magic skill the others possessed, then it would be clear that she had been brought in as a sacrifice. They wanted her heart and nothing more.

"Nothing's happening," Drummond said. "They've been chanting for a while. Shouldn't we see something by now?"

"If this were pure witchcraft," Sandra said, "then absolutely. But the rites and spells from before lacked the focal points we have now. They can be disturbingly powerful but not always the easiest to cast."

"Then we have time. Instead of blundering in there, what if we attack from three separate sides? If Osorio or Brenda was with us, I'd say we each take on a witch, but as it is, three sides will have to do."

Max wanted to jump to his feet. "Sounds like a great plan."

"Doll?"

"Okay. But be prepared for anything. We don't know what…"

As her words trailed off, her mouth stayed agape. Max and Drummond followed her gaze back to the witches. The chanting had stopped, and all four stood at attention facing the north. In unison, they bowed. Max could barely see the figure commanding such respect, and as this newcomer stepped forward, as Max finally recognized this person, he heard LaShanna verify what he saw.

With excited pride dripping through her words, LaShanna deepened her bow. "Madame Ti. Welcome. We are your witches now and always."

Chapter 30

MAX'S STOMACH LURCHED even as his body petrified. Madame Ti. The head witch for Cecily Hull. The powerful witch impatient to rule. Madame Ti. She strolled in with the charisma of a celebrity, the poise of a leader, and the haughtiness of a conqueror. Very much alive. Very much unharmed.

Each witch in turn bowed low and rattled off the same words from the same ancient language. Max couldn't understand it, but the tone betrayed the truth. In any language, he would know they pledged their loyalty, their unwavering devotion, even their souls to their queen.

LaShanna motioned to these witches, and they scurried behind her. "All of us are honored and humbled to be given this great opportunity. We have prepared everything as you wanted, and we only wish we all could see the next day alongside your greatness."

Brushing her fingertips over LaShanna's bowed head, Madame Ti said, "The spirits of the universe are a mystery indeed. I have glimpsed but a fragment of all we can achieve. Fear not. It is my first promise to you, my sisters, that no other of you will be sacrificed. Let us give our dear sister, Emily, a moment."

As all the witches grew silent, part of Max wanted to race down to them and laugh. Madame Ti spoke like a completely different woman. Still full of herself as ever, but she had swallowed the cult leader attitude wholesale.

A disgusted growl crossed her face. A second later, Ruby broke through from the woods carry a large bag. She made a lot of noise while sputtering out one groveled comment after another. Her pink wig sat askew, and her maid costume had torn. She looked like an anime character gone awry. Dumping the bag to the ground, metal and wood and more clattered inside.

"Everything's here, ma'am, exactly as asked for." Ruby bowed, then curtsied, then bowed again.

As if commanding a dog, Madame Ti snapped her fingers and pointed to her side. She waited for Ruby to take the assigned post. After glowering her displeasure, Madame Ti walked with reverence to the northern point of the circle and put out one hand towards Ruby. "You have always followed my guidance. You have always followed my lead."

"Yes, yes. Always." Ruby dropped to her knees, lowering her head deep enough to kiss Madame Ti's feet should it be asked of her.

"You will be allowed to witness history here. I expect your undivided attention and your greatest devotion."

As Ruby muttered her gratitude into the dirt, LaShanna shifted backwards until she stood in the northeast point of the circle. Rosita followed by taking the northwest point, and Sung slipped back into the southeast. Moving with the solemn reverence of nuns in a church, Michon carefully removed each of the central torches. Graceful and humble, she presented a torch to LaShanna, a torch to Rosita, a torch to Sung, and reserved the last for herself as she took the final point at the southwest corner.

Madame Ti beamed over these witches like a teacher watching their graduation. "Tonight, my sisters, we begin a new coven. The Coven of Ti. You will be the founding members and forever known to all. Your names will become legend."

"Better than Hull," Ruby said.

A sharp hiss from Madame Ti, and Ruby pressed her face into the ground, groaning an apology. To the witches: "I had hoped to use the political power of the Hull family to speed the ascent of this coven, to make us the most powerful, to dominate all other witches and lead them to prosperity with a sweeping action. But Cecily Hull lacks the vision of her family's past leadership. Cecily Hull lacks the courage. I do not. I am the greatest living witch, and by being a sister in my coven you will be great, too."

With a nudge of her foot, Madame Ti sent Ruby fluttering to the large bag. From there, Ruby pulled out a covered bucket. She peeled back the plastic top and poured lines of mustard-yellow sand connecting the five witches. Point-to-point within the circle she hustled, regularly glancing at Madame Ti and nodding her head. Max quickly saw a pentagram forming.

"Holy crap," he said. "Am I right about this? Did Madame Ti fake her own kidnapping to get away from Cecily Hull?"

Drummond shook his head. "Madame Ti's plenty strong enough to get away from Hull without all the subterfuge. I think it's worse than that. I think she did it to weaken Hull while sowing confusion and fear in the witch community. People act rash when they feel threatened and can't understand what the real threat is."

"She wants this war? She's priming the engines for this war?"

With her mouth an angry line, Sandra said, "Because it's so much easier to become a supreme dictator when all your opposition is divided against each other."

"The politics, too. Cecily's role was to handle the politicians. With a witch war spilling over into the non-witch world, everyone from City Council members to the Mayor to the Governor will want a fast solution."

"And Madame Ti will be there to fix it all."

Ruby finished the pentagram and tiptoed out of the circle. She returned to her spot with her head pushing into the ground. As Madame Ti lifted her hands high above and the four witches dropped to their knees, Max knew what would be coming next.

He turned to Sandra. "Tonight is all about the grimoire. I've seen you stop all kinds of spells before. If this is something as simple as bringing up the grimoire from underground, surely you can stop that."

"I don't know."

"What's not to know? This is not a time for self-doubt."

"We don't know what she's going to do."

"We absolutely do. She's going to get the grimoire."

"That's what this looks like. But all the spells I researched — not one of them was for something like this. Not one of them looks like this."

With her voice thundering in power even as it seemed to roll like a morning mist, Madame Ti said, "Sisters, the day will come when all witches speak your names with awe. The day will come when all witches bow to you like you bow before me. The Coven of Ti will be the most respected, the most sought after, the most feared coven to have ever existed. And it begins tonight. Here. Now. At the heart of a coven is a grimoire, at the heart of the greatest coven in all of history and all the future will be a legendary grimoire — the Payne Grimoire."

"There," Max said. "Do you need any more proof or can we stop this thing?"

Sandra scowled. "You're not hearing me. It's not that simple. We know what she wants to do, but I still don't recognize the spell she's casting. It makes little sense to me."

Madame Ti continued, "Place your hands on the circle, my sisters. Focus your intentions, and help me give birth to a grand miracle."

Clambering to his feet, Max said, "Let's stick with Drummond's plan. Get down there and attack from three different sides."

"It'll have to be two sides," Drummond said, a disappointed snag in his voice. "Even if those witches didn't have wards, Madame Ti certainly does. I can feel it from here."

"Maybe we should wait," Sandra said.

Max wanted to portray bravery, but his mind pictured the simple math in towering numbers. Two against six. Tamping down these discouraging thoughts, he put his hands around Sandra and kissed her. "We can do this. We've done incredible things before. I trust you and Drummond and us together. Do you trust us?"

"Of course."

"Then let's do this."

Though her chin trembled, she nodded. "Break the circle or kick apart the pentagram. If that doesn't work, go after the women. Kick them, punch them, anything. Disrupt this spell in any way you can. I'll do my best with Madame Ti."

Breaking off in different directions, they ran around the drop-off, heading down the slope on either side, to swing back on the witches casting their spell.

Chapter 31

THE COMBINATION OF MOONLIGHT FROM ABOVE and firelight from odd angles provided enough silhouettes and general fill-light that Max could manage a decent pace without tumbling to the ground. Breaking his neck would not help. He heard the chanting of a new spell and wished he could race faster to stop it, but he knew to have some caution.

The first time he ever met Madame Ti, he saw her capabilities in battle. During the final showdown between the Magi and the Mobley Coven, Madame Ti took her first steps towards prominence. He should have seen it the moment this so-called kidnapping had occurred. She had used a battle to get her career started, she would use an all-out war to take full control.

The Porters could stop her, though. He truly believed that. They had faced strong witches before, and they had faced better organized covens. At the same time, he had to wonder about Sandra.

She acted so hesitant about stopping this spell. Sure, caution was warranted, but it seemed like she wanted to watch Madame Ti in action, wanted to see this grimoire rise from the ground like the awakening dead. There was a hungriness in her eye. Was this the first signs of magic having its influence on her? Should he be worried? With his whole family whirling off in different directions, the idea that she might whirl off, too, unnerved him.

But then maybe he was wrong to think this way. After years of ambling through life, she had discovered her true talent. She had discovered purpose. Even a touch of artistry. He couldn't take that away from her. Besides, as much as he loved and trusted her, if he dared to put her in an ultimatum between magic and their marriage, part of him feared he might lose out.

Up ahead, he saw movement and a stronger flicker of firelight. He stepped to the side of a rough-bark tree and his heart sank. The fire had shifted to down below, Drummond floated in front of him, and on the other side, Sandra jogged forward. They were back to where they had started. LaShanna's spell had struck again.

"Well, that ain't good," Drummond said.

From below, the chanting increased in pace and intensity. Max and Sandra crept to the ledge and gazed over. Drummond floated above.

Undulating with the rhythm of their chant, the witches arched back and rounded forward as if practicing some demonic yoga. Madame Ti's eyes rolled up while she turned her head toward the moon. Behind her, Ruby sucked her fingers with glee, her envious eyes watching every motion of the witches and making weak attempts to repeat them.

Though Max saw only a smattering of clouds, he heard a roll of thunder. The hairs on his arms lifted, and the air felt charged. Each thrust of the witches' bodies pulsed outward, the vibrations hitting Max like waves in a pool.

Drummond tried to lower closer to the witches but hissed in pain. As he returned, he said, "It's no use."

Max said, "I've seen you break through a ward before."

"Yeah, but bashing my head against one ward took everything I had. I usually had help, too. You or Sandra or that time against the Brotherhood, I had another ghost with me. That was always against just one ward. These witches each have a ward, and maybe something else going on, I can't tell. No way can I get through those, and you two can't get down there."

"We're not going to do nothing. We can't let them get away with this."

"There's really nothing bad about what they're doing — digging up an old book."

"You know it's more than that."

"Yeah, of course. It'll give them power, make them a coven, but we're going to have to deal with them in the future. This spell itself isn't good or evil. I don't mean I'm happy about it, just that nobody is getting hurt tonight. I'd love to go down there and stop them. But we can't. Unless you've got a suggestion, I don't see what good we can do being here."

Another roll of thunder on this clear night. Sandra lifted her eyes toward the sky. "Cover your ears," she said, doing as she commanded.

As Max brought his hands up, a bolt of lightning cracked down from the sky, striking the ground in the direct center of the pentagram. Blinding light flashed and sparks spit off. The trees shook from the impact and the massive blast of thunder. Burnt ozone tainted the air.

From below, Ruby's joyful voice cried out. "It worked. It worked."

The witches ceased their chanting. They sat on their knees, looking into the center of the circle with smug satisfaction. Madame Ti walked forward. She bent down at the center and lifted a book as thick as a dictionary, as large as an atlas.

"The Payne Grimoire is ours." Holding the book to her chest, she stepped back to her northern point. "Miss Ruby, would you please get our special guests? We need to begin the next spell."

"Another spell?" Max said, the words shushing from a shocked breath.

Groveling as she backed away, Ruby left the witches behind. That instant, LaShanna motioned to the others, and they prepared the new spell. Michon and Rosita swept away the remnants of the mustard-yellow pentagram as well as the charred marks from the lightning strike. From the bag, LaShanna removed a large hunting knife that she used to cut symbols into the earth along the inside edge of the casting circle. Sung also dug around the bag and brought out five wooden bowls. She placed them in front of each witch, returned to the bag, and produced two small, metal containers. For her part, Madame Ti appeared to be muttering to herself.

"She's prepping a few fast spells," Sandra said. "Either she knows we're here or she's being cautious in case we show."

Max leaned against a tree to keep from falling over. His head spun. Something terrible brewed below, and he couldn't think of what to do.

"Let me see," Madame Ti said, and Sung brought the two containers over.

By this point, Rosita held a second knife and aided in the carving of the spell. Three circles had been drawn in the center. One quite large with a smaller one in front, facing Madame Ti, and an equally small one behind.

After receiving an approving nod, Sung bowed and returned to the casting circle. At the back circle, she removed the deer heart from one container and placed it down. She stepped gingerly to the front circle. Max fought his gag reflex as Sung removed a human heart from the second container and set it in place.

"That must be Emily Dodson's," Sandra said.

"Honey, tell me this is one of the hundred spells you studied. This is blood magic and ancient rites and all of it. What is this about?"

Sandra's face paled. "There are only a couple that come to mind, and considering that Madame Ti spent a lot of time working on transmutations, I'm thinking she intends to have a trial run."

Drummond cocked his head. "They're not crazy enough to sacrifice one of themselves. There's only five of them right now. They still need eight more to make a full coven."

Gazing into the distance, Max said, "Ruby?"

"Could be."

"No," Sandra said. "Madame Ti asked Ruby to get their special guests."

"Then who?"

Stumbling feet cracked old branches as Ruby led two people in. Only one was blindfolded. Max's heart dropped to his gut. Van Horn stood tall and firm. He lowered his head, then his body, in a deep bow toward Madame Ti. Standing next to him, blindfolded and with her hands zip-tied, Cecily Hull quailed, her head turning at one sound, then another, her terror palpable.

Chapter 32

MR. VAN HORN GUIDED CECILY HULL to the center circle. He looked to Madame Ti for permission, and after receiving a nod, he removed the blindfold. Cecily grasped her shoulders, rubbed her upper-arms, and gaped at the witches encircling her. When she saw Van Horn, her shocked expression dropped into repulsion.

"Betrayer." Her voice rose as she belted out the word — rage verging on panic.

Unmoved, Van Horn walked out of the casting circle and took up a position behind Ruby — she still knelt, bowed, and groveled. Madame Ti and her witches watched Cecily, letting the helplessness of her situation sink in. The flicker and crackle of the torches provided the majority of sound.

"This is insane," Max said.

"Keep your voice down." Sandra had her phone out and scrolled through her notes on all the spells.

"She's hardly my favorite person, but we can't let them kill her."

"Be quiet. I'm trying to think."

"I can't believe we're going to see them —"

"Shut up." She closed her eyes, taking a moment to regain her control. Then: "If you want to do something useful, get out your phone and zoom in on the spell they've drawn. Tell me what you see."

Max did as she asked. His heart banged against his chest and each breath hurt in the same area. Panicking. That's what had started to happen. Maybe the witches had a special ward that caused a person to panic if they got too close. But he didn't buy it.

Seeing Cecily Hull vulnerable made her human. The Machiavellian ruler of a family empire had become a woman alone, powerless, staring at her own demise and unable to stop it. A terrifying prospect, and one Max wanted to avoid. Not out of any loyalty to Cecily but out of simple humanity.

With his phone, he started at the closest section and moved clockwise, describing the various symbols. Sandra snagged a branch from the ground and drew the symbols in the dirt. After every few symbols, she would put out her hand to halt him, think for a moment, then roll her fingers for him to continue.

"Was this always the plan?" Cecily said, finally breaking the silence in grim resignation.

Madame Ti gazed down with pity and scorn. "We could have been a powerful team. The greatest. But you are too cautious, too willing to wait a lifetime for what should be yours now."

"That is why you have done this? You were impatient? Please, tell me I am wrong. You are too smart to have thrown away all we have built for this."

"I am smart. More than you, apparently. I see our future, and I am willing to take it."

"At the cost of all these witches?" Cecily tried to make eye contact with the new coven, but they only watched their leader. "I could have handed you all the power you seek without a single life taken."

"Your political games make big promises that never quite come to pass."

"Politics always delivers. If it didn't, the world wouldn't be full of so many politicians. You want power? That's where it is."

Madame Ti's lip curled. "That's where power is in your world. But we live in the real world. The witch world. We have magic, and that is a far greater power. Tonight, you are going to help prove this very point."

As they spoke, as Max continued to describe symbols to Sandra, Cecily appeared to forget her situation. Her voice strengthened, and even her posture straightened. She knew words. She knew debate. Manipulating people, getting others to propose ideas she wanted, using language like a spell to control — that was her way. Max marveled at how these ideas sang upon her slim facial changes.

"I see now," she said, acting as if she had the upper-hand. "I thought you understood how far we had come, how close we are to success. When I've urged you to wait, to be patient, you've been thinking that I meant for years to come when our chance to grasp our goal is only months away, maybe weeks. If I were in your shoes, I would have made a move now, too. I can't blame you for that. I should have been clearer, more open. I tend to play too close to the vest, and I'm sorry I didn't let you know."

Madame Ti's overconfident stance softened. Only a fraction, but Max saw it. She listened, and that would lead her to replay hundreds of conversations over the last years, rethink if she remembered them correctly. Had she misinterpreted the situation? Could she be ruining her best chance at success?

"I know politics can be boring," Cecily pressed on, "but in the next week, I have a meeting with one of our State House members. She is a direct line to the governor. Provided I do my job well — and we both know I always do my job well — I would expect to be handed the very thing we want. Police and other authorities would be instructed to turn a blind eye to our activities. Witches would be safe to practice their spells, but only if we allow it. Go against us, and I could have them arrested. All in the name of protecting the public."

"I have heard this before." Madame Ti's voice did not shake the ground.

"It's not too late. Stop this now, and we can —"

"Go back to before? I know you too well for that. You carry grudges from your childhood. You will never forget or forgive what I have done to you."

"Politics is all about making deals with people who have hurt you before and will hurt you again. It's all about compromising to get closer to what you want. We both want this power, and though we no longer trust each other, I trust in that power. I trust it is enough to bring us together, to let us complete what we started."

Madame Ti dropped her eyes toward Ruby, then lifted to Van Horn, then worked around the circle from one witch to the next. Max paused his symbol descriptions, using the camera to close in on Madame Ti's face. He could see the debate battling on her brow.

After all, if Cecily told the truth, the coven would have a far easier time ahead. The bloodshed clearly didn't matter, but the timing did. Cecily's way promised success in a month or two. Be patient and in short order all that power would sit in their hands. But a witch war — that could take years to resolve. Max saw the realization in Madame Ti's eyes. Some of these witches placing their faith in her tonight might not survive.

Then, a shift. A hard lock of her features. A simple answer.

"No."

What pebbles of bravery had allowed Cecily to speak bold vanished. She hugged herself, diminishing in the circle. Her head darted from one side to the other, seeking escape. Max imagined she even sent pleading eyes to Van Horn, but part of her must have figured out that he had never been working for her. He had been Madame Ti's spy and goon.

"If I listen to you, if you speak the truth, we will gain the power you promise before the year is out. But then you will want to control me."

"What? No, I promise —"

"You have stated that you know politics. You are essentially a politician, and that is a greedy, greedy animal. I think if I play your game, we will end up right here again. But that war — the one that ignites after you have solidified your power — that would be far more costly to the witches. Too many more would die. My way is better."

Sandra drum rolled her hands on the ground. "I got it."

"You know the spell?" Max said.

Drummond whipped over to her. "What are they going to do?"

"I don't know that," she said. "There are still too many spells it could be, and many of them are really closely linked. I'll never know until they start chanting."

"But you said you got it."

With pure, academic joy, she said, "There are about ten transmutation spells that use these combinations of symbols. Different positions, different timings, but in the end, they all rely on the same focal symbols."

Max thought he understood. "You don't need to know the specific spell. You only need to know the weak link."

"Exactly. And I've got it. I can't break their spell as a whole, but I can break that link, that one small piece. Do that, and the rest should fall apart."

They stared at each other, smiling in silence, until Drummond said, "Well, get going on it."

Sandra cleared the dirt with her hand, smoothing out a space to start her spell. Max returned to the ledge to keep an eye on the witches while Drummond bounced between them.

A deep whimper escaped Cecily Hull. "It doesn't have to be like this."

"It didn't — until you allowed the Brotherhood to exist," Madame Ti said. "I warned you about them. I told you they needed to die. The dangers of the ancient rites could not be permitted in the hands of others. You wouldn't listen. I warned you when Sister Sadie poked her insane head into reality once more. The greatest threat to us, I said, but you wouldn't listen. Now she runs amok causing harm to all witches, perverting what we do, and sullying our name."

Tears streamed down Cecily's cheeks. "Please. Please don't."

"Know this — if our casting succeeds tonight, you will possess the strength of the deer. You will prove that what I have discovered works, and in doing so, that knowledge will give the Coven of Ti all it needs to win this war. Traditional witchcraft won't be enough. It didn't help Mother Hope or Grandma Mobley, and it won't be enough to help us. But this spell — this will let us dominate our enemies and usher in an age of peaceful witchcraft."

"I'm sorry. I can make this right."

"This is how you make it right. You embrace the spell, embrace my craft. For a moment, you will be stronger than any human alive. Sadly, for you, Mr. Van Horn will be forced to put you down. Once I've proved my spell works — well, I can't have you running around with all that power."

Cecily continued to plead, but Madame Ti turned away. She motioned to Van Horn. The towering man entered the circle once more and gagged Ms. Hull. When her constant begging became a muted garble, Van Horn returned to his spot. Madame Ti spun back with a gracious smile as she outstretched her hands.

"My sisters, it is time. Let us begin."

Max peeked over at his wife. Deep in concentration, she lit a candle and wafted its fumes over her head. He wanted to warn her that the witches had started but he knew not to disrupt her.

"We can't let them kill her," Drummond said, echoing the thought in Max's head.

"Of course not." Brushing leaves off his legs as he stood, Max added, "Watch Sandra. Protect her."

"What can you do?"

Heading into the woods, he said, "I'll think of something."

Chapter 33

ON HIS FIRST ATTEMPT, Max headed away from Sandra, from Drummond, from the witches, and Madame Ti. He hoped that LaShanna's spell worked by making a person's movements do the opposite of their intention — head west, end up going east. If he went away from the witches, then perhaps he would end up at their casting circle.

No such luck. He simply continued walking away from everyone.

Turning back, he saw the firelight of their torches. That made it easy. He only had to keep that golden flicker in front of him. Walk straight to it.

Yet after a few minutes longer than he had taken when leaving Sandra and Drummond, he did not seem to have moved far at all. The torchlight looked no closer, but the trees had changed. He definitely had walked across some land. The spell had not forced him to remain in place.

Max stopped. He had to think through this better — clearer. If he could figure out —

A gunshot.

The sound attacked from all directions. The echo trailed off everywhere. Max bolted toward the firelight, toward the ledge, toward Sandra.

He whisked by trees and leapt over decaying logs. The dark thickened yet he managed not to fall. Sweat stung his eyes. The moonlight brightened ahead, he pushed harder, and he broke into a clearing with the scorched remnants of the Payne house.

He stared at the rubble, gasping from his run as well as the shock of being in the wrong place. More gunshots. A baby cried in the distance, cutting through the air, scratching into his bones. He spun back to the tree line. A man swung from one branch, his body limp, the noose around his neck taut.

Ducking under the man's legs, Max rushed into the woods. He knew the way from here. He could ignore the false firelight.

Another gunshot. His ears pounded at the sound. That crying, that howling baby — it followed Max. No matter how deep into the forest he went, he still heard that baby. Not even his racing heart banging in his ears could drown out the wailing.

He paused to get his bearings. If he could stay focused on the land, he thought he might find his way back to Sandra. After all, LaShanna's spell had not prevented them from getting to the ledge in the first place.

A shattering scream from behind. Max whirled to catch the shadow of a woman clutching a baby to her chest as she sprinted by. An explosive blast erupted further off, and though Max had never heard the sound before, something deep within identified it as dynamite.

Wiping his forehead, he found his path again and jogged off. The moonlight glittered through the trees. The trees blended into the dark. The dark spun shadows around him. He heard the orchestration of screams, gunshots, and explosives. A distant scent of burning grew stronger.

Up ahead, he saw a bent figure. Sandra? Yes, Sandra. She hunched over her spell. He wanted to call out to her, but those witches were not too far beyond. Picking up his pace, his heart lifted. He burst through the tree line into a clearing with the charred rubble of the Payne house.

He heard the creak of a man swinging from a tree limb. He strained to hold back a scream.

"You are not cut out for this kind of work," his mother said. She stood at a distance to the right.

He rushed towards her, dodging trees and shadows, but when he reached the spot, she was gone. Not far away, he saw the silhouette of a young man.

"I'm leaving," PB said, "and I ain't coming back. Ever."

"Don't say that," Max yelled the words, then covered his

mouth.

From a distance to the left, his mother said, "Who will take care of me when you die playing these games in the woods?"

He dashed over the tall grasses, but she was gone. J had taken her place.

"You pushed out my brother, and you want me to be your servant, working for the Agency so you don't have to."

Max's throat tightened as he moaned. "No, it's not like that."

"The boys love me," his mother said, "but they've got their own lives. Sandra can't stand me. She won't take care of me. All I've got is you, and you are letting us all slip away."

Racing circles around the destroyed house, Max searched for his mother. Her voice trailed off, her words became mush, but he knew she was close by. The Sandwich Boys, too. He had to get to them. Change their minds. They were all near as ever. If he could just reach them —

When he fell, he had no idea until his body hit the ground. Stones dug into his chest and his knees shouted at the sudden trauma. His teeth clashed together, and he tasted blood in his mouth.

The jarring stop left him dazed. He lay against the earth, smelling its deep forest freshness, and tried to clear his head. Pushing to his feet, he rubbed his various pains. And he noticed — no baby crying, no fleeing woman, no gunshots, no hanged man, none of it. His mother had disappeared, and of course, she couldn't have been here because she was in the mountains with the Sandwich Boys. That meant they couldn't be here, either.

Even as his mind suggested that the reality of pain had broken the delusion of a spell — a spell that put horrible thoughts into hallucinations — he trudged directly toward Sandra. Any moment he thought his mind might be losing control again, he pressed a thumb against one of his wounds. That kept him in the real world.

"Back already?" Drummond said, keeping his voice low so as not to disturb Sandra. "You look awful."

"Thanks. You look great, too."

"What did you do out there?"

"Nothing. I tried, but these witches have too many spells going on around us." Max peeked back into the woods, thinking he could hear his mother utter a disapproving laugh, and shuddered. "Too many spells and other things out there."

He checked over the ledge. The witches chanted while Cecily stood in the circle. If she had tried to run, Max guessed that Van Horn stopped her. Or perhaps yet another spell kept her still. Too many spells, indeed. Whatever the case, Cecily didn't try escaping now.

Madame Ti raised a knife. "We offer our blood to unite us, to strengthen us, to bring us together as family."

She cut her forearm and let the blood stream into a bowl. The other witches did the same. Cecily shrieked at the sight while Ruby cheered them on.

After a recitation in another language, Rosita stood with her bowl in hand. She entered the circle, placing each foot with great care, and stopped at the heart of Emily Dodson. Spouting off a few words, she emptied her bowl over the heart before returning to her space outside the circle. Sung went next. Michon and LaShanna did the same, only they poured their blood over the deer heart. Finally, Madame Ti entered and moved directly to Cecily.

"Heart of a human. Heart of a hart. Blood of a witch."

She tipped her bowl over Cecily's head. The proud Hull collapsed to her knees, weeping as her hair flattened and her clothes stained red. Her body heaved when she gasped for air only to bellow out another raging, desperate cry.

As Madame Ti returned to her place on the circle's edge, she started a new round of repeating phrases. Her coven sisters joined in the chant. After two times through, the casting circle ignited with a pulsing red glow.

A shriek. Then Cecily let out whimpers and sharp cries like the sporadic sparks of a campfire. Her body convulsed, and her mouth frothed.

"Not trying to pressure you, hon," Max said, unable to look away from Cecily Hull's terrified form, "but their spell is well on its way."

Sandra took the time to throw an irritated glare before returning to her spellwork. Not as bad a reaction as he expected, but she needed to know. He guessed that she wanted to know, too, despite the interruption.

Another scream from below. Not the same as before, though. The sound still came from Cecily, but it had taken on a deeper, more guttural tone. Cecily's higher shriek had been joined with an animalistic noise that put Max's ancient, primal instincts on alert.

Ruby clapped her hands, rocking and laughing. Max thought Madame Ti might chastise her assistant, but none of the witches noticed. They swayed and chanted and bowed in synchronized, hypnotic movements.

Jerking within her circle, Cecily groaned and huffed, sweated and cried. Despite all the suffering she had caused in her life, Max wanted to stop her pain. Nobody deserved torture. Justice, sure. Measured punishment, yes. But this? This was cruelty. This was wrong.

She flopped over, twisting on her side while her knees still held her hips up. Max watched the horror with a pure desire to look away and a morbid desire to see what happened next. It only got worse.

Her pelvic bones moved under her skin in the wrong directions. She screeched, louder, higher, until no sound came from her strained throat. Even at a distance, Max could hear her bones crack. He thought she would pass out — anybody would have under these circumstances — but the coven must have cast yet another spell preventing her escape into unconsciousness.

He had lost count on how many spells these women managed to keep running simultaneously. Spells of disorientation, spells of delusion, spells to draw their own blood safely, spells to hold Cecily Hull in place, spells to call the grimoire, spells to transmute a human — those were merely the ones he could identify. They probably had more acting in the background that he would never encounter. The five of them proved how strong they were, how skilled, and the terrible thought hit that when the Coven of Ti had a full complement of thirteen witches, they might be unstoppable.

Another series of bone-cracking pops and Cecily's brutal shrieking continued. Her back legs broke at the knees, but she did not fall. They snapped backwards as if locking into their proper place and, though wobbly, held her hips up. Her arms twitched as her rapid breathing slowed. The transformation continued — her ribs pushed outward, expanding the size of her torso, while her spine reshaped into a hideous S — but she no longer howled at the pain. She juddered and convulsed but only gazed out dead-eyed. If she was lucky, the pain had ceased. Max doubted she was that lucky.

Drummond said, "Doll, I think you're out of time. Whatever you got, you might as well cast it."

Sandra tilted her head back and her eyes rolled up — a witch far into the process of casting her spell. Max flushed with pride. He and Drummond assumed she had scrambled for a spell. But she must have figured it out early on because she had been casting for a while now. Had the whole thing ready to go, waiting for the witches to make their move.

"Get ready." Her voice garnered an unnatural whisper. "This isn't a normal spell. This is tapping into their power, and I'm not sure how long I can control it."

She stood, energy crackling off her. She closed her eyes and pointed her hands toward the ledge. The corner of Max's mouth lifted, and he knew his wife would destroy this coven.

But Madame Ti's head snapped up to stare directly at him.

"No," she said.

Chapter 34

A SHOCKWAVE OF ENERGY stampeded through the woods. It threw Max to the ground and knocked Sandra back several steps. When he tried to stand, he discovered that Madame Ti had done more than send a concussive blast, she had cast yet another spell.

Though time continued at the proper speed, Max's body moved in slow motion. Internally, all worked as it should, but outside he strained as if submerged in thick mud. His heart thumped hard, his lungs fought to fill, his eyes labored to see his own wife off to the side. Sandra, too, could not move, and the spell that immobilized them had broken her concentration, stopped her casting. He tried to speak to her, but his mouth would not move fast enough to form words. He only managed a caveman grunt.

As the newly crowned Ti sisters continued, Madame Ti said, "We are close. Stay focused. Pour all your energy into this spell. We are united, we are together, we are one." She continued urging her coven like a basketball coach knowing her team only had to run the clock a little longer to win the big game.

Cecily flipped onto her back. Her nose fused with her upper lip, thrusting outward to form a snout. This time, when she screamed, the sound could not have been called human.

Drummond swished into view. "Both of you, hold on. I've got an idea. I'll come back. I promise." He flew off into the woods.

Sandra uttered her own soft grunt, and Max did his best to look in her direction. His head barely moved. Peeking out of the left corner of his eye, his right involuntarily tried to shut. He saw

Sandra staring back. He wanted to smile, wanted to send her an assuring nod or a loving gaze or any calming expression, but the muscles in his face refused to cooperate. She knew, though. He felt that much even when he could not see her clearly. Their connection, built over years from infatuation and lust to love and devotion — no magic could sever that.

His vision of her blurred. Apparently, Madame Ti's spell did not stop his emotional reactions. A tear dribbled down his cheek.

They had been in desperate situations before. They had been caught in spells, left for dead, and on the edge of dying. As terrible and terrifying as it felt, part of Max — a part that only had time to think this way because of Madame Ti's spell — reminded him that it was good he still felt this way. If ever he became so lackadaisical about the threats they faced, he would have to quit. Nobody in this business — or any business — should take their loved ones for granted. Losing Sandra would never be acceptable, and the mere thought of it would always bring tears to his eyes.

Max had lost his sense of time, too. How long had it been since Drummond left? Perhaps his own thoughts had slowed as well. He knew his partner would not abandon them, yet nothing had happened to save them. Whatever the ghost attempted, it appeared to have failed.

But like a berserker warrior, Drummond roared as he shot in from overhead. Max watched the pale figure race in at full speed, tuck his head, pull in his arms, and slam into the protective ward surrounding the witches. He hit the shield of energy hard enough that dust and dirt danced around the edges where the ward met the ground. His warrior yell crescendoed into a high-pitched squeal of burning pain. Drummond's ghostly form ricocheted off into the distance.

If Max could have spoken, he would have turned to Sandra and asked what the heck that ghost was thinking. This was Drummond's brilliant plan? Instead, Max groaned a long droning sound to express his utter bafflement and disappointment.

Madame Ti held the Payne grimoire in both hands and lifted

it overhead. "I call upon the tragic power within these pages. Hear me, your new master, obey and serve. Give us, the Coven of Ti, your deadly strength. Allow me to be the conduit of your energy, the holder of your sorrow, the bottomless well that you will pour your strength into."

Rubbing his shoulder, Drummond returned, floating through the trees until he reached Max. "You're thinking that I'm an idiot."

The ghost wasn't wrong, but Max would have been more tactful.

"I can't say I enjoyed that, but I had to be willing to do my part and show how it's done." Drummond's gaze shifted to Sandra then back to Max. "You two don't get it, do you? Against more wards, I needed more ghosts. I went back to the cemetery and tried to get the help of the ghosts there, but the Oak Grove dead are too far gone. So, I thought of the next best thing — the Other."

Of course. Drummond had said that those ghosts were nervous, that he had warned them of the coming witch war, and that they knew the witches might try to control them. Fear paralyzed many, but it also pushed many into action.

"Ah, there it is. You're both starting to figure it out. It took a little convincing, and I didn't come back with the army I had hoped for, but I've got about ten with me. Now that they've seen me do as I promised — that I would lead the charge and bash that ward first and survive, even though it would hurt — I'm waiting for them to make their move."

Max strived to glance at Sandra. Her eyes focused in the distance — no doubt where the ten ghosts of the Other congregated. He looked back at Drummond and the ghost nodded.

"I told you to be ready and I meant it. We know LaShanna can be fast with a prepared spell. I'm sure Madame Ti is even faster. When those wards go down, do everything you can. And don't expect anything more from us ghosts. This is going to hurt like hell."

Bellowing another warrior's cry, Drummond shot off into the

ward, hit it hard, and bounced off in pain. But a moment later, Max saw the puffs of dirt around the ward edges on the ground erupt again. And again. They were doing it. The ghosts of the Other were bombarding these wards.

Madame Ti took notice. More hits came. And still more. Thud. Thud. Thud.

Flinching as if given a static shock, Sung Park halted her chanting. Her hand reached for the ghost ward in the pocket of her cloak. When she brought it out, it had cracked into pieces.

Drummond soared in for another strike. This time seven rapid hits followed. The ground surrounding the casting circle vibrated under the constant strain. Michon stopped chanting now. She, too, produced her broken ward.

"Keep casting," Madame Ti said, her conqueror's attitude slipping.

A slew of ghostly attacks on the wards sent Rosita to the ground. She shoved back up, attempting to resume her chant, but even without looking, everybody knew her ward had cracked. The witches looked to each other for support and guidance.

"Refocus," Madame Ti said. "Drop all your spells but the one we cast together. I'll handle the rest."

Drummond led another barrage against the wards, and with it, Max's limbs released from their prison. He flopped forward and staggered to his knees. Ignoring the pain shooting up through to his hips, he jumped back on his feet and turned to help Sandra.

"I'm fine." She immediately lowered to her circle. "I'll recast the spell." When he remained standing, she said, "Go already."

Max sprinted into the woods. This time, he had no trouble keeping an eye on his destination. The spells that had confused him, that had screwed up his internal compass, that had caused him paranoid hallucinations — they had vanished. Excitement surged through him. The Porter Agency had the upper hand now. The witches must have known it.

When he broke through the tree line, however, Van Horn had not received the memo. Like any good bodyguard, he launched into action the moment he spotted an intruder. His big hands grasped Max and lifted him into the air. By the time Max's brain recognized he had been thrown, he sat on the ground with a sore rear.

Van Horn pressed on Max's shoulder. "Do not make me hurt you."

"Stay strong," Madame Ti said, an exultant trill entering her voice. "We are almost there."

Cecily Hull rose on her back haunches — thick, strong legs of a deer with the same thin-haired hide of the beast. Her torso, her arms, and her head had mutated into a nightmare version, both human and animal. Closing her eyes tight, she rolled her head and groaned. Two horns sliced through her scalp, growing with each turn of her neck, each painful moan. They continued to push outward and like limbs of a tree, they branched into multiple lines. Soon enough, Max realized that they were not horns at all but antlers.

Pumping the Payne grimoire overhead as if holding a sign on a picket line, Madame Ti raised her voice above the chanting witches. "We made a deal, Max Porter. Not long ago, yet you have broken it."

"I haven't."

"You agreed to support me should I go against Cecily Hull, yet you are here trying to stop me."

"I never agreed to let you torture her or experiment on her."

"Semantics."

"The lifeblood of any witch deal."

Madame Ti sneered. "Word games won't save you tonight. Do you understand how you have failed? Your ghosts destroyed our wards, but they are exhausted. Most of them have returned from wherever they came. I can feel their energy leaving. You are no match for Mr. Van Horn. And your wife, however powerful, cannot take on five very capable witches. Against us, she is weak and ineffective."

From above, from the ledge, Sandra stood glowing white, eyes rolled back. "Wrong."

Chapter 35

A BLAZE ARCED OUT OF SANDRA. A jagged bolt that shot with purpose like a well-placed arrow. It struck a tree above Madame Ti and whipped along the outside of the casting circle. Jumping from tree to tree, the energy expanded like a sizzling rope, washing out the area with light. It sparked above each witches' head.

Max pulled his leg in tight and kicked out at Van Horn's knee. The brutal blow caused the knee to cave sideways — not broken, but Van Horn would be limping on it for weeks to come. The giant man clutched his knee, giving Max an ample opening.

He rushed into the casting circle and kicked at the blood bowls. The sparking energy above and the sudden appearance of a madman destroying the circle below left the witches in disarray. Michon reached towards Max, but instead of backing away, he closed the distance. Catching her chin with his palm, he continued pressing forward until her legs could not back up fast enough. She fell.

Sandra's spell came together over the center of the circle, building into a static-filled sphere. She had told Max the best she could do was find a weak point. Right before it shot off, he saw it. The grimoire.

The ball of energy bowled straight into the book, knocking it right out of Madame Ti's upraised hands. Sandra collapsed as the last of her spell exited her body, and Madame Ti dropped to her knees, her hair singed, her muscles quaking. Ruby screamed as she snatched up the grimoire, burning her hands. While the witches cried out and hurried to their leader, Max swept his foot across the ground, ruining the careful lines of their spell. He knocked the deer heart out of its circle.

Cecily bleated at him — an angry sound — and he halted like prey before a hunter. Still standing in her circle, she glowered, shifting from one deer leg to the other. Her hands formed fists as her head gouged at the air with her antlers.

Behind Cecily, the witches helped Madame Ti to her feet. Ruby covered their precious book in a coat and handed it over. Van Horn limped to join the coven. During it all, Madame Ti leveled a vicious sneer at Max.

"We worked hard for tonight, and you've ruined it."

Max said, "I'm not apologizing."

As Sung and Rosita gathered all evidence of their witchcraft and placed it in their bags, Madame Ti used LaShanna for support to keep standing. "You haven't won. Only stalled the inevitable."

With the whine of a child, Ruby said, "Let me kill him. Please."

"Go ahead. It might be fun to watch."

Ruby clapped her hands as she turned a hungry eye upon Max. But as she moved in on him, a hoof caught her on the chin. She flailed back as blood splashed upward.

Madame Ti coughed a laugh. "I guess Cecily wants to protect you." She winced. To LaShanna: "I think I need medical attention. Ruby, too." She gazed at her small coven. "Perhaps the rest of us, as well. Come, sisters. Before Sandra can cast again."

LaShanna said, "But the Porters —"

"We'll deal with them. Just not now."

Like a funeral procession, the Coven of Ti and its flunkies shuffled into the forest, letting the darkness consume them from view. But Madame Ti made sure to throw out one parting thought.

"Cecily Hull is a monster of your creation, Max Porter. You fouled our spell and that ruined her. You caused the torture she now endures."

At first, he wondered why she expected him to feel guilt over her pathetic attempt to pass blame. But when he saw Cecily's eyes widened with rage, he understood — Madame Ti spoke not to Max but to Cecily. She wanted to make sure that this creature's twisted half-animal mind lacked the sense to figure out the truth. All Cecily heard was that responsibility for her suffering fell on him. Her back haunches scraped at the ground as she lowered her antlers.

Crap.

Max ran.

He tore off through the woods, weaving around trees, stumbling over the uneven ground. Two thoughts pummeled his brain — lead that monstrous thing away from Sandra and don't die. He felt confident he could succeed with the first one.

Cecily huffed — a deep, husky sound — as she pursued him. The forest slowed her down some, but her real obstacle was her own body. Whenever Max peeked back, he noticed her awkward gait. She had trouble holding her head still — the extra weight from the antlers a new challenge — and she clung to the trees to keep from falling over.

Good thing, too, because Max had no trouble falling. The moonlight kept him from smacking face first into tree trunks and most of their limbs, but the ground became a murky mess of darkness. He stumbled more than ran.

Despite her difficulties, Cecily stayed on his trail. Each time the living plants and dead debris tangled him up, he knew she gained a few feet. Soon, she would catch him. He didn't want to learn how effective she could become with those antlers. Or any part of her. Deer were strong animals, and Cecily had a lot of anger. Those two facts added up to one dead Max.

Coughing as he staggered on, walking more than running, he knew he needed a plan. The stamina of a deer — even a deer-human mutated hybrid — would outlast him. If he could find a way to trap her, hold her, then perhaps Sandra could counteract the spell. Or when Drummond returned from the Other, he could freeze Cecily long enough to secure her. Then they could focus on counter-spells.

But already he wondered how long he had raced through this treacherous forest. The trees all looked like shadowed pillars, confusing his mind without magic. He should have reached the Payne house. Unless he passed it without knowing. Possible, if he never came close to the clearing around it. More possible, if he had gone in the wrong direction from the start.

He heard the clump of hoof against dirt — far enough behind that he dared to pause, get a reading on where he might be. Surveying the mixture of thick darkness and pale moonlight left him dizzy. No wonder so many horrors linked to these woods. Anybody living out here — especially centuries earlier — would be courting madness each day. A simple chore like getting water from the river could send a person beyond sanity.

The river.

Hardly a river. A stream, really. But large enough that a bridge had been built to cross it. That bridge connected to a road, and that road connected to the civilized world. Max had to find that river.

A more human-sounding growl came from much closer than he wanted to admit. He yelled a few foul words, gritted his teeth, and forced his legs to jog. Exhaustion taxed every movement. His shoulders bumped the trees, now. Sweat slicked his body. While his muscles argued for a break, his brain demanded action. No time to rest.

Straining his ears, he sought any sound that might be flowing water. Squinting ahead, he searched for any glint that might be moonlight off a trickling stream. He sniffed the air, hoping for that unique scent of moss and algae and all the components of life-affirming energy that water brought with it. It was a potion that kept plants and animals functioning, and the animal within him could sense its existence through instinctual knowledge.

But a monster lurked in the shadows, and it wanted to devour him.

He checked back on Cecily's progress. He couldn't see her, couldn't hear her. Couldn't —

His foot twisted, and he tumbled. Shifting his body to the side, he let his flank take the brunt of the impact. However, the ground sloped downward giving his head some extra distance to fall. When he thought he should have hit the bottom, he kept going. His cheek bashed into a rock, flashes of light filled his brain and his mouth filled with blood.

He held still. He grumbled as his tongue poked at a tooth — cracked, maybe; loose, definitely. Wonderful. If he lived through the night, he would have to suffer under a dentist's drill.

Pushing back up, he paused. He heard something. A soft shushing.

Water!

Turning toward the sound rising from the bottom of the slope, he missed the stomping of Cecily's attack. She blundered toward him, the speed of her run betraying her gawky control of her limbs. When she lowered her antlers to gore, her unbalanced body and the sudden shift of the sloping ground sent her off-course. Her head missed Max, but her shoulder clipped him in the side.

They both hit the dirt, rolling down, smacking rocks and sticks as they somersaulted to the bottom. When he came to rest, his limbs spread wide, his bruises flared to life. His head hummed. His cheeks burned. Dull aches and sharp slices attacked every inch of skin. Despite all of it, he smiled. Because he also felt water splashing between his fingers.

Chapter 36

WITH A SERIES OF GRUNTS, Max tottered to his feet. He weaved along the edge of the stream, focusing on the next step, trying to find his way forward. Though trees towered on either bank, the water cut a swath that allowed the full moonlight to shine. Max had no trouble seeing his surroundings. If he read the area correctly — not a guarantee considering the abuse his body had taken — he thought he neared the culvert that had once been the covered bridge of Payne Road.

Keep moving. That was all he had to do. Keep moving to draw that creature away from Sandra.

He glanced over his shoulder. Cecily pulled her animal legs underneath and wobbled up. With a shake of her off-balanced head, she ripped free the tattered remains of her blouse. Deer hair covered her body in patches.

Not too far now. If Max could find a final burst of speed — no matter how small — he thought he could reach the road. After that … well, he had no idea. But the big picture didn't matter when trying to survive. Each step forward, each single strategy, kept focus on the bite-sized moments. Then again, how much could he trust his own mind? Perhaps he had been concussed too much tonight and had transmuted in his own way — into a raving lunatic.

She came at him again. He heard the clopping hooves, the splashes of water, the heavy huffing. Calling upon his final reserve, he dashed ahead. Pines and dogwoods ripped by as he half-ran, half-teetered through the woods.

Up ahead, he saw it — Payne Road.

He moaned at the road as if it could save him. Maybe

somebody would be walking by or one of the people living in the nearby homes would hear him. More than anything, he wanted to sleep. His thighs and knees and ankles hated him with each step he forced them to move. His eyes threatened to close after every few feet. Only the ever-present snorts of a mutated beast kept him from stopping.

Shocking him into a heightened level of awareness, the ground kicked upward sharply. The culvert. He had actually reached the culvert.

He climbed onto the road — asphalt — and crossed to the other side. This small sign of civilization inflated his lungs with life. He had a car not far down the road. A short drive and he would be able to find help. If nobody else, then Haven House. Those witches loved Sandra. They would help her.

But Max only managed one unsteady step before Cecily burst through the woods. Rocks, sticks, and leaves flew off like shrapnel. Blood dribbled from the skull wounds where the antlers had broken through. Her white and brown fur had lines of crimson veining throughout. She squatted on her muscular deer legs, arched back, and bawled her rage.

Lunging onto the road, she bared her teeth even as she threatened with her sharp antlers. But the blinding headlights of a car strafed through the trees. Both Max and Cecily halted to look. The growling engine revved and the wheels screeched as the driver sped through Payne Road's snaking turns.

Cecily refocused on Max, but the headlights grew brighter. Closer. Her head cocked toward the car. Mesmerized, her brow dropped low. In a blur, the car slammed into her. The sounds of bones snapping, Cecily yelping, and metal crunching blended into a single, unified punch.

Then nothing.

Silence.

Max peered down the road but found no sign of a car. No red taillights, no engine revs, nothing. The longer he thought on it, the more he doubted if he had seen a car at all. He saw the lights, heard the sound, but no more than that. Turning back to the culvert where the covered bridge had once stood, his skin chilled.

This spot — the most haunted spot on all of Payne Road. But before he could do more than question if the cold came from actual ghosts or the mere thought of ghosts, he heard a mournful whimper.

Cecily.

The mangled mound of limbs covered the road with blood and gore. Her spine had indented to the shape of a front fender, wrapping her top half in one direction and her deer legs in another. One antler had cracked off. Her hooves dug at the road, trying to stand on instinct. Already the stench of her bowels polluted the air.

He waited. She shouldn't have to die alone.

But the minutes dragged on, and her constant pain-soaked mewling aggravated him. She was dead the moment that car hit her. She knew it as well as he did, but still she cried on, unwilling to let go. And if that car didn't exist — if it had been a phantom echo from decades ago — then she suffered greater pains, icy pains, spectral pains, ones that no modern medicine could ever heal.

Either way, her suffering needed to end.

Limping as he trudged down the road, he held his arms close to his sides. That eased the pain of his walk jostling all his wounds. It also gave his mind something to fixate upon because he didn't want to think about Cecily Hull anymore. She was dead. Died the moment she entered that casting circle and the witches worked their spell.

He hoped he could believe that. When he reached his car at the Oak Grove Cemetery, he did believe it. Popping the trunk open, he figured that the creature had to be more animal than human. It had behaved too much like an animal, like a deer. A buck, no less, with those antlers. As he removed his 9mm, he recalled what Madame Ti had said — heart of a hart. He loaded the weapon. A hart, indeed.

Hiking back along the road, the weight of the Glock dragged on his arm. He could have driven the car. He should have. Except he needed the time. To put down an animal was difficult. But he knew that when he reached that abomination, when he held his weapon to its head, he would look in its eyes. Would he see a hart in agony from a car accident? Or would Cecily Hull gaze up at him?

Faster than he wanted, he saw the contorted shadow ahead. Steeling his nerve, he strode directly to the beast and raised the 9mm. He aimed — not that he had to worry about missing at this short distance — and let out a shaking breath. The animal's glazed eye still stared at him, even as it stared into nothingness. He had only shot live rounds into paper targets. His hands trembled.

The creature whined, and Max thought he heard it pleading for his aid. But it did not hold concepts of an afterlife. It did not know that when he squeezed the trigger, it might not find peace and solace. It might be cursed to roam the road like so many others.

"I'm sorry," he whispered as he pressed the muzzle against the beast's skull.

Crunching from the trees. Max swung his weapon to face this new threat. Turned out to be an old threat — Van Horn.

But the lumbering giant raised his hands. "I am not here to cause you any further harm."

"That's good because you'll get shot if you try."

Van Horn gestured toward the dying creature. "I came for them."

"Them?"

"The Cecily parts are female. The deer parts are male. How else should I refer to them?"

Max shrugged. The distinction didn't matter. Both Cecily-parts and deer-parts would be dead-parts soon.

"Please," Van Horn said, taking a step toward the creature. "We cannot allow anybody to find them in the road. There would be television reports, news articles, online discussions."

"So? Only the police and whoever is brought in to clean it all up would know for sure. Most everybody else will come up with some non-magical explanation for whatever photos they see. The story would become another myth of Payne Road."

"Perhaps. But in the end, Madame Ti has ordered me to

retrieve this corpse, and I will do so. I ask that you do not shoot me in the process."

The word *corpse* caught Max's focus. He glanced down at Cecily. The creature gazed back at him — glassy-eyed; dead.

He lowered the Glock and his head. Van Horn took this as acceptance. With a respectful nod, he hefted the beast over his shoulders. He stood still, back to Max, as if he might offer some parting words. But then Madame Ti's man returned to the woods in silence. Max noted the strength Van Horn displayed and hoped they would never have a physical confrontation.

Left alone, Max ejected the single bullet in his weapon. He put the bullet in one pocket, the handgun in another. Its weight pulled on him, trying to guilt him over not being used, but he shook his head. Better that he never squeezed that trigger. He didn't want to know how such an act might change him.

Standing in the middle of the quiet road, he sighed. It was over. For now.

When he reached Oak Grove Cemetery, he found Sandra waiting. The instant she saw him approach, she rushed over. A kiss. An attempt at a hug but he flinched at her touch.

"Where are you hurt?" she asked.

"Everywhere."

Taking his arm with a gentle touch, she led him to the car. "I'll drive."

Once settled in the passenger seat, Max rested his head back and closed his eyes. But Sandra nudged him — right on a bruise — and his body snapped awake. "What's wrong? What happened?"

"Nothing. It's okay. But you can't go to sleep yet. You might have a concussion or something worse. Do your best to stay awake until we get home. I can cast a spell that'll protect you, heal you a bit, until we can get a better look." She started the car. "I'd rather not take you to the hospital and have to explain your condition."

"Afraid you'll get arrested for spousal abuse?"

"More likely they'll put one or both of us in a mental ward."

Adjusting in his seat with the futile hope of finding a position that didn't cause pain, he said, "Yeah, I suppose this is a good case for healing at home."

Sandra backed the car out and drove down Payne Road.

Chapter 37

THEY WERE ALONE. Max sat in their kitchen while Sandra recited a spell at the casting circle she had drawn around him. True healing spells did not exist — not in the magical way of stories or video games. *Drink this potion and a broken bone will be whole.* It didn't work like that. Sandra explained that what witches called healing spells manipulated the energy within a person to strengthen the immune system, boost the white blood cells, even produce more platelets. This, in turn, aided the body into healing itself.

When she finished, she cast another spell that would numb him better than ibuprofen, acetaminophen, or any other over-the-counter pain killers. "Might be better than some of the prescription-only stuff, too." She cleaned up, kissed his cheek, and sat at the table with him.

"Oh, yeah?" Max's body warmed under her touch. "You all going to start competing with morphine?"

"I doubt it's that good. If it was, there'd be a lot of witches addicted to their own numbing spells, and a whole industry of regular folk wanting to hire us like drug dealers. As far as I know, none of that exists."

Drumming his fingers, Max looked around at the normalcy of his house. "You think Drummond's okay?"

"I'm sure he's fine. He's slammed his head into wards before. He knows what he can handle, and he probably has a nice, dead waitress to soothe his recovery."

"If not that, he's been after one of Miss 1800s old friends."

"Really? Do tell."

Max spent a few minutes bringing Sandra up to speed on their ghost partner's romantic troubles in the Other. Taking the time to chat about lighter subjects, to gossip and giggle, helped Max find his foundation again. He thought Sandra looked more grounded, too. Enough so that he dared to bring up the questions plaguing them both.

"This war," he said, swallowing the word as much as speaking it, "where does this leave us? Until a few days ago, I thought I understood how we fit in this world. But now, everything is flipped and spun around and I don't know what to think."

"It won't be like countries going to war. They'll do their best to avoid public notice. Their fights will be much like tonight — deep in the woods, private. That's why Van Horn took away Cecily. They want no evidence to exist for civilians to find."

"You think that'll work in today's world? Social media, video — how are they going to keep this secret?"

"They won't. Collateral damage is inevitable. Once that happens, the public will find out. Not that the public will believe any of it. They'll react like they have in the past. They'll have a scare of demonic groups taking over."

"Like the Dungeons and Dragons nonsense in the 70s?"

"Exactly."

Max perked up. "Hold on. Are you saying that whole thing was a witch war?"

"I'm not *not* saying it."

He chuckled, but only for a second. Sobering, he said, "I wish that gave me an answer, but I'm still stuck with the same point — where does this leave us?"

Sandra did not respond immediately. After a few moments to think, she walked to the refrigerator and brought out the bottle of wine. Placing it on the table with a firm thunk, she set down two glasses. Then she handed him the corkscrew.

"We carry on like we always have."

"I'm not sure I should be drinking."

"The spells I cast will protect you. We'll take the cases that come to us, and do our best to help people with their problems. I suppose business might get busier with all the witches getting up to no good, but at least that means we'll make more money."

"I guess. But with the boys going and my mother's condition—"

"Those things were always going to happen. The witches have nothing to do with it."

"It's just now with this witch thing — everything is changing so fast."

"Not really. All of it — our family, the witches — it's all been building for a long time. With the Sandwich Boys — we've done our best to give them solid ground to build from. It's a good thing they're eager to go into the world and start their lives. Your mother — she's not immortal. Even without the MS, her time will eventually come. It's part of life."

"And the witches?"

"I kind of think Madame Ti was a little right. If Cecily had moved faster, solidified her role controlling magic in the area, this war wouldn't be happening. The void of power can't last empty for this long."

Taking the corkscrew, Max opened the bottle. "And we keep pushing on?"

"As always."

He poured two generous glasses. "You really want to get drunk tonight?"

"I'd rather go to bed and indulge in some life-affirming sex, but I assumed that with every bone and muscle of yours in pain, that wasn't in the cards."

"Honey, you should know better. I'm a man. The only reason I'd ever turn down sex is if … well, I'm not sure there is a reason."

She patted his hand. "Then we better get moving. Our family hasn't left us yet, and I'm pretty sure they'll be home later today or tomorrow."

Groaning against his aching legs as he stood, Max paused to raise his glass. "To the uncertainty of life, and the changes that will come our way."

"My love, don't you know? No matter the changes that come our way, you'll always have me."

They clinked glasses but neither drank. Max gazed down at

the wine before setting it untouched on the table. "You're all I really need."

Lowering her glass, Sandra grinned. As she placed her untouched wine next to his, she took a cleansing breath. "Right back at you."

"To be clear, I'm not giving up alcohol. But I think, well, maybe … I don't know what I'm trying to say."

"That things will be different now."

"I guess. Not all things, I hope."

"Not all."

"Good," he said, leaning on her shoulder. "Because I need you to help me walk."

Snorting laughter, holding each other tight, Max and Sandra headed to their bedroom.

Afterword

Hi folks. Seventeen books in, and I have yet to run out of weird and oddball stories about North Carolina. Sometimes, how I find out about the stories is a story, too. In this case, I learned about the Grandover Resort from my son who had been using the huge building as a quiet place to do his own writing. He's trying his hand at following the old man's path, and I can tell you firsthand that he can write. Hopefully, you'll get a chance to read his work soon. The other main feature of this novel, Payne Road, came from the drummer in my band, Bob Payne. No relation — at least, none that we know of, but he was the first to tell me about this old road with a haunted past.

So, let's get into it.

Everything about the Grandover Resort is true except the most salacious part, the death of Bradley Langan and his witch girlfriend. Those two people are complete fictions. The way the place looks, the PGA quality golf courses, the men that designed the courses, the surrounding homes — all of it is true. Any mistakes in presentation are mine.

When it comes to Payne Road, things get a little more complicated. Payne Road is a real place and is considered the most haunted road in North Carolina. There is a real Facebook Group where people familiar with the road trade stories and experiences. Nearly all the stories presented in this book are accurate. Obviously, they can't all be true, but they are all stories you will come across if you choose to research the road at all.

The only story that is 100% true is that of Milus Frank Edwards — the man who committed suicide via dynamite. The rest contain bits of truth and urban legend, and I tried to have Max explain the real facts and doubts surrounding each tale.

The only major embellishment I injected concerned the devil-worshipping version. While there are some stories suggesting rumors of such behavior, that is where they tend to stop. I added in the greater degree of occultism, the Payne grimoire, and the possibility of townspeople getting involved. All of those are fictions of my imagination.

Max references a YouTube video which you can look up and see the road, the cemetery, the bridge, and even some of the ruined homes that may be related to the stories. Furthermore, in the video, they stop on the culvert that once was the covered bridge, stop their engine, and test what will happen. Spoiler: the car started right back up. However, there are some fascinating ideas as to why this may have worked in older cars from decades past.

Anyway, that hits the big points. I hope you enjoyed this latest story and I'll see you next time with Book 18. Thank you for your constant readership.

Acknowledgements

There is always plenty of thanks to go around in the making of a book. This time, in particular, I'd like to thank Bob Payne (no relation to any of the Payne Road people). Bob is an excellent drummer that I've performed with, and he was the first person to make me aware of Payne Road. So, this book truly would not exist without him. Also, thanks to my early readers. Especially, to Terry who caught a mess of typos that slipped by the rest of us. I always thank my wife and son, and this book is no different. But my son gets an extra shoutout because he brought the Grandover Resort to my attention. I drive by the Grandover Resort at least once-a-week, yet I never gave it much thought until my son pointed out that it would be a cool location for a Max Porter book. And, as always, I can never thank you readers enough. I truly appreciate each of you for participating in this journey with me.

Thank you.

About the Author

Stuart Jaffe is the madman behind the Nathan K thrillers, The Max Porter Paranormal Mysteries, the Ridnight Mysteries, the Parallel Society novels, The Malja Chronicles, The Bluesman, Founders, Real Magic, and much more. He trained in martial arts for over a decade until a knee injury ended that practice. Now, he plays lead guitar in a local blues band, The Bootleggers, and enjoys life on a small farm in rural North Carolina. For those who continue to keep count, the animal list is as follows: one dog, one cat, one aquatic turtle, and three chickens. As best as he's been able to manage, Stuart has made sure that the chickens do not live in the house.

www.ingramcontent.com/pod-product-compliance
Lightning Source LLC
Chambersburg PA
CBHW030519310726
48979CB00010B/1726/J

* 9 7 8 1 9 6 3 5 1 7 1 1 8 *